THE
RIDDLES
OF EPSILON

THE
RIDDLES
OF EPSILON

Christine Morton-Shaw

Illustrated by Neal Packer

HarperCollins *Children's Books*

First published in the USA by HarperCollins Children's Books 2005
First published in Great Britain by *HarperCollins Children's Books* 2005
First published in paperback in Great Britain by *HarperCollins Children's Books* 2006
HarperCollins Children's Books is an imprint of HarperCollins *Publishers* Ltd
77-85 Fulham Palace Road, Hammersmith, London, W6 8JB

www.harpercollinschildrensbooks.co.uk/epsilon

1 3 5 7 9 8 6 4 2

Copyright © Christine Morton-Shaw 2005

ISBN 13: 978 0 00 719982 2
ISBN 10: 0 00 719982 1

Christine Morton-Shaw asserts the moral right to be identified
as the author of the work.

All of the original drawings, maps, charts and Lumic alphabet
in this book were created by Christine Morton-Shaw.
However, grateful thanks are given to Neal Packer who rendered the artwork.

Printed and bound in Great Britain by
Clays Ltd, St Ives plc

For Y

My Diary

Down there, it happened. Down by the ruined cottage. That's where it all began. And I didn't expect any of it – let alone want it to happen to me.

I mean, I'm just an ordinary person. Jessica White, fourteen, no particular skills. So why me? But so much has happened since it all began. So much, in fact, I've decided I have to write it down. I found this huge empty box file in the small library. I'll make a record of the whole thing – the symbols, the flute; I'm even keeping the chat room printouts! I need to keep track of it all. Plus, I'll go mad if I don't. Or maybe I am mad? After all, it's in the family – madness.

Madness is a distinct possibility.

Chapter One

THERE ARE TWO MEMBERS IN THE CHAT ROOM:	Jess
	Avril

AVRIL: So have the Enemy calmed down yet?

JESS: Mum and Dad? Are you kidding? You'd think I'd had tattoos done. It was only a tiny nose ring, for crying out loud! And it was over a week ago, before we even moved here!

AVRIL: Hayley's mum grounded her for a whole week!

JESS: Poor Hayley!

AVRIL: It ended yesterday. She'll be here any minute – we're off to a party.

JESS: Lucky things! Say hi to her from me. Tell them I miss them all.

AVRIL: So did they make you take the nose ring out?

JESS: No way! That's why Dad isn't talking to me.

AVRIL: So what's the new house like?

JESS: Gross. Falling apart. Old. Full of crummy old stuff. My room's OK though – it's the whole attic. Massive. Half carpeted, half bare boards – Dad's put a barre up, and mirrors.

AVRIL: Cool! Your own personal dance studio!

JESS: Well, there's not much else to do in this godforsaken dump. This will be my summer of hell. There are no kids here my age – just toddlers. If I didn't have Domino, I'd die of boredom.

AVRIL: I miss taking him for walks. Mum *still* won't let me get a dog. How's he settling down?

JESS: Oh, he loves it. Lots of rabbits and seagulls to chase. That's all he cares about.

AVRIL: By the way, you left your purple leotard in my room, and your Swat CD.

V HAS ENTERED THE CHAT ROOM

JESS: I've been looking for that CD everywhere! Send it to me?

AVRIL: Oops – doorbell. Hayley's here, gotta go. Talk tomorrow? XXX

AVRIL HAS LEFT THE CHAT ROOM

V: Greetings.

JESS: Hey! Didn't know you could just butt in like that. This is a private room!

V: So you think Lume is a godforsaken place, huh?

JESS: What?

V: For an island, it is a bit remote. But you are wrong. There's a lot going on here.

JESS: I never said I was on Lume. Who are you?

V: V.

JESS: V? What does the V stand for?

V: V.

V HAS LEFT THE CHAT ROOM

Chapter Two

My Diary

It's been sooooo hot all day. And I'm furious. Mad at the heat, mad at Mum and Dad. Sick and tired of this new place with all its stupid "wonderful ancient links".

I don't care about any of that stuff – I just miss Avril. Not to mention swimming pools. Real ones, I mean – clean places to swim, with no seaweed in them to sneak around my legs like green snakes. Yuck.

So today I was determined to get out of doing Mum's latest task. I mean – sanding down another skirting board? Oh, *puh-leeze*! I'd rather sand my own skin than spend another minute doing this stupid restoration work. Big House, my foot! It's just a Big Pile of Rubbish. Mum inherited it but never wanted to live here until now. Well, I wish she still didn't – it's nothing but a relic. The whole place is falling apart. As for Dad, he's just as bad. Mum's nagging him to mend the scullery door – it's almost off its hinges – but all he can think about is *his* latest project.

"Come on, Jess – the chickens arrive tomorrow. We need to dig them a run. Go and get the spade. Chop chop!"

Yes, Dad. No, Dad. Three bags full, Dad.

So I ran away – didn't even take the dog – just went. They can all get lost.

Today I found the only place I like here so far. It's about a quarter of a mile from the Big House, just above the cliffs. There's a small stone seat halfway there, so I can even have a sit-down if I want to on the way there and back – a place to sit and daydream.

Best of all, They don't even know it's here! It's really, really hidden – a huge clump of bushes and trees – you have to really fight your way in. Nettles, too – the place is thick with them. You need to wear jeans, trainers, long sleeves, despite the heat. As it was, I got scratched to pieces.

I'd stolen the shovel from the shed, just to annoy Dad. Hah! Let him look. Serve him right. The shovel was my machete, I hacked my way though. Chop chop, Dad.

Suddenly, I was through. And that's how I found the clearing.

It's quiet in there. A small clearing, circled by trees. Trees like high green walls, all round. You can't see the sea through them, but you can hear it, below in the bay. But apart from that, there's hardly any sound. Just a stillness. Like stepping into a church or a bathroom with nothing in it.

Only there is.

Something in it, I mean.

A cottage. Or what's left of a cottage. Half stone, half rotting wood. Ivy all over it, the roof caved in at one corner. Broken windows. Like eyes. They made the hairs stand up on the back of my neck. And then I had the weirdest feeling — sick, cold, a bit dizzy. It doesn't feel like any normal place. But this afternoon I shrugged the shivers off.

Tumbledown or not, it is a *fantastic* hideout. A good den, where They can never find me.

So. Time to explore.

The door was stiff, half off its hinges. The doorstep an odd black stone, very shiny, like glass. Through the layer of dead leaves and yuck some words shone through. Words, written on the doorstep! Carved, rather. Some English words and symbols of some sort. Weird. Curly signs and straight signs, quite pretty.

The only two I can remember were like this:

Scraping the leaves away, I found the English words:

WHERE – –SILON DWELLS

There were a couple of spaces where some letters were missing, worn away by long-ago footsteps. But still – it looked like part of someone's name.

And I suddenly realised I was about to step into a cottage with a whole history, a house someone had lived in, maybe even died in. Someone with the letters 'SILON' in their name. Man? Woman? Old? Young?

I had to find out. It was time to go in. But the whole doorway was stiff to open and covered in brambles. Chopping away with the shovel, I could sense it behind them – that *stillness*. And the heat. The heat reached for me through the greenery, which is odd really – broken windows, a gap in the roof, lots of air in the place. But *so* hot!

Insects buzzed in the roses that crawled over everything,

inside and out. Climbing roses – they're back at the Big House too, growing over everything. ("They just need taming," Mum had said. "They've just gone a bit wild, that's all." Hypocrite! If you ask me, it's her that needs taming.)

Anyway. The shovel hacked me a way in at last.

Maybe it was my eyes after the bright sun? Maybe I was still feeling light-headed? I'm not sure. But I saw it, clear as day. Just for an instant.

A man stood in one corner. A very tall man, dressed in long, dark clothes. His hand rested on the back of an old, empty rocking chair.

But then I blinked and suddenly he was gone. Not a man. Just an old coat, hanging on a cupboard door. One sleeve draped forward, on to the back of the rocking chair. That was all.

I was scared half to death, I can tell you! But then I stared around and realised what I'd found. The place is fully furnished. An excellent place for a den. Just wait till I tell Avril.

But for some reason it was hard to walk a step farther, to explore. The whole cottage seemed to be watching me – *everything* seemed to be watching my every move. The broken glass on the kitchen cabinet in the corner – like an eye, winking. A dusty mirror on the wall, catching the flash of my eyes. And pots – pots everywhere, on shelves, tables, the floor – pots and boxes of all shapes and sizes. Everything thick with leaves and dust, in shadows where spiders lurked. The whole place felt odd – not unfriendly really, just... Oh, I don't know. As if I wasn't welcome there.

I'm stubborn – or so They tell me all the time. So I whistled a bit, to tell these old walls I wasn't scared. But – I'm not explaining it very well – even the whistling was wrong. A strange tune, a bit oriental, one I've certainly never whistled before – it just seemed to go with the house. I stopped the tune, but it went on in my head, an eerie snippet of Arabian Nights.

That's when I stepped forward.

Something creaked. Something moved. I whirled round.

The chair was rocking!

Ever so slightly, it rocked and creaked. The black sleeve rocked with it, as if a dark hand had set it moving.

It was too much for me – I ran. Out, out, out into the clearing, with the birdsong and the buzzing insects and the sun beating down.

I ran to the other side of the clearing and sat down by an old garden wall. I stared back at the cottage. I was panting, couldn't seem to stop panting. I stared at the door, the windows, upstairs and down. They stared back at me, clouds in their eyes. "Keep out," they seemed to say.

Oh, I know it all sounds crazy, but honest, it was freaky. Really, really freaky.

Like the cottage was... sort of... alive. Or not the cottage. No. Something *in* the cottage, alive and watching and... in charge?

What made me turn then and press my hot forehead into the cold stone wall, to cool it down?

What made me get annoyed at the blasted ivy everywhere and drag a handful away, so my forehead could touch bare stone?

What made me choose that one place – the only place in the wall (I cleared it and found there are no more) with something carved on it?

There it was suddenly, in front of my eyes. An arrow.

My whole stomach turned over; I still don't know why. It was just an arrow, for heaven's sake! An arrow, pointing downwards into the ground. But... what a weird place for an arrow! So close to the ground and pointing nowhere. Just into the earth. Unless...

Curiosity got the better of me. I glanced across at the

cottage, but there was nothing wrong about it now. Just an old ruin, that's all. So I turned my back on it and began to dig.

Leaves first — layers of them, rotted to skeletons. Then the stones and the earth — almost a metre of it. Down, down, directly under the arrow. It was tiring work, I can tell you, but I wouldn't give up.

Behind me, the house now looked snug and cosy, drowsing in the heat. I got the distinct feeling that the house was content again, watching me dig. Crazy — crazy girl! Get a grip! Get back to digging!

But I knew I'd find something. And I did — seconds later, my shovel hit something with a dull thud.

And that's how I found the bucket.

Chapter Three

AVRIL: A bucket? Is that all? I thought you were going to say treasure or something!

JESS: You would. You watch too many movies. This is the real world.

AVRIL: So what's it like, this... er... bucket?

JESS: Dirty. Or at least it was. I cleaned it up later. In my room – didn't want Mum or Dad to see it.

AVRIL: Why not? Why keep a secret about a bucket? That place is getting to you.

JESS: It's wood. And yellow metal, with hoops all around.

AVRIL: Gold!

JESS: No such luck – just brass, I think. Very old. The wood's dark, heavy.

AVRIL: Anything in it?

JESS: Nope. Well – a worm.

AVRIL: Well, what you gonna do with it?

JESS: The worm?

AVRIL: No, stupid – the bucket! The boring, boring BUCKET!

JESS: Dunno.

V HAS ENTERED THE CHAT ROOM

V: Hello, Jess.

JESS: But there was something *carved* on it. On the base.

AVRIL: What?

JESS: A symbol – a bit like half a feather, on its side. And a word. EPSILON.

AVRIL: Epsilon? What's that supposed to mean?

JESS: Dunno.

V: Hello, Jess.

JESS: Just ignore the intruder, by the way.

AVRIL: Intruder? Huh?

JESS: V. He gatecrashed last time too. Probably some nerdy adolescent somewhere. Just ignore him.

AVRIL: Ignore who? Look, I've gotta go – Baz is coming

round, supposedly to do homework!!!

JESS: Baz? My Baz? I've only been gone a week
and you and *my Baz* are doing homework
together?!!!!!!!!

AVRIL: *Your* Baz? Oh, please – pass me a bucket! Hah
hah.

JESS: Oh, very funny.

AVRIL: Well I'll leave you to decide what to do with your
precious bucket and talk tommorra, OK?

JESS: <<...............................>>

AVRIL: OK?

JESS: <<...............................>>

AVRIL: Tsk tsk! Sulky! Bye then XXX

AVRIL HAS LEFT THE CHAT ROOM

V: Hello, Jess.

JESS: Get lost. Stop intruding.

V: Actually, I am not an adolescent as you told Avril. I
am very old.

JESS: So what? Big deal. And what does the letter V
stand for?

V: V is a letter that is not a letter.

JESS: ? Do you always talk in riddles? Oh, just get lost.

V: Wait until sunset. Then put it in your window. Right in
the centre.

JESS: What?

V: The bucket.

V HAS LEFT THE CHAT ROOM

Chapter Four

My Diary

Avril might be a pain, but she's right about one thing. This room's perfect for dancing. Plus, They hardly ever come up here. Private. I can play my guitar as long as I like, spread all my music out. Or pretend to do their boring home-schooling books. Stupid idiots.

I can put on my music, loud as I want – dance the whole length of the attic. They can't even hear me thumping around! There's a whole floor in between me and them. Nothing much in it. Empty rooms, an old bathroom, even a dusty, claustrophobic little library.

Mum and Dad have taken the entire bottom floor for themselves. Mum calls it "our suite". Her art studio's down there, and Dad's darkroom. Then their bedroom, the kitchen, dining room, living room. Two living rooms, in fact, with all our old furniture from home looking lost in the corners. It's a real mess, everything crammed in with stuff that was left here and bought with this horrible, horrible house.

But up here it's much simpler. I like things simple. There was a bed already in here, with a carving of a swan in all four corners of the headboard. It's huge – at least a double. And Dad said it'd be too hard to get down the curve in the attic stairs anyway, so I've kept it. They got me a new mattress for it, of course. Then there's my new wardrobe, the barre, an easel, CD stack, laptop. My desk and PC, my beanbags and bookshelves. Oh, and my globe lamp. And that's about it.

So it's miles and miles of floor space. (My bedroom is the second thing I like here, but I'd never admit it to Them.)

Talking about my PC, I still can't understand it. Avril can't seem to see V when he – or she – comes into the chat room. After I'd printed the whole chat out, I did my own security check, looked in the room history. It said there were only two people in the chat room all evening – me and Avril! Which is impossible. So I had another look at the screen. All my and Avril's chat was still there on the page – but not one word of V's and mine. It had just disappeared from the screen.

Whoever V is, Avril can't see him/her/it. Mum and Dad are always telling me about perves on the Internet, but it can't be one of them. Because whoever comes into a chat room *always* leaves a trace – it's part of the security system. But this V left no trace. It's as if he didn't exist. I'll have to ask Dad – computers are his second love, after all. So he should know.

So – who is V? What did he mean, "V is a letter that is not a letter"? And how does he know I'm on this island? Is V on Lume too?

Gotta go – Mum's calling me, lunch is ready. Smells like leftover spaghetti bolognese from last night. Great. More later.

Chapter Five

My Diary

This is getting weirder! Maybe I *am* going crazy? But hang on, let me start at the beginning.

First off, last night I was grounded. Again. What a rotten day yesterday was! I am so sick of Mum. Her and her skirting boards. She made me do two really long ones, to make up for not helping the day before! Cow.

Dad was still angry – even when his precious chickens arrived. Big deal. Lots of flapping and squawking, I thought at least a hundred chickens had come, but no – there were only two! Noisy little things. Rhode Island Reds, apparently. Still, they are funny. Kinda sweet. Dad put them in the new run – not dug in the right way at all, since I'd stolen the shovel. Which is why he isn't really speaking to me. He has this horrible habit of talking to anything nearby, instead of to me, when he's angry. Last night it was the chickens.

"So, what are you fine auburn ladies called then, eh?"

I nearly threw up on the spot, but the chickens just scurried about, *boc-boc-bock*ing.

"Pardon? What did you say? Your names are Boc and Boc-Boc? Splendid, splendid! I'm sure Jess will come to like you, once she stops sulking. As it is, she can just stop glaring at me and go and make me a nice cup of tea. Can't she, Boc-Boc? And she can do it without that scowl. You'll never lay any eggs at this rate, poor things!"

My dad. He is sooooooo embarrassing.

And so it went on, all evening. Supper was horrible, really strained. Mum's back was bothering her, what with all the painting and sanding. It always makes her bad-tempered. Dad kept jumping up from the table to dash to the back door and snap the sunset (which, I have to admit, does look good against the sea).

Each time he got up, Mum tutted, ever so slightly.

She kept asking me did I like it here, and what did I like, and what did I think of all the old stuff left in the house, and did I want any of it for my room? "For your penthouse suite," she smirked. On and on and on, questions, questions. Didn't I like the patio and gazebo at the back? Didn't I even like the natural swimming pool? Sixteen acres of ancient land: didn't I like *anything at all*, for crying out loud?!

In the end, she just sat still and stared. Dad rushed back, cameras swinging, knocking the salt-cellar over. I went on shovelling in rice pudding, knowing it was coming. Sure enough, here it came: Mum's formal voice.

"Jessica. If you are completely determined to dislike it here, that is quite all right by me. But I refuse to communicate with my daughter in the sulky language of shrugs. If you cannot utter words like a normal human being then take your silence up to your room and sulk alone. Do not inflict it on me."

Same old thing. Her Head Teacher head on as usual.

Not to be outdone, Dad picked up his precious Canon EOS-1n and spoke into it.

"Shutters down again, eh? All systems closed? Ah well. Bed, I think, is the best place for her – don't you, Elizabeth? We'll all try again tomorrow."

So that's how I came to be in bed, stupidly early, watching the sun go down.

And so I saw the message. I don't know what else to call it. I wonder what Avril will make of it? Whatever she thinks, I know what I think. I think this whole place is creepy. And now I can't ignore the fact that something very, very strange is going on.

| THERE ARE TWO MEMBERS IN THE CHAT ROOM: | Jess |
| | Avril |

AVRIL: So what happened then? You said something weird happened! TELL!!!

JESS: Well, I lay on my bed. The walls are slanted – you know, they're attic walls?

AVRIL: Well, yeah. They would be attic walls. Being in an attic. Duh!

JESS: Shut up or I won't tell you.

AVRIL: OK. Get on with it then.

JESS: Well, promise not to laugh.

AVRIL: You have my solemn word.

JESS: Well, maybe I dozed. Maybe the light was playing tricks. But suddenly, something appeared on the corner of the wall.

AVRIL: Appeared?

JESS: Well... kind of... flashed. On and off.

AVRIL: A reflection or something?

JESS: That's what I thought. Like – you know Mum's

crystals? The ones she hangs in every window?

AVRIL: Yep.

JESS: At first I thought it was that. Cos the sun was setting, kind of slanting through the window. But, Avril – there ARE no crystals hanging up in here!

AVRIL: What about mirrors?

JESS: There's only the barre mirror, and that's miles away, all the way at the other end.

AVRIL: And?

JESS: And so I checked the window. But there's nothing shiny there, to reflect lights on to the wall!

AVRIL: Oh, gawd. Is this tale actually going anywhere?

JESS: Listen!!! There's nothing on my windowsill. Just the bucket.

AVRIL: Ah – the famous bucket. <<Yawn.>>

JESS: Shut up and LISTEN! The light flashed again, and this time it stayed. Only there were more of them! Lots of lights, about two centimetres high.

AVRIL: Don't tell me. You have been abducted by aliens and are writing this from the planet Zog.

JESS: Do you want to hear this or not?

AVRIL: Not.

AVRIL HAS LEFT THE CHAT ROOM

JESS: Avril? Avril?

V: She has gone.

JESS: Gone? But she never goes without three kisses!

V: I made her go.

JESS: You little creep! But why? And anyway, when did you enter the chat room?

V: I've been here all the time.

JESS: How come there's no trace of you in the PC?

V: Tell me about the lights. What did you do?

JESS: Why should I tell you? You apparently don't exist!

V: Tell me. Hurry, we don't have much time.

JESS: No time? Who are you? What's going on?

V: The light, Jess. What did you DO?

JESS: OK, OK, keep your hair on. I stood on a chair to see them better, and I worked out where they were coming from, OK?

V: And where were they coming from?

JESS: The bucket. The bucket I dug up from under an arrow at the cottage. The bucket that *you* told me to put in my window. The bucket that is solid wood and brass and has no glassy pieces to reflect anything on to a wall.

V: What did it reflect on to the wall?

JESS: <<...>>

V: Stop ignoring me and tell me – what was it, Jess?

JESS: <<..............................>>

V: Sigh. While you decide whether to trust me or not, can I remind you, we don't have much time?

JESS: OK. Symbols. They were symbols. Thirty-seven of them, projected on to the wall by the bucket, and I stood on a chair risking my neck to see them, and I copied them down, and then the sun went down and they vanished. OK, now will you please tell me what is going ON!!!

V: So – you copied them down. That is good. Well, the rest is simple. Now all you have to do is translate them.

JESS: Oh, yeah, right, is that all?

V: Do it. Hurry.

JESS: How? And why the big hurry?

V: The volcano stone.

JESS: Pardon?

V: The black doorstep, of course. At the cottage.

JESS: Look. Who are you? How did you know about the black doorstep? I didn't even mention that to Avril!

V HAS LEFT THE CHAT ROOM

Chapter Six

My Diary

Still very hot. Headache weather. I'm not sure I can work all this out. It's all happening so fast – first the cottage, the doorstep, the symbols, then the arrow, which led to the bucket, which led to some signs on a wall. To say nothing of V, whoever he/she/it is – someone Avril can't even see in the chat room – and neither can the PC security check! It's all crazy, my head's spinning.

Still, I just ran back down to the cottage, copied down the symbols on the door stone. Had a closer look at the stone itself. It's really unusual – shiny black glass. I suppose the mysterious V is right – it's volcanic. Strange choice for a doorstep – glass!

They think I'm doing my homework now, and anyway they've gone to look for fossils on the beach. So.

1. Here are the symbols from the cottage door-step:

ᖴᑭᑎ ‡ᔓᐯᑕᔕ ⊙ᖯᐯᐯᔓ

2. Here are the English words that are written under them:

WHERE – –SILON DWELLS

3. And here are the symbols from my bedroom wall:

ᖴ⏀ᑭ Ö ⊖ᑎᑎᑕᑎ⊙ ⊙ᑎ⏀⊖

Ö ᔓᑕᐯᐯᑕᖴ⊙ ᔓᑕᐯᔕ⊙

⏀ᑭᐯᔓ ᐯ⏀ ⏀ ᗝᔓᔕ

So there they all are. They look strange in this diary, out of place, like something you might come across in an old archive office. Not something you find in the average teenage bedroom. I'm reluctant to begin working them out.

But I can't just keep on sitting here, staring at them.

OK, I'll admit it. I'm scared. I keep wondering what might happen if I do decipher them.

But I can't *not* decipher them – can I? Who in the whole world would be able to crumple all this up and throw it away? What choice do I have really? No choice at all.

I'm pretty good at puzzles and things. But there isn't a lot to go on. Probably not enough to crack the whole alphabet. I've worked out that some of the little dots and squiggles *under* and *over* other symbols must be letters in themselves. (Vowels, in fact – E and I.) That alone took me for ever – maybe I'm not as clever as I thought. Still, only one way to find out. Here goes…

This is not easy. Like I said – those dots and squiggles threw me for a while. For a start, there are five letters in the word 'where'. But only three symbols in the word carved right above it, from the cottage doorstep.

It's the same with the last word – 'dwells'. Six letters in 'dwells', only five symbols.

So… the funny little dots (or squiggles) *below* another symbol must be separate letters in themselves. Yes. So back to the word 'where'. The dots below must be the vowel E – because there are two of them, just like in the word 'where'.

And so that small curly blob under a letter in the second word must be another vowel – I. (Something something 'silon'.)

Now it makes more sense.

As to the – '– –silon', what else could it be but 'epsilon'? This is the only other word I know connected to the cottage. Epsilon carved on the base of the bucket. That gives me the P also. The As are easy too – a single-lettered word! It can't be I, as the Is are already accounted for.

So what I can decipher of the message so far is this:

WI-H A -IRRORED DREA-
A -OLLOWED SO-ND
-H-S LE- I- -E-IN

So. Going through the alphabet to try out the missing letters; there are some things they cannot possibly be and some things they must be.

DREA- must be 'dream'. It can't be any other word. Therefore M is ⊖.

I- must be 'it', since I already have the N so it's not 'in', and I have S so it's not 'is'. T must be ⇑.

TH-S must be 'thus', since I already have the I, so it's not 'this'. Therefore U = ⇓.

-OLLOWED must be 'followed', since I already have the H, so it's not 'hollowed'. And ⌇ is F.

And -E-IN must be 'begin', 'cause I can't think of another word that fits! Therefore B is ⊔ and G is ⟨.

So even though I haven't got the whole of the alphabet, I have got the whole of this message (or whatever it is). Not that it makes much sense, though.

WITH A MIRRORED DREAM
A FOLLOWED SOUND
THUS LET IT BEGIN

So what's that supposed to mean?!

Oh, sod it! Mum's on the second floor, yelling up the attic stairs. They've found a whole belemnite, whatever that is. Them and their fossils. Gotta go.

Chapter Seven

My Diary

5 a.m.

I've just dreamed of my room. This room. This attic bedroom, but with different furniture. There was this heavy table with a small model boat on it, and a blue-tiled washstand in the corner. The whole floor was bare boards – no swirly blue carpet at this end. Only the bed was the same, my huge bed with a swan carved in each corner of the headboard. My bed. But there was a stranger asleep in it!

It was a boy – a brown-haired boy, about thirteen years old. I keep trying to sketch what he looked like.

He woke up suddenly, sat up in my bed and lit a candle. He leaped out of bed. He was wearing a nightie! He ran to the table. He grabbed a quill pen, dipped it in some ink.

"Quick, quick!" he kept muttering. But he kept fumbling, kept dropping the pen. Three small blots splashed sideways across the paper. He tutted, wiped one of the blots away with his finger, and went on scribbling. No – not just scribbling – *drawing*!

I couldn't see what he was drawing. But whatever it was, he drew it fast, a sketch of some sort. Then he turned the paper over and began to write. More and more words, scrawled fast. Then he ran to the window – my window, only there were these heavy brocaded curtains hanging up – and looked out. Dawn was coming. He rolled the paper up and ran out of the room.

He was still in his nightie.

Down the two flights of stairs he ran, into the scullery. He worked a pump till water came, then he drank straight from the pump, wetting his nightie. But he didn't seem to notice – he just ran full speed out of the back door.

He ran and ran, away from the house, in the direction of the cottage. The sound of his feet thumped the grass, getting fainter. Then another sound came, a soft, eerie sound. Haunting. Like a flute, being played far away. It came from the direction of the cottage.

I tried to follow it, but in my dream I couldn't move any faster, and the sound of the flute grew fainter and fainter.

Until all I could hear was the sound of the sea over the headland.

Then I woke up.

I put on my globe lamp – to be honest, I was a bit scared of the dark, which is NOT like me at all. The strongest feeling gripped me that I had to write it all down in full, sketches too. Then I would put it in the box file I'd found the library. It all seemed so real.

But – sitting here – *I can still hear the flute*!

Very, very faint. All the time I've been writing this, it's been fading, bit by bit. Yet the fainter it gets, it seems to be more and more – oh, I don't know… insistent? Soon it may fade altogether.

It's definitely coming from the direction of the cottage. It's no good. I have to go there before the music stops.

I have to get down there. Now.

6 a.m.

I've just got back from the cottage. Can hardly hold the pen. Still shaking. What on earth is going on? I'm terrified.

The cottage was still in shadow. Cold shadows. Creepy. The birds began to sing – but the flute was the loudest sound now. Coming from behind the cottage door.

The door was closed! I'd left it open, three days ago.

Who had closed it? Maybe the wind? Ridiculous – it was too stiff for the wind to move it at all.

Domino didn't like it either. He wouldn't come close – not even up the little path to the door. He sat in the garden, whined a bit. I called and called him, but he just sat and bristled.

I reached out for the handle, decided to do it quickly – shoved the door open.

The flute music stopped.

But the flute was there. It fell from midair. It clattered to the table. It rolled on to the floor. Because whoever had been playing it had just dropped it. Yet there was no one there.

My legs turned to jelly. Behind my back, Domino growled.

I can't describe how sick I felt, sweaty, clammy. But I couldn't run. I had to go and get that flute! It was as if I had no choice. Somehow I went and picked it up.

It was made of wood. Something was carved on the mouthpiece. The straggly, thin symbol of Epsilon. Like half a feather, toppled over:

It was dry, dusty. It didn't look as if anyone had played it for a hundred years, let alone a minute earlier.

I lifted it to my mouth and blew. Nothing. Blocked –

years of dust and muck. I peered inside. Something was curled up in there. Paper, maybe? I took a deep breath, blew it out. The paper came out with a piercing shriek.

The paper was whispery dry and yellowed with age. It must be fifty, a hundred years old. I unrolled it, turned it the right way round. As I stared at it, my knees went to water. I knelt down slowly, into the dust of the kitchen floor.

It was a sketch. A sketch of a girl.

A girl in a bed. A bed with four swans carved on it.

The girl in the bed was me.

This is what I read on the back of the sketch:

Just now I have dreamed of a girl. She was sleeping in my bedchamber, in my swan bed. Just as Epsilon had said. "Look for a dream that is not a dream." This genteel girl was exceedingly real. I have sketched on the back of this paper what she looked like.

She woke up – reached out in the dark – and the earth lit up at her hand! The earth, but very small, lit up under her fingers. Blue seas, green Africa – oh, everything, very small and bright, brighter than candles, brighter even than the great chandelier downstairs!

And there was a timepiece by her bed – a fine silver thing. Only the very rich have timepieces. And the very gown she wore was silken, with exceeding fine lace, but pale blue.

There was a rug. Blue too – blue like the sea – but it covered half the floor! It reached all the way to the edges of the walls! One rug, or many rugs, cunningly sewn together? I could not tell. But I could feel it soft under my feet.

She wrote something with a pen that was black but did not need an inkwell to make it work. She wrote for a long time, not once needing to dip in. At last she ran to the window and looked out. But the curtains were not the curtains Mama made for me. They were fine as cobwebs – they floated like silver flags. She looked out at the dawn, then put on BREECHES! She was rushing, as if in great alarm.

Then she ran downstairs, where there was a great beast of a dog waiting, a black dog with three white spots along his back. The girl ran into the scullery and drank water from a silver pump that did not need to be pumped! She used the best crystal to drink from, as the gentry do. Then she ran out with the dog, in the direction of the cottage.

But no one else knows about the cottage. Just myself and Epsilon.

Maybe she is magic too? Or whatsoever Epsilon is – maybe she is one of his kind. She has a small pretty face, with hair as black as a rook's wing. In her nose she wore a silver ring. In ancient times, so Epsilon told me, followers of *the 'Borus also wore this ring, as a sign to each other. This sign has alarmed me greatly. I have written down all that I saw, as commanded by Epsilon, who bade me commit all these strange happenings to a journal. Whatever Epsilon is, I think it best to trust him. So I must take this at once to Epsilon and ask him what to do.*

As Agapetos is my witness, so signed by my hand, this fourteenth day of July, in the year of our Lord eighteen hundred and ninety-four. Sebastian Wren, aged thirteen years.

Across the page, splashed clumsily in his hurry, there were three black inkblots. And one smudged fingerprint. A real fingerprint, with whorls and swirls. A real print. Not the print of a boy from a dream at all. The print of a boy whose name I now know.

Because, over a hundred years ago, a boy called Sebastian Wren dreamed of a girl in an attic. A girl who put on her globe lamp and wrote with her ballpoint pen and ran over her fitted carpet and opened her Ikea curtains and drank from an ordinary tap and then ran down to the cottage. As I did, not two hours ago – after dreaming of HIM!

It's easy to work out what "a followed sound" means.

The flute. But now I know what "mirrored dream" means too. Our dreams were the same. The same things happened in each.

I drew him, just as he looked when he woke after dreaming of me.

He drew me, just as I looked when I woke from a dream about him.

What now will begin?

Oh, I can't *can't* wrap my brain around it all. I think I'm going to be sick.

Chapter Eight

My Diary

Haven't written anything in here for the past two days. I haven't done *anything* for two days – apart from run to the bathroom, that is. When I wrote, "I think I'm going to be sick", well – that was an understatement! I have thrown up so many times I feel turned inside out.

Mum fussed and wrung her hands and – feeling guilty, probably – said she'd give me her precious belemnite. (Oh, wow. A baby stone carrot. Why can't she give me a CD, like other mums?)

She even sent for the doctor.

"Thank God there's one on the island!" she said. "What if it's food poisoning? Oh, your dad should never have heated up that spaghetti – I told him not to!"

"Steady on, old girl! This is hardly my fault! How are

you feeling, Jess?"

"Pasta should never *ever* be heated up twice – it says in all the books."

"Elizabeth. You and I ate it too, and we are quite all right. It's not food poisoning, so please calm down."

"Calm down? Calm down? And if it's not food poisoning, it could be anything! It could be meningitis for all you know!"

"Stop shouting. There's the doorbell. The doctor's here."

Thankfully, the doctor calmly sent them out of the room, although Mum insisted on hovering halfway up the stairs. (Standing there arguing over me! It's enough to make anyone throw up.)

Dr Parker is one of these gruff, large men with a big, booming voice who wants to be everyone's bosom buddy.

"Call me Charles, young lady. Call me Charles."

You know the sort. But I can't call anyone Charles when he is a doctor who is listening to my bare chest with a stethoscope. I nearly died of embarrassment.

Well, he did all the icky things that doctors do, then he asked Mum to leave us for a minute. When she'd clattered off downstairs, he sat down next to my bed.

"Well, young Jessica. It's not food poisoning or anything sinister, as your poor mother seems to think. More likely just the heat. Have you been overdoing things a bit? Dancing, maybe?"

He nodded to the barre and then to these untidy pages. "A bit of a writer, too, I see. Working on anything special?"

"No! I mean, yes, I do dance. But I haven't been. I mean, it was too hot. To dance, I mean."

There's something about him that makes me feel all flustered. He has very sharp blue eyes – like he can see right through me.

"So. What do you think of Lume? Bit quiet for a city girl your age, I expect?"

"Quiet? It's dead!"

"Mmm. So – how come you all ended up here? Bit sudden, wasn't it? I mean, we all knew *someone* owned this place, but we've not seen hide nor hair of anyone for twenty-odd years. We thought the whole place would go to rack and ruin! Then suddenly the ferry was full of builders and cement and decorators and God knows what."

And suddenly, I was telling him the whole thing – it just all poured out. How I hated it here and wanted to go back to the city. How Mum and Dad were not getting along. How I never even knew Lume was *here*, for crying out loud, let alone that I was going to be dragged up here to live! How I'd been expelled from school for drinking some beer and smoking some wacky baccy and passing out in the gym. How Mum had said the only way to get me away from Avril and company was to move up here. How they'd not spoken to me when I got my nose ring, just before I left. How Dad's only interested in cameras. How Mum's crystals and her meditating and her 'trying to find herself' has turned us all upside down. How all she thinks about is paints, paints, paints.

"Well – that's her job, isn't it?" he said. "Portraits? So the island bush telegraph tells me, anyway. Doesn't she take commissions, sell them abroad?"

"Yeah, but…"

"But what?"

"Dunno."

"Ah, the famous teenage shrug. Listen, Jess – your mum is a painter and so spends a lot of time with paints. Your dad is a photographer and so spends time with cameras. It's their job! I'm a doctor, so I spend a lot of time with sick people. And your sickness will get better, I promise you. Just try to calm down. Give your mum and dad a chance. Give *Lume* a chance, OK? We're not all fuddy-duddies here, I can tell you."

Fuddy-duddies! Only a fuddy-duddy could use such a pathetic word.

I just stared at him, wondering why he had to talk so loudly. Then, suddenly, his eyes took on a new look. Casual. Over-casual. "So. Where on earth did you get this?"

"What?"

"This bucket."

He walked over to the windowsill and picked up the bucket. Unexpectedly, my stomach churned. I wanted to yell at him, wanted to shout, "Put it down – *Put it down!*" He turned the bucket this way and that – even lifted it up to the light.

"We're having a little garden party in a fortnight," he said absently, his fingers stroking the old wood. "Why don't you all come? It's about time the villagers met you. We were beginning to think you were hermits."

Suddenly, I didn't want him to read the word on the base, to see the symbol carved there. It seemed urgent that he did not. So I was just reaching over, to take the bucket from him, when he quickly turned it upside down and stared at it. We both froze.

Too late. Way too late. He'd seen it.

I had the distinct feeling that as soon as he saw that word, something came pouring out of the upturned bucket. Something invisible but real – something that went on and on, like time, unstoppable. Something that poured out and out, and spread darkly, filling the floor between us, filling the whole room until it could not be ignored. Something like shadows, or darkness. Something that was now free.

We both stayed very still, me watching him, him staring at that word.

"Well, well," he said at last. "Epsilon, eh? Any idea what that means?"

I shrugged and he turned his blue eyes on me. I trusted him – didn't I? Enough to tell him all my woes. But something deep inside me wanted to snatch the bucket back, tell him to get out.

"So where on earth did you dig this up?" he said.

"I didn't. Dig it up, I mean. I mean – I've always had it. I brought it with me. From home, I mean."

He smiled down at me and put the bucket back. Not quite in the centre of the windowsill, I noticed. It annoyed me intensely.

"I see. I see. Well – can't stay here nattering all day. You'll come to the garden party then."

I nodded. It didn't seem like an invitation. It seemed more like an order.

"I'll tell your parents about it. Meanwhile, young lady – no more running about these cliffs in the heat, eh? This is a heatwave, Jessica. Even in the early morning you have to respect it. People are dropping like flies, even on the mainland, and this island is a blasted suntrap. Best take things easy. Rest up. Righty ho then. Drink plenty of water."

Then he was gone.

When I put the bucket back where it belonged – smack bang in the centre – it felt lighter, strangely hollow. Emptied, somehow. And there was something else.

The word 'epsilon' was gone. There was no straggly symbol.

The base of the bucket was bare.

THERE IS ONE MEMBER IN THE CHAT ROOM:	Jess

JESS: Come on, I'm waiting.

JESS: Come on, V!

JESS: Come on, V. I know you're there.

V: How can I be here? After all, there is only you in the chat room.

JESS: Stop playing games. OK then. I know who you *are*.

V: You do? How?

JESS: I solved your riddle. I know your name.

V: Prove it.

JESS: "V is a letter which is not a letter." So V must be a number!

V: Elementary.

JESS: The letter V is 22nd in the English alphabet. Right?

V: <<chuckles>>

JESS: Which tells me nothing. Because it was the wrong alphabet, wasn't it?

V: You are smarter than you look.

JESS: But in roman numerals the letter V means five.

V: Ah!

JESS: Which also tells me nothing. Unless...

V: Unless?

JESS: Unless I go back to the wrong alphabet again! The fifth letter of which is E! So E is your initial.

V: I thought you said you knew my name – not just my initial.

JESS: And the fifth letter of another alphabet – Greek, in actual fact – has an even more ancient symbol. A bit like half a feather, toppled over. And THAT letter is called...

V: Well?

JESS: EPSILON! Hello, Epsilon.

E: At last! I thought you'd never get there.

JESS: But I did. Brilliant, aren't I?

E: Not especially. But you'll do.

JESS: Wow, thanks.

E: So you've been into the small library on the second floor.

JESS: Er... yes. How did you know?

E: Where else would you find a book with Greek in it?

JESS: <<...>>

E: While you're ignoring me, I might as well tell you – you're going to need that library. Use it.

JESS: Look – who are you? I mean, I know your name. And so did Sebastian Wren. But I don't know what you ARE. You seem to know just about everything about me!

E: So why did you decide to trust me?

JESS: Dunno.

E: Don't get all teenaged again. Tell me!

JESS: <<sigh>> OK, your sign. On the bucket. I REALLY didn't want the doctor to read it. Felt all... protective.

E: Good.

JESS: Why good?

E: Good that you followed your instincts. Good you see that the fewer people know about this, the better.

JESS: Yes, but why? Why not the doctor?

E: How do you know you can trust him?

JESS: How do I know I can trust you? Even though Sebastian trusted you.

E: Not enough, as it turned out. Not nearly enough.

JESS: But I must be crazy to trust you! All I know is no one can see you on this page but me. You don't flaming well exist! And Sebastian knew you more than a hundred years ago! What are you – a ghost?

E: <<laughing>>

JESS: Don't laugh at me! I'm scared!

E: Sorry. <<still laughing>> A thousand pardons. But you're right. Maybe it's time for a history lesson.

JESS: You sound just like my mother!

E: Talking of your mother – how can I put this? She is in danger.

JESS: Danger? Ooooh, the plot thickens!

E: This is not funny.

JESS: Not funny? A minute ago you were laughing!!!

E: So why did you just look over your shoulder?

JESS: Pardon?

E: Just then. You looked over your shoulder, towards the window. Why?

JESS: <<...>>

E: Yes. I can see you.

JESS: <<..................................>>

E: But I'm not the only one.

JESS: <<..................................>>

E: Sorry for scaring you.

JESS: I'm not scared. I'm terrified.

E: So I see. That's why you looked over your shoulder just now. Because you don't just feel scared. You feel watched.

JESS: Oh, hell!

E: I told you. This is not funny. And by the way, you still haven't explored the rest of the cottage.

JESS: Forget the cottage. Who else can see me?

E: Someone who knows it has begun. He is watching.

JESS: Who? What's his name?

E: In your language?

JESS: Oh, yes! Pleeeeease – not another riddle. They make me throw up.

E: OK then. Maybe we can call him... the Eye of Miradel.

JESS: The Eye of Miradel? Who do you think you are – J R R Tolkien?

E: <<sigh>> Just go back to the cottage and look for Sebastian, all right?

JESS: Yeah, right. Easy. Go and find sweet little Seb who lived a hundred years ago. Then ask him about the

Eye of Miradel – under a full moon, preferably…

E: You are getting tiresome.

JESS: …with three witches on the Heath and a few wolves howling. Oh and let's not forget—

E: Just get to the cottage and go upstairs, all right?

JESS: …and let's not forget that "Here be dragons!!!!!" <<puts white sheet over head>> WhhhhoooOOOOOOoooooooooooooo!

JESS HAS LEFT THE CHATROOM

Chapter Nine

My Diary

Mum and Dad think I'm resting. And so I am – here, in the cottage. I brought a dishcloth down and a few cushions, and I dusted the rocking chair. Now I'm sitting here yawning in the kitchen, staring at my finds.

Upstairs is cosy – if you can get used to the heat. I had to come down in the end, it was so stifling. Plus, there's only one room I can get into – without risking the roof caving in on me, I mean. The other room is empty anyway, nothing in it apart from a pile of slats and laths from the roof, the odd tile or two. Oh – and a pigeon's nest. (I don't know who was in more of a flap – me or the pigeon!)

But the main bedroom seems safe, and I don't just mean roofwise. It just has this feel to it – as soon as you step into it, you feel different. Like in those sci-fi movies when they step through a time shield or something. The bed is not a bed – it's a hammock, of all things. But the walls are all draped round with thick oriental rugs: pity they're so dusty. At first, I thought I'd clean the place up. I pulled at one of the rugs near the window. It fell to shreds in my hands. So much for that idea.

Whoever Epsilon may be, he was really messy. Pots everywhere, with old curly labels: stuff like BLACKENED THYME and PRESSED LAVENDER OIL, and one that said SPICES FROM THE ORIENT. I had a sniff of that and nearly keeled over – the scent was still there, nearly knocked my head off! Maybe Epsilon was some sort of pharmacist? I keep saying *was*, but of course whatever he was, he still *is*. I keep going round and round in circles about him. Sometimes, I'm convinced that if he's anything at all, he's just a pimply hacker, sitting somewhere on the mainland and having a right laugh at me. But how can that be? I'm in his house. Or his ex-house. Like I said, round and round in circles.

Anyway, there's so much to look at, I almost forgot what I'd come for. For instance, there are two huge star charts on the wall. Old, faded parchment – I didn't dare touch them. One had the usual constellations on it – Orion and the Plough and the Pleiades and stuff. The other had stars I've never heard of: Cygnus and Gienah, and Tau and Sadr. They were drawn by hand, in very fine lettering, and in one corner of the parchment, guess what I found? Epsilon's name, written in symbols, and his sign – that half-feather toppled over! I grinned stupidly at that – felt like I'd found an old photo of a long-lost friend.

There were more things with his name on too – especially on the desk. The desk is one of those old things with compartments and papers, books, envelopes and all sorts of stuff crammed in. I have to admit I'm a bit of a snoop. I gave a little squeal of delight and reached out to rifle through it all.

It was the oddest thing – I couldn't touch the paper.

I tried again and again, but just when my fingers almost had them, something stopped me. I could touch the quills – dry, ink-stained things – and the inkpots strewn about. But not the papers. It's as if I'm only 'allowed' to look at certain things and the rest are out of bounds. Suddenly, I felt shaky.

I hated it – the very thought of someone watching me, controlling my actions. Preventing me from doing something. Epsilon? For the first time in that room, all the hair stood up on the back of my neck. It was as if someone was staring at me from behind.

Uneasy, I straightened up and looked over my shoulder. When you do this because you're nervous, but don't really expect to see someone there, it's an even bigger shock when you do see someone! Because there he was again.

A man stood there – over there by the curtains. A very tall man in a long dark coat. He was standing very still, staring straight at me. I nearly died of shock. Then I blinked and it wasn't a man. There was no one there. Just a full-length mirror in the shadows, and me staring out of it, white as a sheet.

I had to have a sit-down then, calm myself, think. Just me in a mirror. But not me. I had seen him – his long coat. His intent face. Was it Epsilon watching me, stopping me from seeing certain papers, private things? Or – even scarier – was it the 'other one' who was watching me? The Eye of Miradel?

What did the word 'Miradel' mean, anyway? I decided I'd have to find out. Maybe it was just a place name? If I found a map, found where 'Miradel' was on the island, maybe I'd find the other one who was watching me – the one Epsilon had warned me about. But I wasn't sure I wanted to find out. All this was too scary.

But then it occurred to me that even if that *was* Epsilon standing there, he might not mean me any harm. After all,

I'd been invited here. Epsilon had *told* me to come here and find something linked to Sebastian. So that's what I had to do. Eventually, I calmed down enough to carry on my search. Shakily, I went back over to the big desk.

There was a large drawer in this desk. This too was carved with the epsilon. I found I could open that easily.

Inside were three boxes, all neatly lined up. I blew the dust away and picked one up. They are quite small, about twelve centimetres long, all identical wooden boxes, each with a keyhole set in silver. And in the corner of the drawer – the key.

This is a beautiful thing – silver, full of curlicues on the part you hold. I smiled when I saw the actual teeth of the key. What else but the shape of the epsilon?

The key fitted every box. But only one would open. The first one in the line. It opened with a small click. Inside, it was stuffed with more papers. Three of them. I unfolded them all carefully.

One had symbols written on it. One seemed to be the words of a song. The last was headed *DIARY*. And although I'd seen his handwriting only once, I recognised it instantly. Sebastian Wren's.

A strange, cold feeling grew in the pit of my stomach and spread out to my whole body. Sebastian Wren, who had lived more than a hundred years ago, and yet who had somehow dreamed about me. Here in my hand were another few pages written by him – his diary pages, old and faded. It was like a hand reaching through the years, reaching through time to find me, standing there in the bedroom of the cottage. I had the clear impression that what I was about to read would change my life for ever. This made my hands shake as I carried the papers over to the hammock. My legs were wobbling so much, I needed to sit down, and the cushions of the hammock looked cozy and comforting.

I settled down into the hammock and started to read.

First I read the page of Sebastian's diary :

I am sitting writing quietly in the hammock. Epsilon has just gone, once again bidding me write all this down. Although he is making as little sense as he usually does, about this girl. My name for her – "the girl with the world in her hand" – made him laugh outright. "And thou callest ME a riddler!" he said. He told me there will be wondrous things in later times, such as candles a person does not have to light; he said they will light up whole rooms at the touch of the hand! But I do not believe much of what he says. This girl, he also says, I must assist when the time comes. But how can I help a girl from within a dream? Although I would sorely like to assist her — she looked troubled and had the air of one bent under a great weight.

He keeps telling me also to look after Mama. This worries me greatly, for I fear she is indeed ailing in some way. She stares into the candles, she sighs and does not speak; she goes for many solitary walks down to the shore; she comes back looking as lost as when she did set out. Epsilon tells me all is not well with her. Papa, of course, barely notices. I dared this last evening to knock upon his door. I asked him to send for a physician to Mama. But he became angry at once, saying that Physics cost much money and there is none nearer than the mainland and please to go out and refrain from invading his privacy, they do not call it the <u>*withdrawing*</u> *room for nought.*

Meanwhile, the villagers are all preparing for the Greet. They sometimes let me partake of their busyness, although always I feel the outsider, after seven years of dwelling here! But Master Cork from the end cott is not like the rest. He does not mock me for my "elegant" voice and ways, and I have spent much time at his hearth. He lets me sit quiet while he whittles the tall pole for the Aroundy dance. He calls the pole his Coscoroba, and the way he fusses over his wood is remarkable to see. He tells me tales too, and sings as he works, or his grandam does when he falls quiet. Master Cork has a fine deep voice and sings the old songs well. But old Mistress Cork's voice is not so fine!

My favourite of his songs is called 'The Ballad of Yolandë', for it has a tune peculiarly soothing to the ears. It has many strange words, yet the music makes them all flow together as if with no seams. And since Epsilon told me to search well in the old ways, and to mark in particular any mention of Yolandë, I did write the whole sweet verse down late at night. As I was smiling down at my paper, Epsilon then appears and makes me fly up in fright and upset my whole inkpot! He says he is come to warn me that, "Shining stars may be cold to the touch," and to read this song with care.

I am getting weary of his old-fashioned mannerisms and his great need to be ciphering, for then he announced: "The key of this ballad is V then V then V then V." The which has given me nothing but a headache this whole long day.

Mama is sore pressed to prepare her share of the banqueting table, and so is taking some of her ready preserves to the Greet instead. She said, "Oh, Sebastian, I be too wearied to knead the bread, what with all the shells I am working to gather!"

I wish very much she would stop gathering these shells,

since no one has set her this task but she. But there she is, every sunrise, turning the whole shoreline over in the bay. And back she comes, her aprons full, and she tumbles the shells and stones all together into the garden, where they flatten Father's hollyhocks.

What work is it that you do, Mama? What is it you seek? (I asked it of her, tired of her hand-wringing and sighing.) But she turned her tired eyes upon me and said, "Why, nothing, son! I seek nothing at all but peace."

Meanwhile, she walks her bedchamber at night and hums. 'Tis strange, as she hums 'The Ballad of Yolandë', although where she has heard it I cannot tell, nor will she tell me.

I must put away this, my paper. Papa will be waiting for me back at home, pacing the hallway and frowning as usual. I must help him load the kitchen benches and settles into the hand cart, to take over, ready for the Greet. Also, the task has been given me of taking Mama's preserves tomorrow, the which she is busy labelling. They are heavy enough a burden to push over the miles and will be in grave danger of shattering before I ever reach Milton House. Then Father will be displeased with me again, no doubt. But then again – when is he ever not?

It was the freakiest thing in the world, to sit in the same hammock Sebastian sat in and read something he wrote so long ago – about me. The girl with the world in her hand. My globe lamp. I suppose if he was only used to candles and oil lamps, me switching on my globe lamp must have seemed like magic to him. Or sorcery.

It gave me a bit of a start too to see that soon – in his time – the Greet is coming up. Just like here and now. It's like I've slipped into a time warp or something, watching things happening to him in 1894. Yet the events seem to be a bit too similar for my liking, too close to my own life. For instance, Epsilon is trying to help him, too. And the Greet is coming up. And Sebastian is, like me, trying to work out what on earth is going on. Each time he learns a bit more, he writes another diary page. Just like I'm doing now.

I sat quite still for a while after reading it. Then I turned to the other two papers in the box. The first had the words of a song, written in Sebastian's fast, spidery handwriting.

The Ballad of Yolandë

Of the heather will I sing, its purple chimes.
Awake! Oh, the music, loud in those pipes!

And see – the hooves shed, long before time
    began –
I see all of them, hidden in the dark roots.

In my silvered choices I dance unchained.
Yet I hear the catted night stir.
I dance in celebration in the moonlight,
While calling my blue svelte night!

Winter's wrath will fade.
I search for the sweet tooth
Of the honeyed summer –
All the treasures of her pale fingers of wheat.

Her stories tighten the landscape,
Her standing stones, deep shadowed by children:
They are laughing.
They chant their hidden apple slumbers.
They run from their cradles!
They embrace my cobwebs and cool dew.

Eyes blink in the wintergreen –
The magical light where infant workers
Smiled, last summer.

Singers of songs, players of harps –
My wise babies with no enemy!
With silver pens they are writing at casements,
All busy with charm!

Their knowledge I will sing of,
I will flute them to owls,
Call them to seals,
Spreading my song!

At last, the faithful plumes of princes come out,
Parading past crowds!
Then from the castle door, the east will rise
And the west will slumber!

The icy north will hammer the door
And the Lemon Squire turn south.

Squire, let me sing, I pray!
Let the sea sip the shore.
(He in weakness has to open up
Like limpets!
Though hungry for nectar, he has no choice.)

Crush petals, O my hand!
Honesty seeds – heather blossom –
Singing to release their scents!
No dust of winter will ignore my perfume.

Dwelling in his bone castle
He reaches empty hands, filled with no music.
Bring me my harp that lies chiming in heather –
Sing and dance, but not of death!

To life itself will I sing.
To life itself must I step.
Let winter possess all her heady scents,
My own musk is not black or cold.
My dripping heart of summer brings seeds:
Sows them even over the ruin of December's earth.

Listen to the owl in the ruin of the keep.
He is weaving the boughs together.
My heart swells with his delight.
In his eyes, the mark of the moon.

Arise, my songs! My ballads
Are chanting all seedlings near –

Tiny travelers on wind or feather,
Flee now and take root!

From your growth I take my melody.
From you, my song swells.
From the summer of life,
The songster of beauty.

On the bottom, Sebastian had scrawled the clue Epsilon had given him, when he came to warn him about this ballad:

V THEN V THEN V THEN V

I stared at the name in the ballad: Yolandë. Aloud, I tried to say the name a few times. The dots over the e make me think it's spoken with an emphasis on the e – so that it rhymes with panda. It looks like an archaic spelling of Yolanda to me.

I read the ballad over and over, trying to think what "V then V then V" might mean. But it was no use – it was all beyond me. So finally I turned to the last paper, which Sebastian had labelled *THE KEY*.

Here it is.

I stared at all the symbols until my eyes went fuzzy. They were the same sort of symbols as had appeared on my bedroom wall – and I'd managed to decipher those. Surely this was the same process? I just needed to set my mind to it.

It was then that I realised just how tired I was: from the heat of the room, and the rich scents of the spices and the perfumed candles standing around – not lit, of course, but still giving off this heady scent. I've smelled something like it before, I think – Mum's endless incense sticks or the smell in a church. But this smell is richer, older; you can almost taste it in the air. And the drone of insects, and a lost bee in the window, trying to push out the pane of glass with its forehead. And above it all, the endless *Rhroo-hoo! Rhroo-hoo!* of the pigeon in her nest. I felt half hypnotised.

Anyway, I couldn't stop yawning. I felt dizzy too. I remembered the doctor's warning about the heatwave. So I returned the boxes to the desk and came downstairs to have a rest, to think and doze in the rocking chair.

I like this place now. It feels creepy at times – but it also feels like it's mine. Like it's for me to use. Any minute, I keep expecting to see Epsilon – the real Epsilon, not just glimpsed shadows – suddenly appear in a corner. I wonder what he really looks like. I wonder if I'd be scared. I've never seen a ghost (although he laughed like mad when I asked him if he was one!). I want to meet him.

I stopped writing, looked all round the room. "When can I meet you, Epsilon?" I asked the house out loud.

The pigeon stopped cooing. But then a new noise started. Outside. A sort of flapping. Like wings, but huge wings – it can't be the pigeon, she's too small. Like great birds, coming nearer.

I've just been outside and searched the sky for birds. Nothing. Just the sun beating down on the top of my head, and the hushing of the sea in the bay below.

It's no good – I have to get out of this heat. I'm going back. I'll take the documents with me and decipher the symbols at home. Mum will go crazy if she sees me up and about – I'll have to sneak in. She'll still be in the kitchen, I know – she's promised the doctor she'll bake for the garden party, or the Greet, as they call it here. Though how she can stand being near the stove in this weather is beyond me.

OK. I feel sick again. Time to go back.

I am strangely reluctant to leave.

Bye, Epsilon.

Chapter Ten

THERE ARE TWO MEMBERS IN THE CHAT ROOM:	Jess
	Avril

AVRIL: You're making all this up! What are you like? You always exaggerate!

JESS: I'm not doing that now – honest, Avril.

AVRIL: So let me get this right. Now you've met a ghost. Correction – *two* ghosts!

JESS: No. Yes. Oh, I don't know.

AVRIL: And one is a little boy, and one is a man called Epsilon, who is named after a bucket??? Oh, puh-*leeze*!

JESS: He is *not* named after a bucket! The bucket just had his name carved on it.

AVRIL: Why? And why was it buried in the ground, under an arrow? Come on then – tell me!

JESS: I don't *know*.

AVRIL: So ask him! Ask either of them – the teeny-tiny ghost or the great big ghost.

JESS: Epsilon says he's not a ghost.

AVRIL: Well, he's either a ghost or a figment of your imagination. Either way, you can still ask him. Like, "Hey, Mr Figment-of-my-Imagination, what's all this about buried buckets and hidden hammocks? Tell me quick cos I'm driving my friend Avril totally crazy!"

JESS: I knew you wouldn't understand.

AVRIL: You knew right. I'M GOING. I'll catch you again sometime. But next time, do me a favour?

JESS: What?

AVRIL: Try to talk about something normal, OK? No more exaggerating. This is getting boring.

AVRIL HAS LEFT THE CHAT ROOM

JESS: Epsilon? Are you there?

E: Of course I am.

JESS: Yeah – eavesdropping as usual.

E: She thinks you are telling lies. Why would she think that?

JESS: She's stupid.

E: "Making this up," she said. "Exaggerating."

JESS: Forget her. She's horrible.

E: So you have a bit of a reputation for telling lies?

JESS: OK, OK – so what if I do? I'm bound to tell lies, aren't I? I mean, it's inherited. I get it from my precious mother.

E: And what does your mother lie about?

JESS: Not "does". Did. Lied and lied and lied. She is such a hypocrite! Saying they'd come up here to get me away from Avril and everything. Rubbish! Dad wanted us to get away, all right – away from Mum's *boyfriend*. Away from the fact she'd just had an *affair*. Away from all the lies she told. Lie after lie after lie. But I found out. I found her with him. Told Dad.

E: I see. So you came away for a new start all round.

JESS: OK, so now you know. Can we change the subject?

E: Your dad sounds like a very forgiving sort.

JESS: Dad? He's a doormat. Pathetic.

E: Is all this why you spend less and less time with them?

JESS: Suppose so.

E: And why you've moved half your things down to the cottage?

JESS: *Now* who's exaggerating? I only moved my laptop and my home-schooling books.

E: And your files and your favourite quilt and lots of other stuff. Running away from them won't help matters, will it?

JESS: Oh, stop lecturing me. Let's change the subject. I just like spending time there. And I've got a million questions to ask you.

E: As you wish.

JESS: So – you used to sleep in a hammock? Cool!

E: No. I *do* sleep in a hammock. Present tense. Although I don't really sleep as such – just rest. But in that hammock, yes.

JESS: Present tense? You still live there?!????!!!!!!!!

E: Of course.

JESS: But – you never leave any footprints in all the dust!

E: Haven't you gathered by now, you are dealing with something that does not follow the rules of the world?

JESS: Tell me then. I need to know. What *am* I dealing with?

E: You'll understand much more when you read the documents in the second box.

JESS: Aha! So I was right – the boxes ARE in order!

E: Of course. The key will fit the others when the time is right for you to learn more.

JESS: And why am I learning all this weirdo stuff?
I mean, why me?

E: Because of your mother. Because of the danger that
she is in.

JESS: Oh, not back to her again. I'm not talking about
her, all right? I just want some answers. Like – when can
I see *you*?

E: But you have seen me.

JESS: Not a coat on a door, not glimpsed in a mirror!
When can I really see you? Sebastian did – he said you
appeared in his room – in *this* attic room – and made
him spill his inkpot. So if he did, why can't I?

E: You will. In a fortnight. At the Greet. Maybe even
before that.

JESS: You'll be at the Greet?

E: I'll be around. You will see me. You will see a friendly
enemy. You will see a hostile friend. You must not get
them mixed up.

JESS: Oh, gawd – more riddles. Why can't you just tell
me what's going on?

E: Hidden things need a place to hide.

JESS: Why? I mean, why all the secrecy? Why can't you
just tell me what's going on?

E: Don't forget – there are others watching, waiting,

listening in all the time. They want to solve all this too. That's why I can only tell it to you piece by piece. They might find one piece of it, or a few pieces, but they must not find the whole. So we have to keep things hidden.

JESS: And that reminds me – *who hid the bucket?*

E: Sebastian, of course. He buried it.

JESS: Why?

E: Because he got scared.

JESS: What of?

E: Of you, mostly.

JESS: Look, Epsilon. I am asking you really nicely. Please, please tell me what is going on? What's so important about the bucket? Where did it come from? Why did it have your name carved on it?

E: Because I made it. And signed it.

JESS: You made the bucket?

E: I made it out of special wood – bog oak. There's a lot of it lying about here. It's ancient – that's the important thing. Ancient materials have always been used on this island. A message *from* something ancient *about* something ancient.

JESS: What on earth is *bog* oak?!

E: Bog oak is wood that has been covered in peat. It

preserves it. It lies there for centuries – whole tree trunks, whole stumps. It carves well. And if you're going to make a special bucket, you might as well use a special wood.

JESS: A special bucket?

E: Part of my job is to guide you. I tried to guide Sebastian too. So I implanted the symbols into something I knew he'd use, down at the cottage. He spent whole days down there; hot, thirsty days – I knew he'd drink from the well. I hoped he would find the symbols.

JESS: The symbols that were reflected on to my bedroom wall? About "a mirrored dream" and "a followed sound"?

E: The very same.

JESS: And did he find them?

E: Not at first. At first he just played with the bucket. He sailed little paper boats in it. Kept his pet frog in it – that sort of thing. This was when he'd first met me, when he'd first found the cottage.

JESS: And then?

E: And then he started dreaming about you. He started getting the messages. He saw the symbols, just like you did, reflected from the bucket. He got scared. Even of me. For a time, he just hid everything to do with all this. Hid everything, in all sorts of places.

JESS: Hang on – reflected on his bedroom wall by what? How can anything reflect from solid wood?

E: I keep telling you. You are not dealing with something that follows the rules of this earth. It was more a matter of time. It was time for the message to be seen. So – you saw it. Both of you.

JESS: But then he got scared? And buried the bucket? Why didn't you just dig it up again, if you knew I needed to see it?

E: Because there was no need. I knew that whoever carried on his search – his work – would find it anyway. Once power comes to the surface, there is no stopping it. But I gave you a bit of help. I carved the arrow into the wall.

JESS: Don't tell me – you also rocked the rocking chair to make me run out of the cottage and down the garden. You scared me half to death!

E: Of course I did.

JESS: And the symbols? The symbols on the volcano stone – the doorstep? Did you carve those too?

E: Yes.

JESS: To leave a code, to help me decipher the symbols?

E: Yes.

JESS: So why volcanic glass?

E: I told you – I am not from your time. I deal with ancient things. Things that have been around since time began. I like to surround myself with reminders of those times. Bog oak. Volcanic glass. Fossils. Have you seen my kitchen floor, for example?

JESS: Seen it? Of course I have – I've walked on it.

E: Look closer next time you go. And make it soon. Tomorrow. There are some interesting things in my room. Go and take a look.

JESS: Oh, I now have your royal permission to snoop about, do I? You wouldn't let me, back at the cottage! Why, thank you, O great one!

E: No! Please do not call me that! I am just a worker of the One.

JESS: What One?

E: Come back to the cottage tomorrow.

JESS: Epsilon… who is the One that you work for? What is his name?

E: He is the One.

JESS: One? Is this another clue – like, the number one?

E HAS LEFT THE CHAT ROOM

Later

Sebastian's diary has upset me a bit. I keep reading it over. Epsilon warned me about my mum, Epsilon warned Seb about his mama. Seb is going to go to the Greet; we are going to go to the Greet. Seb's mum began acting strangely. And this is what's bothering me more than anything else.

Mum.

Much as I hate her, I can't help worrying. She's been busy baking for the Greet, cakes and scones and stuff – the freezer is full of them. But she keeps stopping what she's doing and staring out of the window. Like she's far, far away; like she's not here at all. Then Dad will get cross and have to repeat himself. "Elizabeth!" he snaps. Then she comes to herself again and goes on working. But she keeps sighing, sighing all the time. And doodling. Endlessly sketching. (Which is not unusual in itself – after all, she is an artist.) But she's doodling the same weird thing, over and over.

I keep coming across it up and down the house – the same image. In her sketchpads, over and over. On the table napkins. On the steamed-up kitchen window.

A face.

A faintly drawn woman's face, staring out from behind something like a net curtain. Or from behind wobbly glass.

Big, scared eyes and such an expression – such a desperate, pleading look, it wrings my heart. Over and over, the same face, and she draws it all the time.

I can't work it out. Last time she got all far away, last spring, it was all because of That Man. Her boyfriend. The toyboy, as Dad called him. Days and days of it: every time you looked up, there she was, sighing, staring into space, listening to soppy music – all that icky 'in love' stuff. And sneaking off at all hours, telling lies all the time about where she was. So here we are on a remote island and I keep thinking, is she at it again? But who on earth with? Dr Parker, maybe? Then I remember how brash and jolly he is, and besides – it feels all different. Not like she's pining for a new man at all – more like she's getting sick or something.

At least my dad is a bit nicer than poor old Seb's! My dad would send for the doctor straightaway if Mum got ill. So that's all right.

As to the ballad, I have to agree with Seb. Yolandë's song is cool! Why all the dire warnings about it? I don't know. Keep racking my brains about all the "V then V then V" stuff, but I'm no wiser than Sebastian about it.

The page full of symbols was easy though. I had it translated in a jiffy. I had to fiddle around and add punctuation, but I managed it in the end. It says:

The Key

In the space below the well
A map to the tooth lies hidden.
The space is marked by an infidel
Whose hand reveals what's bidden.

Through merrow hair
In Neptune's lair
Past thirty fingers pale –
Then hark for a river in the dark
And reach for the spout of the whale!

So there it is. Clear as mud. And there are more clues, written in English on the back, I almost missed them.

Lemon Sq
Galeria 5
Cloves – tooth

Which tells me absolutely nothing!!! Apart from the fact that the Lemon Squire is mentioned in Yolandë's song.

Galeria sounds a bit familiar, but I can't think where

I've come across it before. I looked it up in the dictionary and it's not there, so it *must* be a name.

As to cloves and tooth – well, on the other side of the paper, 'The Key' mentions a tooth – a map to the tooth.

Gotta go... Dad's yelling upstairs, yakking on about garden chairs or something. Why can't they just leave me alone?!!! Back soon.

Later

Oh, no. What's happening?

Just ran downstairs, to find Dad in the garden, pulling stuff out of the shed.

"So there you are! At last – didn't you hear me calling?"

(Yessss!!! He's talking to me again! Thank goodness for that.)

"Need a hand, Dad?"

"I'll say, kitten. Just wriggle your way in there, will you? You're thinner than me. Gotta get those deckchairs out. Sorry, but they're all the way at the back."

They were too – seven, eight, nine, *ten* deckchairs! And one old bench.

"What you doing, Dad? Having a party?"

"Not me, worse luck. The doctor and his flaming Greet thing. Been here the whole week – every time I turn round, there he is again! Wants us to take these over, says half the village'll be sitting on their thumbs if not."

I thought of Seb's benches and settles going to the Greet. My mouth went dry.

"What's up, old girl? Still feeling sick? Maybe I shouldn't have asked you to do this... Your mother will probably have a fit!"

"I'm fine. Really. So – don't you like the doctor then?"

"Like him? Course I like him! Seems like a decent chap. Just want to get on in the darkroom; I've films waiting to develop. No rest for the wicked and all that. OK – that the last of them?"

I handed the last deckchair out. Just then, the garden gate went *sneak! sneak!* on its hinges, as it always does. We both turned round and watched Mum come up the path carrying a plastic shopping bag. She was wearing a dress! In the day! Now that *is* a first is all I can say.

"Tsk. Must oil those hinges," muttered Dad. He stared at her, a little frown between his brows. Then she looked up and saw us watching.

"Hello, you two! Just had a lovely walk with Domino – right along the bay! His tongue's nearly lolling out of his mouth, poor pet, and I could do with a cup of tea myself. What about it, Jess?"

I was just about to say "Oh, why me?" when she opened the bag and tipped it upside-down – right over the flower bed.

Shells came pouring out – hundreds of shells, of all shapes and sizes. She smiled down at them fondly. Dad's mouth fell open.

"Did you have to dump them just there?" he said quietly. "I rather liked those hollyhocks."

Chapter Eleven

THERE ARE TWO MEMBERS IN THE CHAT ROOM:	Jess
	Avril

JESS: You must be CRAZY!!!

AVRIL: Oh, listen to you – after all the bull you've been going on about for weeks, I'm the one that's crazy all of a sudden?

JESS: Yes, but – to smoke pot at your mum's house – *no wonder she went berserk!*

AVRIL: Oh, don't you start! How was I to know she was going to come back a day early? You should have heard her: How dare I throw a party when she'd trusted me to stay here alone, and that your parents had the right idea, sending you away from it all and getting rid of the problem once and for all. She didn't stop yelling for an hour!

JESS: They didn't send me away.

AVRIL: What?

JESS: My parents. They didn't send me away.

AVRIL: Course they did!

JESS: They came with me.

AVRIL: Yeah, more fool them. I mean, I can always *send* you some wacky baccy. Where do they think they are, Timbuktu? If you want some drugs, I'm your man!

JESS: Avril, have you ever come across the word 'galeria'? Or Galeria 5?

AVRIL: That a drug? Never heard of it. Do you want me to look it up? Baz has a copy of the *Druggies' Bible*. He'll be here in a minute – I can ask him.

JESS: I doubt it's a drug – not up here.

AVRIL: So why you asking? Sounds more like a plant to me – or a herb.

AVRIL HAS LEFT THE CHAT ROOM

E: You are following a red herring there. Just thought I'd tell you.

JESS: Sigh. Did you *have* to kick Avril off just to tell me that?

E: No. I had to kick her off because your mouth is too big.

JESS: Well, thank you very much!

E: You are welcome.

JESS: Look, what do you want?

E: I want you to reread Yolandë's ballad. You haven't much time – the Greet is getting nearer. You need to understand the words.

JESS: Why?

E: And I told you before, you also need to go back to the cottage.

JESS: Why?

E: It is time to open the second box.

JESS: Admit it. You work for MI6.

E: I work for someone far more powerful than that.

JESS: Don't tell me. Scotland Yard? The CIA? Captain Kirk of the Starship *Enterprise*?

E: You are being foolish. Just read 'The Ballad of Yolandë' again.

JESS: I can't boldly go where I've *gone before*! I've *read* it. Time and time again.

E: Read it once more. It is important – take it from me. From Epsilon. From E. Or should I say, from V? *From V!*

JESS: .... Oh, RIGHT!!! Five! How incredibly stupid of me!

E: I agree.

JESS: I find the fifth word, then the fifth word after that, and so on?

E: At long last! Well – what are you waiting for?

JESS HAS LEFT THE CHAT ROOM

My Diary

So. Back to, let's see… page fifty of this rapidly growing file!!! 'The Ballad of Yolandë'.

"V then V then V then V." Start at the fifth word, then the fifth after that, then the fifth after that. And so on! Easy peasy, lemon squeezy!

It started as fun. This Yolandë with her lovely song. (I had actually wished I could hear the music – thought it'd make an amazing dance!) But now the words are starting to look plain nasty.

So this is what I got. Every fifth word of the Yolandë song says something quite opposite to the words of the song itself.

> *I awake in the time of dark choices*
> *I stir in my wrath*
> *For the treasures of the deep*
> *Are hidden from my eyes.*

The workers of my enemy are busy.
I will call my faithful out
From east, west, north and south.
I sip weakness like nectar –
Crush honesty to dust.
My bone hands bring lies and death.
I must possess!
My black heart sows ruin;
To ruin is my delight.
Mark my chanting, travellers—
Flee from my song of beauty!

Oh, YUCK! Whoever this Yolandë is – I'm dreading meeting her.

Two days later

Just when I think I can handle all of this, something else happens that really freaks me out.

It was last night. Mum and Dad had gone to bed early so I sneaked downstairs for a midnight feast. All that working out the "V then V" bit left me tired and hungry. But halfway through a packet of chocolate biscuits, I heard it. The weirdest, eeriest singing I've ever heard. Muffled, as if behind several doors. It set my hair on end.

I opened the kitchen door very quietly – and there was Mum, sneaking out of the front door. She had her dressing gown on. She was humming in a secret, happy way. Instantly, rage rose up inside my chest and grew and grew. Just like before – sneaking off to meet someone. And I'd followed her that time last summer and caught them at it. Told Dad. So I followed her again.

In the moonlight, she walked straight down the drive and out of the big front gates. Here she turned left, taking the path that leads to the lake.

I followed at a distance, keeping to the shadows. But even when the clouds came to cover the moon so that I lost her for an instant, I always knew where she was. Because she was humming that same tune, over and over. A haunting tune, and what with the wind whispering in the trees and the creeping about in the dark, it started to really spook me.

Along the lake path she went, not even shivering, although there was a white mist over the water and I was a bit chilly. I had to clench my teeth together to stop them chattering. Then, suddenly, she left the path and walked straight across the open ground. Now we were going uphill.

I kept slipping and stumbling on stones, but Mum seemed to be able to see in the dark. She didn't trip or hesitate – she just walked with an eerie sureness of foot, as if she knew this path and had walked it many times before.

I stopped a minute to catch my breath, trying to get my bearings. I've only been out of the grounds a few times since we arrived, walking Domino – usually I just take him down to the cottage with me. So although I've seen the lake from a distance, from near our big front gates, I'd never been out this far before. Suddenly, I saw where she was heading. The moon came back out – lit up the whole of the hillside.

There, at the top of the hill, was a tower. She was already halfway there.

As I struggled to catch up, I thought about what I knew about this tower. Precious little. But Dad had taken some photos there and showed them to me. "It's the oddest place, kitten," he'd said. "A folly. You'll have to go and take a look. No door. No windows. No way in, no way out. Must be solid. Just a solid tower with no purpose, with four nasty looking gargoyles on top."

As I reached the top of the hill, I looked up and saw two of these gargoyles, moonlit and gleaming against the sky. The other two were hidden round the far side of the tower. Ugly things with open mouths and bulging eyes, they stared outwards in two different directions – east and north. The north gargoyle had its scaly hands – or were they wings? – up to its eyes, as if peering intently through the dark.

It occurred to me that this north gargoyle faced our land, and I got the sudden impression that even though it was made of stone it could see our house and our gardens. And had been watching us, all the time.

But the thing that scared me the most was – now that I was standing right at the foot of the tower – I could hear voices. Not Mum's voice, not her humming. She wasn't humming at all now, anyway. She just stood at the base of the tower and stared back towards the lake. Her eyes were open, but now I saw why she'd been able to walk so calmly, so sure-footedly, even without a torch. Her eyes were glassy and fixed.

She was sleepwalking.

She didn't even notice me as I crept up to her. She just stared with those wide, eerie eyes into the darkness, towards the lake. And all around those voices rose and fell. Male voices, chanting, singing, speaking and then answering one another. Behind these sounds, another – a sort of low *shhhing*. Like... running water? But lots of water, not a trickle – a great body of water, whispering to itself. At first these sounds seemed to be coming from the air or the earth itself – but then I realised that they were echoing out of the gargoyle heads.

Even though I knew that wasn't possible, I stared up, looking for a way to *make* it possible. Maybe there was a space at the top of the tower where people could gather? A kind of hidden parapet all around? But even if there was, the sound of those people would be very different from this. Their chants would come straight out, cleanly, into the open air. As it was, it was as if the very depths of the tower were chanting.

I put my ear to the round wall. The sound intensified.

Men's low voices, mumbling strange words. Speaking and answering, and chanting. A low, echoey chant going on and on, but it was hard to understand the words. Something about the "time of dark choices", about the "eyes of the four compasses". Something about Yolandë. But the voices didn't sound as if they were coming from just the other side of this wall. They seemed far away, echoing – as if they were travelling from somewhere else and were being distorted along the way. It just didn't make sense.

Round the tower I went, puzzled, feeling my way. Nothing. Nothing but nettles that stung my hands, and the wind carrying those voices away, and a faint whistling hum from the top of the tower, like some giant was blowing across the neck of a bottle and making it vibrate.

I moved underneath the west gargoyle and heard the

voices rise and chant – "Yolandë, Yolandë!" Round to the south gargoyle, with its stone mouth wide open in a vicious snarl. Round to the east gargoyle, which seemed to have only one eye in the centre of its head. Back again, to the other side of where Mum stood, staring, her dressing gown flapping in the wind.

Then, as the wind dropped, I understand more words. They chilled me to the bone.

> *"Ours is for the Ouroborus!*
> *Ours is for to be empowered.*
> *Tooth to tail we chant in chorus –*
> *The innocent will be devoured!*
> *One is nought and One is dead,*
> *Because the tail is at the head!*
> *Ours is for the Inverted Law.*
> *Ours the jewel from Cimul's jaw."*

Mum heard them too.

At first, she just gave a small moan. I stood up then, went and stared up at her face, not knowing what to do. You should never wake a sleepwalker, I thought. Never. But how to take her away from this eerie place with that awful chanting, rising and rising?

When the chant began again, Mum looked up. She saw the gargoyles with their ugly mouths agape and their eyes wide open. Her lips began to move. I leaned closer, trying to hear what she was starting to whisper. It was the same words, and as the men's voices rose and grew in urgency, Mum's whisper also grew.

"Ours is for the Ouroborus! Ours is for to be empowered!" she said, and her voice grew too.

"Shh, Mum! No – they'll hear you!"

A huge, sickly feeling grew and grew in me, along with the voices and Mum's whispering. A feeling of danger, of evil. Whoever these men were, they met in secret and did not want to be seen or heard. Somehow they knew the way into the tower that had no doors and no windows. Somehow they met in a hidden place and chanted dreadful words. They must not hear Mum – they must not find us up here, eavesdropping.

"Mum! Wake up – be quiet! Oh, please be quiet!"

But she couldn't hear me at all. Her voice rose and rose and then abruptly stopped. But the voices of the men went on with the next line of the chant.

"The innocent will be devoured!"

Hearing those words, Mum gave a hideous scream. It echoed out over the lake, coming back creepily to where we stood.

The men's chant ceased abruptly. Then their voices rose, disturbed, confused, questioning – the sound of a gathering of people taken by surprise. They'd heard her.

I dragged her by the arms then, pulled her from the tower, pulled her back down the hill, quickly, quickly! But she kept stumbling and falling; she couldn't seem to hurry. I dragged her back down the slope towards the lake. Back into the mist around the still water. She stumbled and fell a dozen times, and each time it took her an age to get up and start again. I had to almost hold her up – her legs kept giving way.

"Come on, Mum! Stand up! Run!"

But it was too late. Someone was coming – but not from behind us, not from the tower. Our way was blocked. Someone stood in front of us. Someone with a torch.

I stopped still, hung on to Mum, panting and gasping for air. Footsteps came closer. Two sets of footsteps. Two beams from two torches.

"Jessica? And Elizabeth? What on *earth* are you doing out here?"

"Who are you?" I yelled, blinking into the torchlight.

"It's OK – it's only me – the doctor. Me and Ely. Here – give her to me." He strode forward and lifted Mum into his arms.

"What are you doing here?" I asked.

"Fishing," said the doctor. "This lake's full of pike. Ely, take my torch, help Jessica back."

The man called Ely took my arm to guide me back over the path. He was very old; his wrinkled face seemed kind and calm. But I saw no fishing rods in their hands, not a sign of fishing. And I realised the doctor was finding it hard to speak.

He was panting hard – they both were. They'd run here from somewhere else.

Had Dr Parker just lied to me?

Chapter Twelve

My Diary

The doctor gave Mum a tranquilliser and we put her to bed. And then in the kitchen Dad fussed about as he made cocoa, saying he'd never get over the shock of the four of us spilling through the door like that – it almost gave him a heart attack on his way to the bathroom! And the doctor asked Dad a lot of questions about how long Mum'd been sleepwalking, had she been having any headaches, any other funny behaviour at all?

Funny behaviour? I stared from the doctor to Ely and back to the doctor, my eyes seeing it all – those guarded looks, the closed-up faces. The jolly, bright smile of the doctor flashing on and off. He asked Dad whether we had any salve and made me put some on my nettle-stung hands. I watched him all the time I was rubbing it in.

"What bait were you using, Dr Parker?"

"Bait?" He took a sip of his cocoa.

"For your fishing. The pike."

"Oh, that. Mackerel, mostly. What about you, Ely?"

Ely nodded up from Mum's armchair, his eyes smiling my way. His eyes are very clear and blue – a forget-me-not blue. Disturbing. Baby-blue eyes in a wise man's face.

"Yes, mackerel. But I wasn't having much luck."

"So where are your rods?"

"Still on the lake bank," said Dr Parker. "We heard your mother scream and came running. Why do you ask?"

"Which bit of the lake? I mean, I'd just walked *past* the lake. I never saw you there!"

My voice sounded sullen, too suspicious. I knew it, but I couldn't seem to change it.

"No? Well, we were holed up in the reeds on the far side. Didn't see you either, come to that. Didn't even hear you. I expect that was because of the wind. It rustles those reeds all night long, enough to drive you mad."

"Yes, that'll be it," said Ely. "The wind, that's why we didn't hear you pass."

I stared from one to the other. I knew I looked sulky. I always get sulky when I think people are lying to me. Suddenly, the doctor put down his cup.

"What's up, Jess? Don't you believe us? What do you think we were doing out there in the dark then? Smuggling or something?"

All three men laughed, but I just went on staring.

"So why were you panting?"

"Panting?"

"Yes, panting. You were both panting like you'd been running."

"Jessica!" said Dad, looking horribly embarrassed by my accusations. "What on earth is the matter with you? I'm terribly sorry, doctor…"

But the doctor waved his apologies away. "Oh, don't you worry, she's had a bit of a shock, hearing her poor old mum yelling like that. It gave us a fright, let alone her! So we ran round the lake and helped them home. *Ran* round the lake, Jessica. We are not as young as we once were – Ely here is over eighty! I think we are entitled to sound a bit out of breath, don't you?"

Ely's blue, blue eyes nodded my way. He gave me a warm smile across the room. Then the doctor said I should get to bed, that was quite enough excitement for one night, and he'd come by first thing in the morning, see how Mum was getting along.

Dad saw them out, and just after he said goodbye and

was locking the back door, I glanced out of the kitchen window.

The doctor and Ely both walked a few paces down the garden path, then turned towards each other at the same moment. They stood still and stared with grim faces. Dr Parker shook his head.

Then they strode away into the darkness, and Dad came in to turn out the lights.

I slept really badly. I dreamed the gargoyles flew into my room and stole the epsilon bucket. It seemed so real that when I half woke, I grabbed the bucket and fell asleep again, the bucket by my side. But it was the same all night – all my dreams had terrible gargoyle faces in them, with stone mouths open and that dreadful chanting coming out. I kept waking up and putting on my globe lamp, feeling uneasy. I couldn't stop thinking about that north gargoyle, shielding its eyes with its hands – or were they wings? – staring my way. Bulging stone eyes, open all the time. Eyes that never close.

As soon as it was light, I gave up trying to sleep. I got dressed and picked up the bucket that had started all this. Just a bucket – yet a special bucket. I had a silly, sentimental feeling about it. Like I wanted to take it back to the cottage, return it to the place Epsilon had made it.

On an impulse, I gathered together a few bits and bobs and scooped them into it. Just my personal treasures, from under my bed. My fifty-pound note. Granny Libby's jet necklace. Mum's belemnite. The photo Dad took of me when I was six. Last year's letter from Baz, asking me to go out with him. And finally the packet of cigarettes – a goodbye gift from Avril. I laid them all in the bucket and covered them over with an old pillowcase. It'd be nice to hide them down at the cottage instead of under my bed. Much more secret.

I ran down to the cottage, feeling jittery all the way. But before I went into the house itself, I retraced my steps down the garden path. Over to the garden wall where I'd run to that first day, when Epsilon had rocked the rocking chair and scared me half to death.

I stood looking down at the little arrow carved at the base of the wall. This was the place Sebastian had buried the bucket, more than a hundred years ago. The place I'd dug it from, weeks ago now. Already it was overgrown with weeds, hidden. With a funny sense of satisfaction, I placed the bucket – with all the bits of junk – back into the hole I'd dug. I wedged it in and buried it over. It seemed fitting.

Like I was giving something back to Epsilon and to Sebastian.

And now that I'm here in Epsilon's room, I'm trying hard to tell myself I feel safer. But I keep coming back to the fact that I'm not sure really who Epsilon is at all.

All I know is that a group of islanders met last night somehow at that closed-up tower and chanted horrible words about being devoured, and about tails and heads and something called the Ouroborus. Someone on this island knows many secrets and is looking for the same thing as me – Epsilon had said so. Looking for the answer to the same questions. About something ancient, Epsilon said. But Epsilon himself could be leading me astray. What is he – a ghost? A spirit? A teenage computer hacker? A wise old man?

I thought of Ely with his bright-blue eyes. Maybe Ely *was* Epsilon? His face was very kind and calm. Full of wisdom even. But Ely had – I suspected – been at the tower, along with Dr Parker, muttering about the time of dark choices. Or had they?

Maybe they had been fishing for pike after all? Hiding in the reeds on the far side – it was at least possible. I saw a show on TV about fishing once, and the way the anglers sneaked about on those riverbanks was ridiculous, as if the fish were snipers with AK rifles and any minute they'd all be killed by a fishy bullet.

Death by pike. I giggled, then caught my breath. Even the sound of my own voice unnerved me. Overwrought. Paranoid. Crazy.

I lit all the candles – all twelve of them – and sat in their soft mellow light, thinking. Calm down, calm down. You are safe here, I told myself. Then I went over to Epsilon's desk and opened the bottom drawer.

There were the three identical boxes, except one was now empty. I reached for the cool silver key and opened the second box.

Inside was a sheaf of pages – Sebastian's diary papers – the longest entry yet. At a glance, I saw that he was writing his diary while copying down an ancient myth of the island. At first, his writing was just the same as ever – scrawly, spidery, but tidy and evenly spaced. But the longer he wrote, the more his writing changed and got tighter and smaller and more sloping on the page. Until in the end it was all over the place.

Once again I settled into the hammock and began to read.

It will be a long night, from the sounds of it. Nobody has so far slept, what with the wind howling fit to take the roof off, and the thrashing of the rain at every casement.

Papa greatly dislikes the thunder; he says it gives him his "storm headache". And Mama, of course, is terrified of any loud noise.

But from my bedchamber, high in the house, I can watch the lightning over the whole ocean. Any boats out in that water will surely perish, for the waves boil and surge as high as the Miradel, as far as the eye can see. But mercifully, I cannot see any little boats. Just the grey sea heaving. The lightning seems to burst downward from its clouds like hands, jabbing their fingers into the water.

Papa has coughed and harrumphed for three hours straight. Earlier, I heard him call out to Mama to fetch his headache remedy.

"Where are you, woman? My head is fit to burst!" called he, thinking not at all of her fear and quaking, but only of how she could serve him in his own distress.

Mama gave no reply, so I shivered my way down to the scullery and found his wretched remedy at last (behind the pudding basin) and carried it up to him. He thanked me not a bit, but snatched it from me and slammed the door in my face, his eyes as black as devils.

Even from where I stood I could smell the brandy.

Mama gives no answer to my knocking on her door, even though I have knocked as loud as I dared. I will go to her in another hour by the clock. I will take her some strong China tea, for I noticed that the range was still just glowing in the kitchen and it will take short work with the bellows to get up a lively flame. But not quite yet. I will let her hide her head under the pillows until the worst is over.

Meanwhile, I find myself drawn here, to the small library. I have set my candle on the tiny shelf table. There are no curtains in here, just broken, gappy shutters that creaked and groaned when I closed them. But still the gusts of wind reach in, setting the candle flame flaring and leaping. So I must light two, lest a solitary one dies on me and I find myself in utter darkness, unable to find the door. The very thought of this makes my mouth go dry.

This room is chilly indeed. No fire has been lit in here for many a year, judging by the skeins of cobwebs hanging thick above the grate. Papa allows no one in here, although I have never discovered why. Sometimes, the menfolk of the island come to the parlour and talk with him about old things. Men come from far away too, farther than the mainland. They talk about myths and the old tales – then Papa comes up here and fetches curly maps for them to pore over downstairs. These men oftentimes take books away or bring books back. But he lets no one in – just briefly visits this room himself, and never asks Mama to have the fire lit.

So I have taken the fringed silk covering from the armchair and wrapped myself up. It is bright gold and crimson, quite as fine as any prince's cloak from Persia – so I can study these old books and maps very cosily. There are rows and rows of old tomes here, many with intriguing titles and gold-edged pages. Two catch my eye especially: 'The Mythology of the Small Islands' is one, and 'The Cartography of Lume' another.

And so I shall discover more and will copy into my journal whatsoever I find, in readiness to ask Epsilon tomorrow.

If the morrow will ever come, that is, and this infernal night end!

Long ago, the mythology says, Lume was a gentle place, inhabited by seals and ermine and wild birds. These creatures dwelled in the caves and holes in the cliffs, and they made their own wild music.

But there came an ancient time when a great

king rose up in that place. His name was L'Ume, and his heart was filled with melody. So wondrous was his music that it was given a name – the Lumic.

L'Ume's rule was perfect, and he made his kingdom perfect. So his subjects loved him greatly.

Just now – a great crash came! I leaped to my feet, and the wind rattled the shutters so violently that BOTH candles almost expired. So I have stolen the lamp from the dining room and now sit here in a steadier shine. The candles I have also left lit, strangely reluctant to be in any gloom. I fear that a tree has come down in the garden, but have no wish to open the shutters again to look out.

And L'Ume sang songs so enchanting that the creatures of the sea would gather all around the shores to hear them. Whales and porpoises and dolphins would swim close to listen. And some say they sing those songs still, one to another, deep under the oceans. And, says the book, "that is why the island is steeped in such powers, and why on its shores to this day can be heard the singing of the ancient songs of L'Ume, with all their peculiar beauty".

I have never heard this singing. But Master Cork told me once that some of the old ones in the village have heard it when the sun is setting and the sky red. They have come back from the shore entranced, unable to speak because of what they have heard.

Now into this time came one subject, young and vigorous. He was beloved of King L'Ume, who made him into a prince. The king taught him much of his music and some of his beauty. The prince grew lordly, with high bearing and a haughty head. But he also grew restless.

He was jealous of L'Ume's melodies! He wanted his own music to enchant the whale and the porpoise and to be carried by them into the depths of the sea.

The chimney is wailing. In the cold hearth, old ashes stir and resettle. It is as if someone is stirring them with an invisible poker. Who sat here before that fire long ago, in this room where nobody comes? Whose old books are these, that men come from far and wide to open them for their secrets? Maybe I am intruding? I wish Epsilon was here. Sometimes, he arrives of a sudden – I look around and there he is. Just as easily, he vanishes away again into nothing. As fearful as I am of him, I do so hate to be solitary in this creaking room.

So the haughty prince crept alone one night, deep into the hidden tunnels of the island. He sat behind a veil of water and dwelled on his hatred. And he devised a plan that would turn the whole of L'Ume's kingdom inside out.

The wind shrieks. The cobwebs above the grate belly out... in... out. I sit shivering before a great oval looking glass, and in it my right hand becomes my left hand.

As the prince sat alone in the dark bowels of Lume, his hair grew long. His teeth grew into fangs and his heart grew sour. He knew that his own melody had no enchantment. Since he could never match the Lumic, he sought instead to invert it. So he sang a new song – a Song of Inversion.

Then out of the prince's mouth came a song so monstrous that the great creatures of the sea rolled in terror and the seas rose up. For the song held only unspeakable ugliness. And that is why we call *him Prince Cimul – or the Lord of Inversion – for he dared to invert the beauty of the Lumic.*

Cimul – the Lord of Inversion! This name stirs me strangely. I feel hot and chilled at once. There is no space between the lightning and its thunder. They arrive together. In the face of the looking glass I am captured, a bright-lit scribe.

So out crept the Inverter from the secret seams of the earth, and he broadcast it far and wide, in cunning whispers, that L'Ume's kingdom was anyone's for the taking! He planted his vile song – the Cimul – into the ears of all.

Yet look – the lamp! It throws my own shape large against the wall. I am a grey giant with a grey quill, scribbling on a grey parchment. Then the lightning cracks and lights me up again, scribbling. There are two scribes – one bright, one dark!

So a great unrest rose up, and a hunger not known before – a hunger for the songs of the dark. This is why we call him the Dark Peril.

That feeling is back again – that I am being watched. I swivel around. I cannot seem to stop doing it, looking for something I dread to see. It is as if there are eyes in the walls, at the shutters – as if someone peers in at me from all sides. But such fanciful thoughts will not help me with my history of Lume. Enough, Sebastian! Write!

Then Cimul walked out on to Long Beach, and he challenged King L'Ume outright.

"Look," said he. "Your subjects have never before had two songs warring within them – they have only known the Lumic! But I have created the Cimul, and your people are no longer at rest. So ask them, one by one – whom would you serve? The king who brings them one song – or the prince who brings them choice?"

The gaps between the thunderclaps are longer now. In his room, Papa coughs and paces – the level in the brandy decanter will be falling. And a new sound – very soft – what is that? It is coming from along the corridor. A footfall? But now the thunder is back; it drowns it out. It is my fear anyway, only my own fear.

Then all of Lume quivered, as did the mighty sea creatures swimming and listening. They waited for the king to stand and slay this Cimul, the Lord of Inversion. But he did not. Instead, King L'Ume raised his hands up to the sky. His beautiful hand was scarred by ugly marks – tooth marks, as from a vicious bite.

I am not imagining it! Footsteps approach, soft sounds, like someone creeping along the corridor. No, no!

And this utterance came from the mouth of the king: "My beautiful heart is breaking, on this Day of Dark Inversion. But let each one now decide, and then live with his deciding in the coming days, whichever it may be."

Then each mortal turned their back either on Cimul or upon the king, who alone had ruled them all. So Cimul gathered a great army that day, the day King L'Ume let each decide.

I am a grey scribe, listening, listening. Then the lightning flashes and the bright scribe turns and listens. I am split in two. And I swear it – the sound comes nearer, soft along the corridor. No, no! I must dip into the ink, I must write. Here I am, dipping my quill into the ink. I will ignore it all.

But King L'Ume still had his hands raised high, and lightning forked from his fingers. The lightning reached out to Cimul, and as it smote him in the mouth, King L'Ume said these words:

**"From your mouth has come this
inversion of innocence.
Now in the name of Agapetos I declare you bound:
Nothing else can you plunder, from this day!
Only that gifted to you by innocent hands
will you possess!
Your tooth has been your weaponry,
and I tear it from your jaw!"**

In the garden, a crashing, a mighty tumbling. My eyes seem to see through the shutters: the wooden bench has been torn from its plinth; it rolls over and over; it splinters into the orchard wall. In the corridor – silence.

At the sound of the name Agapetos, Cimul screamed a terrible scream. Then out of his open mouth fell one tooth, sharp as a dagger, and it fell to the sand on Long Beach. Cimul turned tail and fled then, and all his followers fled with him, on to Coscoroba Rock.

They start again – the footsteps. They are coming closer; they are very stealthy. Write! Write!

But one of Cimul's followers – a foolish youth – reached back to snatch the tooth and carried it to his prince. This was the very first time the tooth was "gifted" unto him. Cimul raised it high in triumph and sang this cursing song in reply:

> *"If we possess the tooth, we too can curse.*
> *If we can curse, we too can rule.*
> *If we can rule, we too can misrule.*
> *Long live the Inverter, Lord Cimul."*

My heart leaps in my chest, it bangs so! I cannot open that door to see who is approaching. I can only scribble, faster, faster.

But Cimul had forgotten the faithful listeners, the creatures of the sea. And as Cimul raised the tooth high above Coscoroba Rock, a shining porpoise leaped from the waves – and caught it in his jaws.

Write write write I am not listening not listening not listening.

Then the dolphin and the whale and the porpoise carried the tooth deep into the secret places under the ocean, where its powers of cursing lie hidden to this day...

A sigh – just now – right outside the door –

Yet some say that Cimul's followers are rising up in force, are gathering once again, to find the tooth and invoke the cursings Prince Cimul spoke over it...

Enough! No more! It is written. And the storm is done also. From outside – silence. From behind the door – silence. My hand shakes so, I can barely write.

IT IS NOT REAL, ANY OF IT! It is a story, a legend,

written in a quaking room in a quaking house in the middle of a terrible storm. That is all. It is just a myth. I will open the door now. I will open the door calmly, and there will be no pale eyes there, watching. There will be nothing waiting – no dark creatures crouched there, gathered.

I will say a word to help me do it. A word, to make me brave.

The word will be 'Agapetos'.

Go now, Sebastian.

Chapter Thirteen

THERE ARE TWO MEMBERS IN THE CHAT ROOM:	Jess
	Avril

AVRIL: So what *did* he find when he opened the door?

JESS: Dunno. Haven't even found that bit yet.

AVRIL: You're seriously telling me that all these spooky things are about a fang? A *tooth*?

JESS: Apparently.

AVRIL: And who do you think the men are? The men meeting in secret at the tower thing?

JESS: Not sure. But from what they were saying, they are up to no good.

AVRIL: Jess. You sound like an Enid Blyton story.

JESS: Avril. This is no story.

AVRIL: *The Island of Adventure!*

JESS: I'm scared.

AVRIL: No need to be scared.

JESS: No?

AVRIL: Noooo. Just make sure you have lots of yummy picnics and wash everything down with lashings of ginger beer – then it will all come right in the end. According to the gospel of Enid Blyton.

JESS: I HATE IT WHEN YOU DO THIS!

AVRIL: Well, come *on*! Every time I talk to you, you go on and on about ancient myths and ghosts, and here am I expelled from school again and what do you care?

JESS: You've been *expelled*?

AVRIL: Yesterday.

JESS: Why?

AVRIL: Drinking. Smoking. Usual things. Not that you care.

JESS: But I didn't know! How can I care if I didn't know? That's not fair.

AVRIL: Not fair? All you talk about is yourself and your spooky new mates, and you never even ask about me at all. Why should I tell you – you don't care about me – it's all you, you, you.

JESS: I'm sorry, Avril. Really. I'm just so – freaked out.

AVRIL: Can I remind you of something? Like, why we all

fell out with you last spring?

JESS: I'm not sure I want to hear this.

AVRIL: Hard luck. We all got so sick of you going on and on and on about yourself. Your life, your mum and her stupid affair, on and on and on. You might be the centre of your own little universe, Jessica White, but you are not the centre of mine. Thank God or I'd die of utter boredom. You are the most boring person I have ever, *ever* met.

AVRIL HAS LEFT THE CHAT ROOM

E: Ouch! I saw that!

JESS: Go away.

E: No. I have to show you a picture. A round picture. In a square frame. Down at the cottage.

JESS: A picture? Don't tell me – another snippet of the whole. Why can't I see it all at once, instead of this stupid... *puzzle*?!

E: Sometimes jigsaws are entirely necessary.

JESS: Epsilon. Read my lips. I do not like jigsaw puzzles. I do not like any jigsaws. I especially do not like this jigsaw. This jigsaw freaks me out.

E: Nevertheless, you are as involved as Sebastian was.

JESS: Oh, and you really cared about him, didn't you! I mean – where were you when he needed you? Poor little boy, stuck in a scary library with dark things creeping down the corridors. Where were you?

E: Working elsewhere.

JESS: On the island? This horrible, spooky island?

E: On the island.

JESS: Which reminds me – what is that tower thing? And who are the men I heard doing all that horrible chanting?

E: They are workers of the Dark Ones who are watching you. They sense that the time of dark choices has arrived again. They sense that their ancient relic has come to light again – the tooth. It has been lost for many, many years now. They want it.

JESS: So… this is all about a tooth?

E: <<sigh>> Not at all. It's all about a *curse*. They want to invoke the old curses spoken *over* the tooth.

JESS: I get it. Not.

E: You will. Just stay close to me.

JESS: Oh, yeah! Right! How the hell do I stay close to someone I've never met? Get real.

E: Use your mind. And go to the small library. Tonight.

JESS: The small library?

E: I believe that's what I said.

JESS: Tonight?

E: I believe that's also what I said.

JESS: Alone?

E: I believe I did not actually say that. But the inference was there – yes.

JESS: Are you *kidding*? You must think I'm crazy!

E: You'll be fine. I will protect you.

JESS: You'll be there?

E: In a sense.

JESS: <<sigh>>

E: It shouldn't take you long anyway. Just go and look for the other book.

JESS: Other book?

E: I wish you would stop repeating everything I say. The other book – the one Sebastian didn't have time to read.

JESS: The cartography thingummy?

E: The very same. It's time for maps. Talking of which – you are not a hermit, you know! Tsk tsk! Lazy girl!

JESS: What's that supposed to mean?

E: You should get out more. Go for a walk. Get some exercise.

JESS: So. You want me to find a map of Lume? Then go and explore?

E: You are learning.

JESS: Wow, thanks. Anything else?

E: Yes. Take a bit of interest in your mother's artwork.

JESS: Mum's artwork? You cannot be serious! After all the panic it's causing? Have you *heard* my dad lately? He's foaming at the mouth!

E: I fail to see why.

JESS: You're a little slow, aren't you – for an invisible being? She is supposed to be a PORTRAIT PAINTER!

E: So?

JESS: Well – it's her career! It's what we live on! Not all this weird black and white stuff!

E: You disappoint me. You sound just like your father.

JESS: <<..............................>>

E: I see I have hit a raw nerve.

JESS: <<..............................>>

E: Well – you DO sound like him!

JESS: Oh, just SHUT UP!

JESS HAS LEFT THE CHAT ROOM

Chapter Fourteen

My Diary

Epsilon is driving me absolutely crackers! But I suppose he's right.

First – Mum's artwork.

Always before, it's been portraits. Men, women, children, pets. People pay a small fortune for them. Her desk is littered with photographs sent from all over the world. She peers at them through magnifying glasses; she paints them, huge and exact. Japanese girls in blue silks. Toddlers in kilts and sporrans. Grandmothers holding tiny babies. She paints them all, muttering. ("I wish they'd take their ridiculous glasses off! How am I expected to see their eyes? It's all reflection!" and "Oh, *no* – not another Polaroid!")

But lately, all that stuff has disappeared. The tools of

her trade – gone. Which is why Dad's panicking. It's the money, really – his photos just bring in peanuts, and he knows it. He's always desperately trying to win some famous photography prize, but he never quite manages it. So he worries about money all the time.

Anyway, it started two days ago. All the paraphernalia of paints, tubes, brushes, turpentine – vanished. Just one minute brush left – an eyelash of a brush, I kid you not! And a single pot of black drawing ink. She keeps making funny little sketches in black. But she won't show me those. Yet she leaves the others all over the place – the ones of that haunting face. A woman's face, staring through strands of cloud or cloth or something. The same face, over and over.

"What's up, Mum? Where's all your portrait stuff?"

That shrug. That sigh.

"Nothing's *up*. Just felt like a change."

"So who's this woman then?"

"No one. Just an idea. Leave me alone."

Later, I noticed the tubes, photos, the half-finished grandma – all bundled together in the bin. Mum! Who freaks out if I move one tiny paintbrush one centimetre along the desk!

It's as if these storms have got inside the house somehow

and swept through her studio. The garden has the same look – the trees scoured bare, the lawn a mess of strewn boughs and clothespegs plucked from the washing line. The wheelbarrow, upside-down in the mud. Even the wooden bench, smashed to smithereens against the orchard wall.

As for Dad, he's actually just as bad. He's been jabbering on for two days about a swan on the lake – a black swan. *Click-click whirr* – he puts in a new roll of film, winds it, dashes back out again. He must have filled ten million rolls by now – all for one swan! Big deal.

I think they're both cracking up. I really do.

Meanwhile, I sift through this growing file, sort the clues, re-read Seb's diary pages.

It's all right for Epsilon. He's fine and dandy, floating around or whatever it is he does, safe and sound! Me – I feel stalked.

All I can really gather is this: somewhere there is an old relic – a tooth – from a mythical being called Cimul. The ever-helpful-stupid Epsilon said that it's not the tooth that matters – it's the curse. So. Let's see.

King L'Ume cursed the tooth he'd zapped from Cimul's jaw. His curse also said that Cimul could never again *steal* anything – he had to be *given it* freely, in order to possess it.

And Cimul spoke another curse: that if he and his followers possessed the tooth, they would use it in order to rule.

So whose curse is THE curse? The one that this is all about?

Pass.

Anyway, old L'Ume sent a bolt of lightning and Cimul's tooth dropped out and then a kleptomaniac porpoise, of all things, grabbed it and took it under the sea and now dark thingies are looking for it.

Well, all that might be high on Epsilon's agenda, but it's not the highest thing on mine. Like… staying sane is! Because whatever's happening to me now happened to Sebastian, last century. And Seb seems to be somewhat losing it.

And Mum seems to be obsessed with shells. Just like Seb's mama. But why are they both collecting shells? Why shells? Are they both cracking up?

But I suppose the tooth does keep cropping up in the documents. Let's see… how many times so far?

1. In 'The Key'.

> *In the space below the well*
> *A map to the **tooth** lies hidden.*

The space is marked by an infidel
Whose hand reveals what's bidden.

Through merrow hair
In Neptune's lair
Past thirty fingers pale –
Then hark for a river in the dark
And reach for the spout of the whale!

So the tooth is hidden somewhere under a well. No, no. The *map* to the tooth is hidden under a well. Which well? *The* well, it says. Unhelpfully.

2. In 'The Ballad of Yolandë'. This is a bit more vague, but...

Winter's wrath will fade.
I search for the sweet **tooth**
Of the honeyed summer—
All the treasures of her pale fingers of wheat.

Which, when you link it in with her hidden message, ties in with:

I stir in my wrath
For the treasures of the deep
Are hidden from my eyes.

So she appears to be looking for something, and it seems to be the tooth. But who is Yolandë anyway?

3. The chant I heard at the tower:

Ours is for the Ouroborus!
Ours is for to be empowered.
Tooth *to tail we chant in chorus,*
The innocent will be devoured!
One is nought and One is dead,
Because the tail is at the head!
Ours is for the Inverted Law.
Ours the jewel from Cimul's jaw.

So – two mentions of 'tooth' again. But what is an Ouroborus?

Pass. But at least I can now link up these tower men to the myth that Sebastian wrote down. "Ours the jewel from Cimul's jaw." Cimul was the haughty prince, the Lord of Inversion. The jewel from his jaw is obviously the tooth, lost now under the sea.

But Epsilon had said that these tower men are workers of the Dark Ones. That they sense the relic has come to light somewhere. I wonder...

If the relic was hidden for years and years under the sea, maybe it's been washed to shore? Maybe it has finally just turned up, dislodged from under the sea, and now is lying somewhere on the beach?

Hang on... beach. Shore.

OH, I GET IT!

At least – I get one tiny bit of it! What do you find on a beach? What is brought on to the shore, all the time, by the tide? Shells! And who has been sifting through shells since all this began? Mum – and Seb's mama before her.

Both mothers are somehow trying to find the relic on the shore.

But who told them to? The mysterious Yolandë? Is that why Mum hums that same tune over and over? Is it the same tune Seb's mama sings, the one he knows well? That would make sense. Seb has heard the tune – sitting at the hearth of Master Cork while he carves the pole for the Aroundy dance, ready for the Greet. His Coscoroba, he called it. And Mama sings the same ballad – 'The Ballad of Yolandë' – night after night in her rooms. And now Mum is humming a tune, over and over. Is that also 'The Ballad of

Yolandë'? I wish I could find a copy of the music, then I could compare the tune.

And the face that Mum draws, over and over? It must be Yolandë – surely? But who *is* Yolandë? Oh, it's driving me crazy. All I know is, whoever it is, they have somehow involved both mothers in all this.

4. Finally, scribbled in English – not symbols – on the back of the document called 'The Key':

> *Lemon Sq*
> *Galeria 5*
> *Cloves – **tooth***

B-I-G S-I-G-H!

The other thing is the name Agapetos. I knew I'd come across that before, and sure enough, I found it at last – in Sebastian's very first diary entry:

As Agapetos is my witness, *so signed by my hand, this fourteenth day of July, in the year of our Lord eighteen hundred and ninety-four. Sebastian Wren, aged thirteen years.*

So Sebastian knew about Agapetos before he read the history, and used the name not just to "make himself brave" but to bear witness to the truth of his writings and diary. So, to Sebastian at least, Agapetos was no myth – he was real.

(I wish Dad would stop knocking on my door. *When* will he ever get the message? I've told him a zillion times! If he knocks and I don't answer, it's because I DON'T WANT HIM TO COME IN! Mum doesn't even knock – she waltzes straight in. They are both driving me insane.)

Talking about gathering shells – Mum was at it again this morning. Only this time she didn't even dump the bag out into Dad's hollyhocks. No.

She tipped the whole lot out on to the kitchen table, yakking away all the time as if it was normal! When Dad jumped to his feet (toast in one hand, butter knife in the other), she stared at him in astonishment. As if *he'd* just done something weird!

"Whatever's the matter with you lately, Richard? You're so... odd!"

Dad stared at her as if she was crazy. Which she is. "Odd! *I'm* odd?!"

She watched a blob of butter slide slowly off his knife,

tsked and wiped it carefully away with her napkin. Among all that mess!

"Yes, Richard – odd. Dashing off at all hours to photograph ridiculous swans. Jessica, close your mouth. You look quite foolish."

Dad and I stared down at the tablecloth. Shells, stones, bits of seaweed and sand. Sand everywhere, even in the butter dish.

Dad lost it. "Well, I do beg your *pardon*, Elizabeth! I mean to say, I thought it was quite normal to sit at the table and eat breakfast, I thought that was what tables were for – didn't you, Jess?"

"Don't bring me into it!"

"But no! I am quite wrong, quite *odd* in fact. After all, what is normal about a wildlife photographer photographing wildlife? Very weird, I do agree. Whereas your behaviour is most rational. O*ho*, here comes Mrs Neptune carrying half the beach! By all means, dear, come and tip it all over the breakfast table. Be my guest, I mean to *say*!"

I was staring down at the tablecloth, fascinated. From under a piece of seaweed a minute crab scuttled, tapped its tiny pincers together, then froze. A second later, another, which ran and hid under a spoon.

Mum saw me staring and looked down. She clicked her tongue and a look of huge concern came over her face. Then she reached down and picked them up – one, two – one in each hand, delicately, between thumb and forefinger.

"Silly little things… let me take you back!" she said. Then she was gone, and Dad hurled his toast against the clock and stabbed the butter knife right into the bread, where it stuck like a dagger in a head.

"Blasted *women*!" he yelled. "I'm going out!" And he did.

So I sat there alone and stared down at the scattering of coastal specimens. It looked like a school nature table. Then I began to laugh. I laughed till I cried, till tears rolled down my cheeks. I mean, miniature crustaceans and marmalade! I kept thinking of Avril and her wacky baccy. My parents don't need drink and drugs – they're spaced-out enough on their own little planet as it is.

(Oh, hell! It's no good – he's back. I will kill him if he won't stop knocking on my door. Back later.)

Back already. Well, it wasn't Dad. It wasn't anyone! Just a neat little posy on the floor. Five tiny white flowers and one big black feather stuck in.

A peace offering from Epsilon? Awwww! But maybe also a nudge. A bit of a prod. "I need to show you a picture," he'd said. "A round picture in a square frame. Down at the cottage." And while I'm there, I may as well have a look at that kitchen floor.

To say nothing of trying to unlock the third box, to see if it will open. You never know.

Chapter Fifteen

My Diary

But I never did get the chance to open the third box. Not just then anyway.

By that time I couldn't even have picked up a key – let alone fitted it into a tiny lock! My hands were shaking too much to be able to do *anything*. They still are. But I'm getting ahead of myself.

It was odd that all the way there I felt so uneasy. Different. Not just watched – that feeling's there most of the time now. It's hard to explain, but I felt like a watch spring that was being wound tighter and tighter. A sense of urgency that was getting bigger.

I must have looked round a dozen times, expecting to see someone following me. But there was only Domino, leaping about, sniffling for rabbits. He seemed fine, so I told myself it was just me, just my imagination – like poor old Sebastian getting freaked out in the small library.

It's a bit cooler now, after the storm. But only a bit. The cottage kitchen is always cooler than the bedroom – it must be the stone floor that does it. Talking of which, Epsilon had specifically told me to take a closer look at it. So that's where I began.

At first, nothing seemed obvious. Just a floor made of small stone slabs. But wait – not stone exactly. Not like the stone of the walls. More like... slate?

Also, the slate slabs were not very big at all – not wide and long, like floor slabs usually are. These were smaller – small squares of slate, each one only about twenty centimetres across.

It seemed an odd, fussy way to lay a floor. I felt there was something I was missing here – that the floor had been laid like this for a reason.

I couldn't see the whole of the floor until I'd moved stuff to one side. The rocking chair. The heavy table – it took me ages to shift that. Then the two faded rugs at the far end – I dragged them out of the back door and temporarily dumped them in the garden. Then I went back inside and looked all round.

Then I saw them. Here and there, in the floor, were little

indentations or shallow bumps. Kneeling down, I peered at one more closely. A curly thing, lodged in the slate, about the width of my hand. Tiny coils, all snuggled together in the slate.

Fossils.

I thought back to Mum's book on fossils, the one she'd used to identify the belemnite. (The usual wave of dislike swept over me as I thought of her. *Oh, wow. A baby stone carrot. Why can't she give me a CD, like other mums?*) These fossils weren't long and thin like the belemnite, but round and coiled up. Ammonites. The remains of shelled creatures, fallen into the silt millions of years ago. Lots of them – but not dotted about evenly at all.

They were roughly in two groups. One group spanned one corner of the room, the other the opposite corner. The spacing of each group seemed random. Nevertheless, I got the distinct feeling that the layouts of the two groups were quite deliberate, with that definite gap between them.

Staring at the floor, I suddenly wondered if the reason the slabs were cut so small was so that the floor could be more easily laid into this pattern. Some of the ammonites were quite close together. This would be hard to do if you were working with large slabs of slate, each with just the odd fossil in it. So the slate would have to be cut smaller, the ammonites carved out of the larger pieces and joined together to make the pattern work.

But what was the pattern? Looked like nothing to me.

I shrugged, baffled. All I could do, I decided, was to copy down the spacing of the fossils and put it in the box file, in case it was important.

So I did just that – had to stand on the table, risking my neck, to get a decent overview. But I managed it in the end.

So here are the two sets of patterns from the kitchen floor. One a set of ten fossils, the other a set of nine.

THE AMMONITE FLOOR

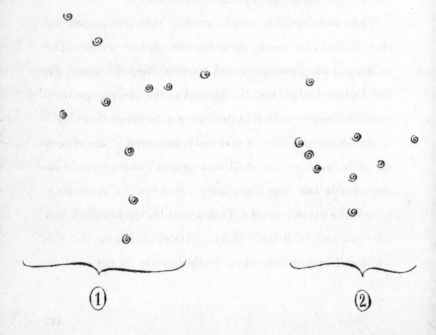

When I'd finished and had replaced the rugs, I had a slow prowl all around. "I like ancient things," Epsilon had said. Now, as I looked around, I saw that the place was crammed with them. On shelves and in corners, stuffed everywhere in fact, were things made long ago by the earth itself. Things made over millions of years, formed below ground.

A huge lump of fossilised wood, with the scales of a pine tree clearly etched into it.

A split-open rock with what looked like purple quartz inside.

A big wobbly blob of fossilised lava, laid on a shelf as if at any minute it would pour off and drip to the floor.

A long slender stalactite, laid along the top of the bookcase.

And – on the large shelf – a carving I'd not noticed before, dusty and dark. It was a dark piece of oak, as big as my head, and carved into a perfect letter O. The whole thing felt heavy and dense when I picked it up, and had an unusual feel to it. "Bog oak," I whispered to myself. But so perfectly carved into that smooth circle.

Was it the letter O? Or was it a number – zero? Maybe Epsilon just liked round things. Round ammonites. Round rugs. Round pictures on the walls.

Suddenly, I remembered what I'd come here for. "A round picture in a square frame." I turned my attention to the pictures on the walls. Down in the kitchen – pictures of herbs and plants with long Latin names. All the pictures were round, but none was held in a square frame.

So I came up to the bedroom and saw it at once.

Just above the star charts, sitting all alone. A large round picture in a square golden frame. I went closer and lifted it down from the wall. I dusted off the glass and stared.

It was nothing. I mean – nothing like I'd expected. Disappointing. Just a circle painted in gold on a black background. Again, the middle was missing from the circle. Just a letter O, drawn in gold. The same shape as the carved O downstairs.

I stared at it, wondering. Something kept stirring at the back of my mind. Not just one thing – several things. As if I'd come across a reference to this shape quite a few times, but couldn't quite bring them to the front of my mind.

The frame was getting heavy. So I carried the whole thing over on to the hammock. As I tilted it to heave it on, I noticed something on the back. Another picture. Another circular thing. But this time done in *black* on a *gold* background. The same image, but with its colours in reverse.

I laid it flat on the hammock and bent over it. It was a snake. But a snake curved into a perfect letter O. Only not quite perfect – I could see that now.

There was a tiny gap in between the head and the open mouth. The mouth had fangs curving out of it, and the snake in the picture was about to eat its own tail. Two words were written in scaly lettering under the snake:

The Ouroborus

Looking at that snake made me feel sick and weary. The very air seemed thick and grey. And there was something else. The distinct feeling of a pair of eyes on me. Not the usual feeling of being watched at all. The absolute certainty that I was no longer alone in this room. That someone else was in here with me and was now staring at my back.

Slowly, I turned round. It was by the desk.

The shape of a man. A tall man, standing still and staring straight at me. He was all dressed in dark shadows.

One hand rested lightly on the desk. Just hovered there, as lightly as a fallen leaf lies on the surface of water. But the eyes of this man were not like any eyes I have ever seen.

"Welcome," he said.

What do you do when you see a ghost? Or a spirit, or a being from another time, or whatever he is? I don't know what anyone else would do. I just know what I did.

I screamed. Then I clapped my hand to my mouth.

"Do not be scared," he said. "My name is Epsilon. I see you've found it at last."

He pointed towards the snake picture then looked at me with enquiring eyes.

I nodded too. (Yes-I've-found-the-snake-picture-now-go-away-because-I-think-I'm-having-a-heart-attack.)

He moved towards me. But it wasn't ordinary 'moving' at all. It was like watching shadows gather in a cloud. All the edges of him were fuzzy, like he was trailing whips of mist behind him.

He bent down and lifted up the picture. He turned the Ouroborus side towards me, then the O side, then back to the Ouroborus.

"Notice," he said, "the one is the inversion of the other. This fact will be important for you. That is the only reason I have allowed the image of the Ouroborus in here."

He replaced it on its hook – with the snake side facing the wall. "But we can at least turn its face away," he said. "I much prefer *this* side to the other. Don't you?"

I blinked. Nodded. Stared.

He walked over to the window and looked out over the sea. Even as I stared at him, he seemed to be evaporating. Getting even fainter. He gazed out of the window for a moment, and even though his eyes stared only at the sea, I got the feeling he was actually seeing something else. Seeing many things. Then he turned back to me.

"Your father is at the lake, taking a photograph you need to see," he said. "Your mother is in her studio, drawing something you must find. It is time for you to return to the Big House."

I cleared my throat, tried to speak. It came out in a strangled little squeak. "Now?"

"Now."

I stood up, my legs very shaky. I still couldn't take my eyes off him. He was there – yet he was not there. I couldn't see anything about him clearly at all, like his clothes or his hair. Just shadows, moving all the time. And even as I stood up, he was getting fainter. All except his eyes.

His eyes were still clear. They shone. They were like – oh, I don't know. Like deep water. Or crystals – like the lights inside crystals. Clear and multifaceted and hard to look away from.

As the rest of him faded, his eyes went on looking at me,

until they were all that was left. Those disembodied eyes stared at me for a long, long moment. Then they too vanished.

I burst into tears and ran sobbing down the stairs and out. I cried with sheer terror all the way home.

Chapter Sixteen

My Diary

Bedtime

So I didn't get to unlock the third box – not just then. Right now, I feel like I'll never go back to that cottage again. I mean, there is scared and there is *terrified*. Epsilon appearing like that almost made my heart stop. I want this to end now – whatever this stupid quest is. I never asked for it anyway, didn't want anything like this to happen to me. Why me?

"Because of your mother," Epsilon had said.

And that's another thing. His thoughts. Things he's said to me in the chat room. They keep intruding, they keep sliding in and out of my head. Like he's got inside my head somehow and reminds me of things there. Prods me. Prods me into a direction I'm not sure I want to go.

Earlier, when I got back to my attic room, I still couldn't

stop shaking. I kept thinking of the bucket. The bucket that started all this.

The epsilon symbol and his name had been there on the base, as clear as day – until Dr Parker picked up the bucket and read them there. He'd gone very still and intent – like he recognised the word 'Epsilon'. So what has the doctor got to do with all this? And Ely – who is Ely anyway? I mean, what does he do on the island? Were they both really there at the tower that night? If so, why? They seemed to be summoning something. A rite. A spell. This made me smile. Ridiculous – the very thought of Dr Parker muttering spells! Get a grip, Jess.

Thinking of the tower made me remember that Epsilon had told me to go to the small library. Tonight. "It's time for maps," he said. But my nerves are so on edge – I feel I can't take any more. The wind is rising and thunder, very distant, rolls, far out to sea. I don't think I could be in the library in a growing storm. When Sebastian did that, something came creeping along the corridor outside – something I still don't know about.

I'm not sure I have the guts for this.

Yet… if Epsilon can appear to me at the cottage, he could appear to me here. After all, he did appear to Sebastian in this room – he made him spill his inkpot in fright. He's obviously powerful enough to appear when and where he likes. So I can't really get away from Epsilon anyway. So I might as well do what he asks. Whether he's good or not, I still have to try and work all this out.

I'll have to find my torch – I'm not risking the storm causing a blackout! I'd die of fright. I'll take this box file too, so I can put anything I find straight into it.

Poor Sebastian. I know just how he felt. He needed a word to make himself feel brave. "Agapetos," he'd used.

Me? No way am I going to utter any word around here until I'm sure what that word means. The workers of the Dark Ones are watching me, Epsilon said. If they can see me, maybe they can hear me too. Plus, so far Epsilon is the scariest thing of all – so why should I trust him? And so on, round and round and round. It's all one big circle.

I'm putting it off. Come on, Jess! Go to the small library. Now.

When in doubt, eat chocolate. That's what makes *me* brave.

So I've brought loads with me. Four bars, in fact. And two bags of crisps, a Coke, a packet of biscuits and two packets of mints! Could have done with a backpack to carry it all, what with my box file and everything.

Mum and Dad were in bed hours ago. It all feels secret and creepy, like being some kind of spy. The room isn't much different from when Seb was here, which makes it all worse somehow.

I remember coming in here with Mum when we first arrived. She loved it. She just kept spinning on her heel and staring all around. "Why move it all out?" she said at last. "Why change it? These books have been here for years and years. Some of them must be quite valuable." So she'd talked Dad out of stripping the whole room bare to use as his darkroom. They decided on the old scullery downstairs instead – it was cooler for his photography chemicals: they'd store better.

Come to think of it, that was the first time Mum said something a bit odd in this house. In here, on that very first day. She ran her fingers along the spines of the massive books. She stared up at the tall shelves.

"Poor old house. We're already ripping every room apart," she said. "This feels like its heart. I think we can leave it its heart, don't you, Richard?"

And oddly enough, Dad agreed.

Now I'm sitting here staring nervously all around, finding things Sebastian found that night, more than a hundred years ago.

Sure enough, over there is the little shelf table he set his candlesticks on. And nearby is the grate. (No cobwebs, though, not after the cleaning Mum gave this place when we arrived. The spiders wouldn't dare!)

The armchair he sat in is here too — although the crimson-and-gold coverlet is gone. And, of course, the books — rows and rows of them. Floor to ceiling!

It's a bit stuffy, but I've opened only one of the shutters — it creaked so much, it scared me half to death! And the thought of doing exactly what Sebastian did, last century, is just too much for me.

So I've laid out all my comfort food on the table (it looks like the snack shop at school) and I've already eaten the chocolate bars. Maybe that's why I feel so sick now.

Mmm… and maybe not…

Sebastian was right about these books. Great fat things with leather spines, all inlaid with gold. Books on Egyptology. On astrology. On prehistoric art. Foreign books, with titles written in what looks like Hebrew. There are thousands of smaller books too, many laid on their sides or slanting, willy-nilly. *A Discussion on the Evolution of the World* and *Essays from Portugal, Volume IV*.

At last, very high up — how on earth did he climb up there? — *The Mythology of the Small Islands* and *The Cartography of Lume*. Side by side, as if Sebastian had only just put them back.

So just now I dragged my chair over to climb up, just like he must have done.

I nearly broke my back getting the cartography book down! And I fail to see how he actually *read* it, in candlelight. Even in electric light (and I've put three on, no fear!) I'm struggling with the small script.

The maps are so old. Such tiny, slanty writing, full of curly bits, and each S is an F! Hang on – I've just remembered Mum's magnifying glass...

Later

A lot of the cartography book is fascinating, but pretty useless really. Like page 367: *THE IFLAND OF LUME, by Mafter Marcuf Siffonf – fketched from fight whilft fitting in a fmall veffel, 1643.*

Sorry, Master Marcus-Sissons-who-sketched-from-sight-whilst-sitting-in-a-small-~~veffel~~ vessel, but your map is way too old. Plus, it bears little resemblance to the actual shape of Lume, so your fmall veffel muft have been failing on an unufually ftormy fea!

But there were two things stuffed in the index pages. A loose map, hand-drawn. And a tatty old letter, tucked just behind it. The map was marked in one corner – 1894. This was exactly how the island looked when Sebastian lived here.

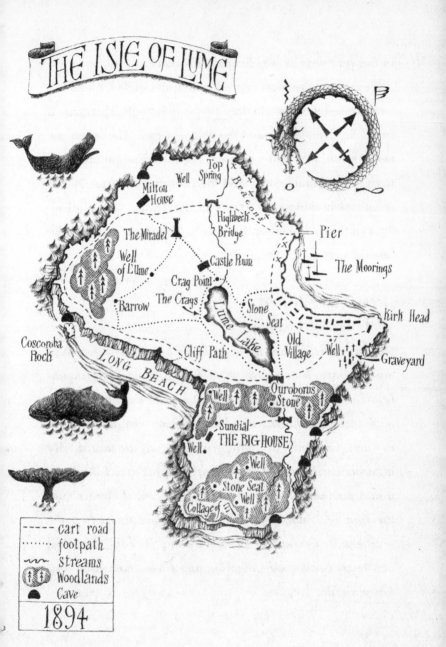

In the very year he was keeping his diary!

I examined the small printed writing and smiled. I wouldn't be surprised if Sebastian drew this map himself. There was a small clue, hidden around the compass rose. The letters for north, south, east and west were not in English at all. They were in the Lumic code. And the compass rose was not the usual type of thing at all. It was an Ouroborus.

And this is the letter that was hidden in the index of the book of maps.

Lume, 28 July 1894

My darling Sebastian,

I write this in some haste while my headache is gone and my thoughts clear. I write it in the event something should befall me, so that you may know what to do. Should your papa succeed in having me placed "for my own safety" in an asylum, you will be quite friendless in the world. My allowance will be utterly at your disposal, but I doubt he would disclose this fact unbidden. However, if you write to my firm of London solicitors and enclose this letter, the excellent Mr Greenwood will advise you. He can be reached at: Messrs Greenwood, Adamson and Greenwood, Esqs, 113 Lincoln's Inn, London.

If all things unfold as I suspect they may, your papa will no doubt place you in school as a boarder. If that be the case, I beg you to make the best of it, my dearest boy. Obey your masters and learn hard, being especially diligent with your language studies. For the speaking of varied languages is the key to escaping all that is dreary in this world! The allowance my own dear father left me is enough to enable you to travel, when you have completed your studies. Indeed, I heartily encourage you to do so, for there are many wonders abroad on the earth that will remain quite beyond your reach unless – in fact – you reach for them!

My last will and testament is also lodged with Mr Greenwood, who is a fine man, greatly to be trusted. As you will eventually see, it is my wish that this house (being left solely to me by Father, and not being in the ownership of your papa, whatever he may state to the contrary) remain in this family for your heirs. Dear and attentive boy, this is a good and even a great house, and I ask that you guard it from falling into disrepair.

If I should leave you suddenly to dwell elsewhere, I ask you to have a steady and stout heart and, in effect, to wipe me gently from your day-to-day tasks. For it is true indeed that some sickness has come upon me, and my mind is much absorbed at times, folded up in a world none can see but myself.

But we may safely state that if this sickness proceeds, I shall be so unlike my former self that – darling boy – I shall be lost not only to you but to my old life also! Some afflictions of the mind offer much comfort, Sebastian, as I have witnessed for myself with my own dearest mother, who quite happily dwelled to the end in her private dream world, oblivious to my own distress. Thus, what would be the purpose of you mourning my absence? No doubt I would be similar, quite satisfied with my new life, as I pray that you will learn to become stoic and satisfied with yours.

I have left you also many diverse trinkets that came to me when my own parents left this mortal world. Alas, there is nothing of any great value, and indeed, what does a small boy want with paste baubles and lockets and hat pins and the like?!

Yet a fine young man, abroad in the world, might return home at some future time to gain comfort and rest from the things of his past. In that event, I ask you to ever hold them tenderly, in cherished memory of she who penned this –

Your most loving

Mama

Well. I've found a map, just as Epsilon wanted.

And I've found a letter that made me want to cry.

What else did Epsilon ask me to look for? He said in the

cottage, "Your father is at the lake, taking a photograph you need to see. Your mother is in her studio, drawing something you must find."

So. I'll go to Mum's studio first. Then to the darkroom, to see what I can find.

1 a.m.
Mum's studio is creepily different. All those paintbrushes gone, all those photos, and no huge canvas. Just endless bits of paper strewn all around. On almost every one that face. The woman's face, peering out through cloud or thin gauze or something. There must be hundreds of them!

But then I found something else. Two weird sketches in black and white.

As I picked the first one up, a great wave of weariness rolled over me. Something is happening here, and Mum is now more than involved. Even at a glance, I could see what she'd drawn. I didn't recognise the castle or any of the winding paths, but the place the paths lead to is clear enough.

The tower. On the map, it is labelled 'The Miradel'. And Epsilon had said my watchers were called the Eye of Miradel. So the tower is definitely the place I'm being watched from.

And I have another addition to this growing file. This is Mum's first sketch.

In the castle where nobody dwells, the flags are flying in readiness.

They are coming soon, the Dark Ones!

Long of neck and black of foot, they gather at a path rising from no path.

Oh search the deep waters with your sharpened eyes,

O You who live in the skies!

As to the words she's written along the bottom scroll, they make me feel queasy, although I don't quite know why.

In the castle where nobody dwells, the flags are
flying in readiness.
They are coming soon, the Dark Ones!
Long of neck and black of foot they gather at a path
rising from no path.
Oh search the deep waters with your sharpened eyes,
Oh you who live in the skies!!!

What it means I don't know. But it's clear that whatever 'began' that night 'with a mirrored dream' and 'a followed sound' – whatever it is, Mum somehow senses it. Something took her up to the Miradel that night. Something is making her gather shells and hum that strange tune and draw that face over and over. Something is making her sketch the Miradel and write words that echo what the men were chanting – that something is being summoned here. Something is gathering. Something dark and ancient and scary.

As if to confirm it, I turned to the second sketch and went cold. Her second sketch shows a woman standing above a cliff. The same castle is in the background. The woman's arms are held out, and she is also summoning something.

This is Mum's second sketch.

Come forth!

Come forth!—
The Dark one is awakening
from my hand of bone beckons you.
My hand where your webbed feet land.
—You know my flock of Cygnus
Come to me now, the flock of Cygnus
I call you back to me—from every compass
layers of bronze & golden skies
I call you by name—from out from your

These words bothered me even more.

> *I call you out from your layers of bronze & golden*
> *skies*
> *I call you by name – from every compass*
> *I call you back to me – you know my voice well*
> *Come to me now, the flock of Cygnus –*
> *My hand of bone beckons you from where your*
> *webbed feet land*
> *The Dark One is awakening – come forth! Come*
> *forth!*

Who is this woman summoning her faithful to her? Why do they appear to be swans? "The Flock of Cygnus." I know that Cygnus means swan. After all, a cygnet is a baby swan.

Is Yolandë's the face Mum keeps sketching, over and over? Yolandë, who the old ones sang about in Sebastian's time? Or is it someone else?

I read the words again, thinking hard. "In the castle where nobody dwells, the flags are flying in readiness." Where is this castle? I stared at the Miradel in the drawing then compared it with the map.

Sure enough, there are the ruins of an ancient castle just near Lume Lake. And looking at the contour points of the map, the woman in Mum's sketch must be standing on top of the Crags. At the place marked the Viewpoint on the map. Over her left shoulder is the ruined castle – the castle where nobody dwells. And – checking back to the first sketch – over the shoulder of the ruined castle (so to speak) is the Tower of Miradel in the distance.

So the woman must be standing on the Crags at the Viewpoint and looking out *over the lake*. The same lake Dad's been visiting for days now. He was nattering about it: *"There's a swan appeared on Lume Lake, kitten. A black swan! Quick, pass me that roll of film. This could be the very set of wildlife shots I've waited all my life for!"*

Right. Time to check out Dad's darkroom.

Dad would kill me if he knew I'd been in his darkroom. It is utterly forbidden, especially when the small red light is on, when the developing process is under way.

But I knew the red light wouldn't be on tonight – he's snoring his head off in the next room. So in I went.

I love the smell of the darkroom. All those funny chemicals – it so reminds me of Dad; he carries a whiff of that sharpness around wherever he goes. I stood there sniffing it in, looking all around.

On the table his cameras lay neatly in a row. I'd never

touch those. His files too. Too many negatives to look through – I'd be here for ever. So I went to the latest of his prints. To the two rows of newly developed images, all pinned up on the double drying line.

Swans.

At least – one swan. The same swan, the black one, over and over again. Two separate films, each one hung on its own drying line. One whole film was of the swan feeding. Dabbling in the reeds. Sticking its long black neck under the water. Instantly, I heard the lines in my head.

Oh search the deep waters with your sharpened eyes, Oh you who live in the skies! And another phrase: *long of neck and black of foot, they gather...* This made me feel odd, dizzy, as if something shifted in the room slightly, as if something stepped closer.

I had to grab hold of the table to shake it off. Then I turned to the second roll of film. This time, a whole series of flight images – a time-line caught on paper. The black swan beginning to taxi over the water, walking the surface with its black feet. Farther along the lake, gathering speed. Taking off. The black swan in flight over the lake. Flying up to the Crags. Coming down to land at the Viewpoint. Almost landed. Landed.

I could tell that Dad kept lengthening the zoom,

following the swan as closely as he could. But he must have been finding it hard to keep it in shot because the last photo was a bit blurred and smudgy.

The swan was just touching down on the Viewpoint, flapping its enormous wings. Or… hang on. *Was* it the swan?

There it was, silhouetted against the white cloud. The black swan with its wings spread out to either side in a great V. But… it was much too large, surely? And those wings didn't look quite right. I looked again and felt all the blood drain from my face.

It was not a swan. Not a swan at all. It was a *woman* standing on the Crags, with her arms held out wide.

I compared it to the sketch Mum had drawn – looked from one paper to the other. It was the same woman, her arms held out to the sky.

One, drawn by Mum in her strange, disturbed state. The other, captured by Dad on the very last smudgy frame of his roll of film. *When his camera had been pointing not at a woman at all – but at the black swan.*

I sat down shakily, engulfed by a steady, gnawing fear.

Chapter Seventeen

My Diary

I've walked and cycled and staggered up so many hills, I'm exhausted! But at least I know the lay of the land now. And I've met some of the other villagers.

It seems that the weekend's Greet has got the whole village into a spin – flags on every cottage; flowers cramming the church; the Maypole thingummy on show in the village, ready to carry down to the beach.

Mum is ready for the Greet too. Early this morning, she ordered me to take six tins of scones and stuff over to Doc Parker's. Lent me her cranky old bike with its ancient wicker panniers – just wouldn't take no for an answer.

She's not in the best of moods as it is, on two accounts. First, the missing drawings. And second, last night's sleeptalking – or whatever it was that scared Dad half to death.

She spent half the night standing muttering by their bedroom window, Dad said. Just standing there, staring out. "Come on, old girl, come back to bed!" Dad said. "What are you looking for out there in the dark?"

Until at last she turned to him and said, "Her! I'm looking for her!" But her eyes were shut.

"She couldn't even see *me*," he whispered to me before he went out, "let alone whatever was outside the window! I tell you, it gave me the creeps!"

Mum didn't seem to remember anything at all – didn't mention it anyway. Just looked bleary-eyed and pale.

As to the drawings, good grief, you'd think someone had swiped the crown jewels! She almost ransacked the place. "But you *must* have them! I know I left them just here, last night. It's the same with my magnifying glass. Have you been in here again?"

"Me? No way!" (The drawings, in fact, were folded up in my jeans pocket, along with the map.)

Eventually, she bundled me outside and crammed tin after tin into the bike's panniers. I hate it when she tries to get rid of me.

"Stop sulking, Jessica, it won't kill you to get rid of a bit of that puppy fat! Now, you can't miss it – turn left at the gates, follow the lake path to Crag Point, go past that tower thing, and you'll see the track to the doctor's house."

"But Mu-um, how *far* is it?"

"Oh, for crying out loud, not far! Now when you get there, the quiche in the *blue* tin needs to go straight in the freezer until tomorrow – it's prawns – make sure you tell Charles."

"Charles?"

"The doctor. Dr Parker."

"Oh, I see. First name terms now, are we?"

"Don't be childish, Jessica. Now, don't bother with the doorbell – it doesn't work. Go straight to the back door and yell; you'll have to be loud – he's usually in his study on the top floor."

"Oh, he is, is he? Usually?"

"Yes, Jessica, he is. Usually. And take this roll of film to your dad. He's on that wretched lake as per usual. Well, go on! I'm busy!"

Busy doodling another black and white creepy thing, no doubt. Or another ten zillion sketches of that woman's face, staring out through ribbons of cloud. I tell you, I'm the only sane person left in our house.

Anyway, just before I left our land, I tried to find the Ouroborus Stone that was marked on the map. I felt it could be another clue. But the thicket was too dense. It was a mass of brambles – impossible to get into. I gave up in the end and went on to the lake.

And, true to form, there was Dad, furtively hidden halfway up a tree on the far side of the lake. The whirring of the camera gave him away.

"Gotcha!"

"Shh, Jess! You'll scare her away!"

"Her who? Here's your film."

"The black swan! Trying to get some shots of her preening. Come and see. Climb up, there's room for two."

"Shift up a bit then. Give me a hand. Anyway, how do you know it's a her?"

"Because she won't cooperate. Typical female, fidgeting about half the blasted day, just won't stay still."

"Dad. It's a swan. Swans move about."

"Yes, worse luck. Ow! That's my foot! Now then – over there, see? Got her back to us, as usual."

It wasn't worth the climb. Not really. Last night, if I'd seen this swan, I'd have freaked out totally. But in the cold light of day, I saw it was just a swan. Just a small smudge of black in the middle of the silver water – and every so often, she stuck her head under and showed us her backside.

Dad clicked and whirred away anyhow, muttering all the

time ("Come on, show me your pretty face!" and "Oh, blast – not another posterior shot!").

It was fine when I was there with Dad. But as soon as I left him and pushed the bike round the lake, suddenly there it was again – that watched feeling. Nothing had changed – the same birdsong, the same lapping of the water, the crunch of the pebbles underfoot. Yet this growing feeling of eyes on me, watching, following me.

But every time I turned round, there was nothing – just the swan in the distance, facing my way.

Just a *swan*, Jessica, I told myself. Not a woman at all.

Well, it's exhausting. It's not really such a small island!

Pushing my bike up to Crag Point nearly killed me. I swear I almost dislocated my legs. At the top of the Crags I saw the ruins, just up ahead. The castle. I stood panting with my bike, above a little dip in the path that led to the castle. The way to the ruin went downhill from this point, then slightly uphill again. At the top of the next incline was the castle.

Or what was left of the castle. Which is not much – a few cornerstones, half a turret. And just one main wall still standing, with two slim windows intact, and the bright-blue sky framed in them.

Why walk when I could ride down? I climbed back on my bike, stood on the pedals and rode the path down the little dip.

Big mistake. This was no path – it was *corrugated*!

The bike went bumping down and down into it, skidded sideways and threw me off. I lay on the ground in the dip and watched the front wheel, still spinning awkwardly. I'd managed to buckle the wheel. Great.

As I crawled over to assess the damage, I realised that everything sounded different. Once in the dip, all the sounds around went dim and dull, as if I'd fallen into a hole or something. It wasn't a very big dip even – maybe three metres across, with bushes all around. But as I knelt there, I felt cocooned, wrapped up in a special heat, removed from the rest of the island. Peaceful, even.

Time for a Coke. I settled down in the dip, looked all around as I ate my chocolate. No sound from the lake below. To my right and left the stone flags of this old, old path. Now that I looked closer, I fancied they were *tiered*. And the stones were old and worn, sagging in the middle from the passage of many feet. The whole area was massively overgrown and mossy, but suddenly I could see what I was looking at.

This was not a smooth path at all. These were steps. No

wonder it had felt corrugated! Steps, leading up on either side. At my back, behind a tangle of shrubs and trees, the hill with the tower.

Then in a flash, I realised where I was. I was sitting right in the middle of Mum's first sketch!

Unfolding the sketch, I felt that shivering start again — the same as at the cottage, that first time. Hands shaking, hairs rising on the back of my neck.

It's only a sketch! I told myself. But it didn't help. And as I looked at it, I saw I was sitting on the lowest step of all in the dip. To either side, the funny paths led away — as if this low step was the *start* of each path. Somehow it didn't feel like one path but *two* paths, both starting here.

And when I read the words again, I felt dizzy and sick.

> *In the castle where nobody dwells, the flags are*
> *flying in readiness.*
> *They are coming soon, the Dark Ones!*
> *Long of neck and black of foot **they gather at a***
> ***path rising from no path.***
> *Oh search the deep waters with your sharpened eyes,*
> *Oh you who live in the skies!!!*

Mum had drawn this place as it had looked long ago,

when the castle was still standing, but derelict. Because the closer I studied the drawing, the clearer it all got: the ivy, crawling in and out of the windows. The windows with no glass or shutters. She'd drawn it as it must have looked a hundred years ago or so. As it would have been when Sebastian and his mama were alive. It was a castle nobody dwells in because it was a ruin even then.

So there I sat, on "a path rising from no path", where the Dark Ones were going to gather. I had the distinct feeling they already *had* begun to gather. In fact, I was totally jittery, convinced someone or something was creeping up, then and there.

A thought occurred to me. If this step really was significant – if it was the start of the two ancient paths (one leading to the ruin, one to the Miradel) – maybe it would be marked in some way?

I bent down and began to pull up the long grass. Under the weeds, moss. Scraping it off with my fingernails, I uncovered first one letter, then more and more, of a text carved there long ago. It was hard to make out, as each letter was worn and crumbling. But I managed it in the end.

> *ONE LADY she be,*
> *ONE LADY we be,*

ONE LADY be he-without-trace.
For he be ONE LADY,
And she be ONE LADY,
And we see the ONE LADY's face.

I thought again of Mum's picture of the woman standing up here on the Crags. One Lady. One Lady who seems to crop up time and time again. Mum had drawn her. Dad had photographed her. Last night, Mum was standing asleep at her bedroom window, "looking for her".

Then I looked again at the carved letters. Funny that the words 'ONE LADY' were written in capitals each time. Or maybe not. I stared at the words, puzzling.

Then suddenly I saw it – the letters of ONE LADY, rearranged, an anagram. I spoke the name aloud. "YOLANDË!"

As soon as I said her name, something changed. That slip, that lurch – like I was falling and falling into something dark and deep. I closed my eyes, shook my head. Opened my eyes again. I was still here, still kneeling on the path – quite steady. Yet everything was different. Something ominous had arrived. Something unstoppable.

My chocolate wrapper rustled in a tiny breeze and made me jump. The reeds at my back bent and whispered.

Reeds? Reeds grow near water, don't they? Yet the lake was far below!

Peering closer at the picture, I realised that above the path Mum had drawn the suggestion of a small pond, before which I now sat. In her sketch it was all cleared and visible. Now it was a tangle of shrubs and matted reeds. I could smell it, though, as I shoved my way in – that whiff of old, still water.

With my hands, I tore and ripped a gap in the greenery, a little spyhole, that's all, barely wide enough for my face.

I looked through the gap – yelled out with shock. A face looked back at me. On the other side of the gap, framed perfectly – the face of the black swan. Her sharp little eyes were fixed on me intently.

Then, as I reeled backwards in fright, a loud crashing began behind me. A massive, ungainly flailing. I leaped up, alarmed.

A swear word. A scrabbling in the reeds. Someone struggling on the ground. Then the swan was flying into the air, huge wings loud and flapping. Higher, higher she went, then was gone in a great curve over the lake.

"Jess? Can you believe that?! Hang on... help me up. I've grazed my face; didn't realise these were steps!"

"Oh, *Dad*! What the hell are you *doing*? You nearly scared me half to *death*!"

"I got it all! A whole film!"

"All? All what?"

"You and the swan! The swan followed you – she came after you straightaway – must've thought there was food in the panniers or something—"

"There is, but—"

"That'll be it then. She must've smelled it, come after you soon as you left the lake. All that time, there's me perched up a tree all morning and just a glimpse of her backside in the air, then up you waltz – and bingo!"

He was fiddling all the time, out of breath, taking out the film, packing up the camera, cheeks flushed and shiny beads of blood on his face where he'd fallen headfirst on the path.

"Dad. You're bleeding."

"Am I? Must go, got to develop this film – see you later. Tell Mum I'll be in the darkroom all afternoon. Bye, kitten!"

And he was gone.

Chapter Eighteen

My Diary

It's hard to run away when you're pushing a bike with a buckled wheel. But I did it at breakneck speed.

Taking the path round the ruins, I hurried off, panting, thinking of those horrid little eyes peering at me through the greenery. Stalked by a swan. Now who's cracking up? Then I staggered up the hill to the tower.

In the day, the tower isn't half as creepy. But the sound was still there, somewhere in the background – that strange, faraway rushing of water. Yet there was no river nearby. No water at all.

It's no wonder my hands were so stung though – as I said, the base of the tower is thick with nettles. Nothing much else – a few small white moths flitting about, that's all. So I turned my attention to the gargoyles themselves.

Well! Talk about secrets written in stone! The gargoyles leered down and seemed to be mocking me. I walked all round the tower, staring up at those stone faces.

First, the north gargoyle, the one overlooking our land. I had glimpsed it correctly in the moonlight – those weren't hands at all, framing that ugly face. They were wings. Swan's wings, curved about a birdlike head. A horrible, gaping beak. The top curve of the beak looked as sharp as a scimitar. And around its neck – the Ouroborus, draped like a necklace. The eyes were enormous in the birdlike head. With sharply cut pupils, they bulged out obscenely. And on its breast, the letter N. N for north.

So... a hideous swan, permanently overlooking our house. Great. After my experience at the pond, this was the last thing I wanted to see.

I walked to the back and looked at the next gargoyle. W for west. This one stared out to sea – a watcher of the ocean, I could tell that from the face. It was a huge fish creature, scaled and all writhed up in itself. Seaweed dripped from its fins. Round, fishy eyes and barnacle skin, and an anchor and chain around its neck. Yuck.

S for south. The south gargoyle was lovely compared to the others. It was a beautiful woman, with her hair streaming out behind her. A bit like the figurehead of a ship. Her eyes were dreamy, with a calm, gentle gaze. Held in the crook of her elbow was a lyre. A musician.

Around her neck, a necklace of delicate spring flowers. Her slender hands were held at either side of her mouth, as if she was about to call out to someone. To someone directly ahead, but far away. Looking at the map, I searched for whatever lay in the direction she gazed towards.

Just a large house. Milton House. Dr Parker's house.

But the east gargoyle was the worst of all. It wasn't just ugly. It was evil. Even the E carved on its chest was horrible, made up of small, writhing human figures, their tiny mouths stretched open in agony. This gargoyle was in the form of a devil, with a face so appalling that it made me start to shiver. Its eyes held a look of great cunning. It was a gloating, leering face with terrible, all-seeing eyes that glared outwards towards the east. Its open mouth had fangs rather than teeth. But one of the front fangs was missing; the other curved down, sharp and glinting in the sunlight. Even its hands were horrible. They were talons, and the forefinger of the right hand pointed to something far away. The left hand held one end of a noose, which dangled down under the whole figure. In the crook of its arm, a mirror. And round the gargoyle's neck was a necklace made of tiny baby skulls.

So. A swan, spying on us.

A fish creature, watching the western sea.

A lovely woman – Yolandë perhaps – watching the doctor's house.

And a creature with one fang missing, watching the east. Who else could this be but Cimul? The Lord of Inversion, carrying his mirror.

I checked on the map for what he could be pointing at. Coscoroba Rock. The place he had fled to in the myth, after he had been cursed. The same rock the tooth had been taken from, snatched from his hand by a porpoise long ago and carried into the depths of the sea.

The wind touched the tiny nodding grasses around the tower and made them shimmer. Such a peaceful place. Such a strange tower, with terrible stories told in its stone. I remembered something Dad had told me once, about gargoyles. That some believed they awoke at night and left their stone plinths. That they had the power to fly, to cause mischief, but they were always back again by sunrise, to sit the day through in total stillness. Meanwhile, the tops of their heads caught the rain and spat it out of their open mouths, down to the ground far below. So they watered the land they watched over, the land they flew out over each night.

I was glad to get away.

*

I was pretty shaky by the time I got to the doctor's, I can tell you. And it didn't help when I saw the plaque on the front door – MILTON HOUSE. I remembered the first time I'd seen this name – in Sebastian's first diary entry. Seb had been taking settles and benches over to Miltons' place. Which is now the doctor's place, where the garden party is going to be held tomorrow, apparently. Then later, we'll all go down to the back for a massive barbecue and for the ceremony of the Coscoroba pole. Just like Sebastian did, more than a hundred years ago. Just like people have been doing on this island for hundreds of years before that even. An ancient tradition. A ceremony. To celebrate what?

I stared up at the plaque and felt scared. Whatever it was, the Greet was *tomorrow*. And I sensed that something would happen that couldn't be stopped. "Once power comes to the surface, there is no stopping it," Epsilon had said. That was what I felt like now – like I was just one small cog in a great machine that had been set in motion and could not now be switched off.

Finally, I left the plaque and did what Mum had said. Round the back, park the bike, unpack the bags, through the gate (stroke the cat), up to the back door, take a deep breath – *yell*!

"DOCTOR PARKER!"

"Great heavens! You scared me out of my wits, girl!"

Poor Dr Parker. He wasn't upstairs in his study at all – he was right behind the back door!

"Good thing I have a stout heart, isn't it?" he said, looking weak with fright.

"Sorry, Dr Parker. Mum said this one has to go straight into the freezer – it's prawns."

"Charles. Call me Charles. Makes me feel old, all this Dr Parker stuff. What have you been up to then? You look as white as a sheet."

"Oh… just walking."

His freezer was filled to the brim with small packages wrapped in newspaper. Hundreds of them, in fact. He saw me staring down at them and grinned.

"Every fisherman in the place seems to bring me a share of his catch. Mackerel, mostly. The stuff makes me ill. I give Mrs Shilling most of it, or use it for pike bait. Here – cram it in!"

Pike bait. So maybe he had been fishing that night after all? I started to relax a bit. "Don't you like mackerel then?"

He stared down ruefully at all the fishy parcels. "Hate the stuff. Allergic."

That started me off, and him too. I never thought an

adult could laugh like that. For such a big man, he has this daft little giggle that makes you want to join in, just to hear it again. It was the same all afternoon. He took me driving round the island on his rounds, said the bike looked like a death trap, and anyway, he could do with the company. We laughed at anything and everything. It started as soon as we set off in the car.

"So how old is Mrs Shilling?"

"Oh, her. Eighty-seven."

"Eighty-*seven*?!"

"Mmm. Didn't know you'd even met her!"

"Yes. She was sitting on the back gate when I came in."

The car came to a shuddering stop. "Mrs Shilling was sitting on the *gate*?!"

"Yes. Having a good scratch. She didn't look all that old, though – even in cat years!"

He bent over the steering wheel and started to wheeze. That giggle, it built up and up till it exploded with a giant snort.

"What? What have I said?" But I could hardly get the words out for laughing.

Finally he calmed down. "Mrs Shilling isn't my cat. She's my housekeeper. She gets to eat the fish. Well, she can barely chew anything else – she has no teeth!"

"Oh! Oh, I *see*. I thought… with you saying about the fish… and I'd just seen the cat and— Oh!"

I'd forgotten what a good laugh felt like. Even when we were back on our way, driving to the village along the top road, he kept quivering and snorting and we'd start off all over again. He laughed till he cried.

"Sorry, sorry! I just keep thinking of Mrs Shilling, sitting on the back gate, having a good scratch. Oh, God! Stop it, stop it, I'll crash this thing! You'll know what I mean when you meet her." And I did. The first cottage we stopped at.

To the door came the smallest, most bent, most wrinkly, most smelly, most *ancient* old hag I have ever seen in all my life. She sniffed at me when the doctor introduced me, then looked up at the doctor with suspicious little eyes.

"I hope you're not getting a cold, Doctor? Your eyes are rather watery."

A twitch of his mouth – a sort of hiccup. "Me? No, no, no, Mrs Shilling – it's you I'm worried about. Left your medicine again, tsk tsk tsk. You can remember to put my whisky and soda out each night, but can't remember to take your stomach medicine. It will not *do*!"

She glared at me, as if something major was my fault. "Well, I suppose you'd better come in."

The inside of her house was like Mrs Shilling, only

bigger. Smelly, crumpled and every stick of furniture old and rickety. Each chair looked incapable of holding anything heavier than a bird.

Talking of birds – they were everywhere! Pictures and ornaments, robins and swallows on the wing and eagles swooping on to rabbits, and blue tits and herons, on every mantelpiece, every shelf. If they'd all been alive, the noise would have been totally deafening. I stared at them as the doc took her blood pressure, though she informed him it was all stuff and nonsense and there was nothing wrong with her at all, just a bit of indigestion.

When he went to wash his hands (don't blame him either – she stank!), she spent the time glaring at me as if I was a particularly revolting bit of dog poo. I sat on the edge of a very filthy chair and tried to smile at her.

Suddenly, she said, "Well, girl? Have you found it yet?"

"Found what, Mrs Shilling?"

"There is no need to shout, child. I am not in the slightest bit deaf."

"Sorry. Found what, Mrs Shilling?"

"You know what, young lady. Here. This should help, if you have half a brain. Pretend it's a boy."

I blinked, startled. She'd quickly risen out of her chair, crossed the room, as nimble as a child – and now she put into my hands one of the small bird pictures. It was grimy and torn, a curled bit of card.

"Uh… thank you! I… er…"

She stared down at me and gave a sniff of utter derision. "Just as I thought. Stupid as they come!" she snapped.

Then the doctor was back, and he boomed his goodbyes and gave her a parcel of frozen mackerel, slamming it on to the sugar-strewn table as he passed.

"See you tomorrow, Mrs Shilling. I'll come by bright and early to pick you up – lots to do, what with the Greet and everything."

"Will *she* be there?" Mrs Shilling asked.

"Oh, yes – guest of honour, in fact! Now then – two spoonfuls tonight, just before bed, and no forgetting. Now do I make myself clear?"

"Clear as crystal, thank you. Now go away – the pair of you. You make me tired."

Back in the car, I turned to him immediately. "That? Is your *housekeeper*?"

"I know, I know. She's completely gaga and I cannot get her to wash! But she arrived one day a few years ago, insisting she make me cups of tea – and I drink coffee – and oddly enough, she's a very good cleaner. She's harmless and kind enough."

"Kind! She said I was as stupid as they come!"

He roared with laughter when I told him what she'd said. "What does she think you're looking for then? God, she's as mad as a cat in a sack! But I keep my eye on her."

I didn't tell him about the card. I'd slipped it into the back pocket of my jeans and realised that if I got it out, out too would come the map – and Mum's drawing. If he thought Mrs Shilling was as mad as a cat in a sack, what might he think of my mother, gathering shells and doodling ancient castles?

"What's up, Jessica?"

"Oh, nothing. Where next?"

"A tour. Meet a few more people. We should walk really – it's only a few hundred metres. Getting lazy. Anyway, Jerry C's next. Arthritis. Hands. He's a carpenter, too; needs his hands. He's been trying a diet rich in tomatoes. Here we are."

Outside Jerry C's house, a small crowd stood. They were admiring a tall carved pole, propped up by the door. The doctor nodded to it as we climbed out of the car.

"The Maypole thing. Well... we call it that, even though it's not May at all. Can't really call it a *July pole*, can we?"

I went close and stared at it, and it instantly happened again. That sudden lurch, that sideslip in time. It was as if

Sebastian had stepped closer out of the past and was whispering something urgently in my ear...

"Master Cork... is not like the rest... I have spent much time at his hearth. He lets me sit quiet while he whittles the tall pole for the Aroundy dance. He calls the pole his Coscoroba, and the way he fusses over his wood is remarkable to see."

I leaned against the wall and steadied myself as I looked up at the Aroundy pole. It was truly amazing – the intricacy of that carving! A thick pole of wood, about fifteen centimetres in diameter, and all the way up it fish creatures and snakes and swans and flowers. Hundreds of them, all intertwined in high relief. And another thing – the swans were in the very same design as the swans on my bed. The same stylised curve of neck, the same overcurved beak, the same sharp little eyes.

At the very top of the pole, holes were carved deep into the wood, like so many tiny caves, for ribbons to be threaded into. And sure enough, some of the women were uncurling long coils of ribbons from their pockets and reaching up.

I turned to the old man standing at the door. And suddenly I fancied I saw him – Sebastian Wren, standing just behind Jerry C. A little boy wearing hot, itchy knickerbockers and a thick jacket. A boy who dressed differently and sounded too English to the islanders. A boy who didn't fit in. An outsider, like me.

Then I blinked and Sebastian was gone. There was just the old man, Jerry C, smiling down at me.

Instantly, I knew that this was the very same cottage Sebastian had come to, to sit at the hearth. This man was a descendant of Sebastian's Master Cork.

Jerry C, the doctor had called him. C for Cork. Both men were carpenters, sculptors; both men carved the Coscoroba, each in their own time. Before I could think, I'd blurted it out. "You are Jerry Cork," I said weakly. "And one of your ancestors carved my swan bed. He carved the Coscoroba too."

Jerry Cork reached for my hand and shook it. Arthritic fingers curled over my own. "That he did, young lady. That he did. There's his carvings all up and down this island. But only this family knows the design for the Aroundy pole, for the pole gets burned every year and never copied down, so it's all kept up here." He tapped his head proudly.

But even as I smiled up at him, I started to feel dizzy. The doctor came up and took my arm. He made me sit down, and they brought me a drink of water, very cold and pure from the well, and I began to feel like I was in a long, long dream. I went on chatting somehow – the village women all said hello and called others from their cottages until there were too many people to talk to at once. Then, inexplicably, I started on a long series of massive yawns. Once I started, I couldn't stop.

The doctor bundled me back into the car and – incredibly – I fell asleep. I was passed out all the way back to his house. I woke up only when the doc dropped my bike when he was putting it in the backseat and bashed one of the panniers. Then he drove me home, scolding and tutting and saying I needed iron ("Iron, young lady! You tire far too easily – good thing I have some in stock!") until we bumped our way back past the lake.

No sign of the swan, but I twisted round to look at the Miradel. "Doctor. Who built that tower thing?"

"Mmm?" (He was avoiding a pothole.)

"Back there. I mean – no doors, no windows – who on earth built it?"

"Oh, that! That's just a folly. Our ancestors were very fond of follies. Had more money than sense, some of them. It serves no purpose."

"Is it true that there's no way in and no way out?" I asked.

"Way in? There's nothing inside it to get *into*. It's solid. I've investigated every inch of it. Had to – it used to be on my land. Couldn't risk it falling down on someone's head – they'd have sued me for every penny I've got."

"Who built it?"

"Mmm? My great-great-dunno-how-many-greats-grand-father."

"Really? What was his name?"

"Milton. Milton C Parker. He built it as 'a place of rest', according to family legend – but how you rest in a solid building is beyond me. Some say he was buried nearby. Maybe that's what he meant."

"Milton! So your house was named after him?"

He nodded, then slowed the car down to negotiate the turn into our front gates. "Awfully interested in history all of a sudden, aren't we?"

"Me? I just like old things. So who does it belong to now?"

"The Miradel? Why – all of us, I suppose!"

"The whole of Lume?"

"The whole of Lume. Here we are then! I'll just pop in – have a word with your mother, give her these iron tablets and make sure you take them."

But just as I said bye and started to push the bike round

the back, he stopped me and held out something. Something small and grubby and curled up at the edges.

"Jessica? You dropped this."

It was Mrs Shilling's little card, with the picture of a bird on it. I reached out to take it. But he didn't let it go. We each hung on to one end of it and a familiar look came over his face. That casual look – overcasual – like he'd had in my room that day when he'd first seen the bucket.

"By the way, Jess," he said, "how did you know that the Aroundy pole was called the Coscoroba?"

I stared down at him, blushing beet red. I'd given myself away. "What?"

"You said it to Jerry Cork. You called it the Coscoroba. But that's a very ancient name for it. An old island name. However did you come to hear of it?"

I racked my brains. He still wouldn't let go of that card. "I... read it. I read about it somewhere. In an old book – the house is full of them. The same word is on the map too."

"The map?"

"Coscoroba Rock. It's a rock that sticks out. At the end of Long Beach. Everyone knows about it – you must have heard of it?"

"Of course I have. That's where we'll burn the Coscoroba pole tomorrow. It's an old custom, to cast it into the sea from Coscoroba Rock."

"Well then," I stammered, "that's how I heard the name." There was an uncomfortable pause.

"Jessica. Are you… worrying yourself about anything?" he asked.

I stared up into those crinkled, kind eyes. Longed to tell him everything. Longed to trust someone with all this.

"Worrying about anything? No." For some reason, I let the card held between us go.

He glanced down at the bird picture and I swear he did a double take. Then he flipped the card over on to its information side. He read quickly, his frown deepening. Finally, he looked up again and smiled at me.

"This is a small island, Jessica. It's full of old stories, old legends. But that's all they are – legends. It wouldn't do to get scared and all upset about legends now, would it?"

"Upset? Why… no. It wouldn't. That'd just be silly."

"You would come and tell me, wouldn't you? If anyone had been upsetting you at all? You can trust me, you know."

Unexpectedly, a huge lump rose up in the back of my throat. I could have sat down then and there and cried my eyes out, telling him everything. But something stopped me.

"I'm fine, Dr Parker. Really I am. I'm just not feeling

very well. That's all. But thanks anyway."

Finally, he nodded and handed me the card. Then he strode away to go and find Mum. I stared down at the tiny picture in my hand – the bird card.

Not just any bird, I saw now as I stared down at it. I flipped the card over and read the back. *LATIN*: TROGLODYTES TROGLODYTES said the card. *Common name: Wren. A very small European bird, much loved for its loud, melodic song.*

What had Mrs Shilling said? "Pretend it's a boy."

A wren. A boy. A boy called Sebastian. Sebastian Wren. She knows.

Chapter Nineteen

THERE IS ONE MEMBER IN THE CHAT ROOM:	Jess

JESS: Are you there, Epsilon?

E: I'm down here at the cottage. I'm waiting for you.

JESS: Will I... I mean, will you... will I see you? Please don't do that thing with your eyes again.

E: I won't harm you.

JESS: I'm scared of you.

E: I know. But I won't harm you. Come down and open the last box. Then I will appear. There is much to tell you before tomorrow. Will you come now?

JESS: I don't know. I'm *scared!*

E: Bring your whole file. It's time we started putting some of the puzzle pieces together.

JESS HAS LEFT THE CHAT ROOM

The cottage looked peaceful, nestling in its corner of garden, surrounded by the singing of early evening blackbirds. But looks are deceiving.

As soon as I walked in, I felt it – a sort of crackling in the air. An energy, an expectancy. The sound of my footsteps seemed amplified as I climbed the stairs. Epsilon's room was empty and still.

I stood at the door a moment, looking at the round picture in its square frame. The golden O. Behind it, I knew, was that round black snake, about to devour its own tail. Taking nourishment only from itself. The thought of it hanging there, hidden, was horrible. Hurriedly, I lit a candle.

I crouched by the desk and opened the drawer. As I took out the third and last box, I wondered if I was about to discover what Sebastian had found that night when he finally opened the library door – that night of the storm, when he'd heard someone creeping down the corridor towards him. I stared down at the box, my mouth dry. I wasn't sure I was up to any of this. Wasn't sure I wanted to find out. But what choice did I have? None really. None at all.

The third box unlocked easily. Inside it were three different things.

Four pages of Sebastian's diary, hastily written in his spidery scrawl.

A letter from Martha to Sebastian.

And finally, a yellowed newspaper cutting, folded into a neat square.

First, I read Sebastian's diary papers. This is what he had written:

I stared at the door for an age, willing myself to open it. Finally, I turned the handle and pulled.

Someone was standing there, pale in the lamplight. But I almost did not recognise her, those eyes...

"Mama?"

Her feet were bare; she wore the thinnest of nightgowns. She held it gathered before her, and held in the gathers were many shells. They chinked together softly under her fingers. She chose a shell and held it up.

"Look, Sebastian – this one was me, all coiled up!"

"Mama!"

She chose another shell. "And this one, this one, look! Your smallest fingernail when you were born. And the same tiny pink!"

"Mama, what are you doing?"

But she put her finger to her lips and bent down. She placed the little pink shell delicately on the floor. "Look what I have made!" she said. She turned and pointed away, back into the dark corridor.

I raised my lamp and stared. The lamplight shot along the corridor. Hundreds of tiny gleams lit up along the floor; they ricocheted away into the darkness. A long thin row of shells, each one set agleam by the lamp! And suddenly, a memory leaped from nowhere – last summer, high on the west cliffs, watching the fishermen hurriedly light the beacons, one by one, all along the coastline.

A beacon of shells. A path, to light the way through fog. For what? For something approaching; something coming nearer.

"Mama – what have you done?"

She leaped up and tugged at my sleeve. "Come with me, Sebastian – let's follow it!"

"No, Mama."

"But you can hear the sea in it! Come, you'll see." She would not stop tugging, her fingers plucking at my sleeve.

"Very well, Mama. But you are shivering. Come, we will follow it – but only back to your bedchamber."

But the shell path did not just lead to her chamber. It meandered all over and split into two roads, then three. At every turn, more and more, leading into every corner of the house. But the one she wanted to follow – she was adamant, there was no stopping her – led to Papa's door, and there she stopped and stood as if waiting.

Sure enough, Papa's door flew open. He saw it all in a glance – the hair loose, the wild look of delight, the path of shells leading away.

"What in the name of…?!"

But Mama leaned forward and pressed her cold finger to his lips. "Shhh!" she said. "It's too late, Edmond."

He went still. "Too late? What is too late?"

"She has already stepped on them."

"Who has? Stepped on what?"

"On her stepping stones. You cannot stop her."

"Stop whom? Who the blazes are you talking about?" said Papa. But in his eyes a quick, keen look.

"The One Lady." She gave a little laugh. "My lady."

At that, Papa began to roar at me. I must get my crazed mother back to her bed – I must clear up these infernal shells instantly – he would write to the asylum in the morning – she was just like her mad mother – get her away from his door – he detested the very sight of her wild, mad face and her hair all over like a common gypsy!

But I had the sudden suspicion that he was <u>acting</u>. That he was pleased with what she had said. But… he could not be. Could he?

Mama only smiled as I led her away. Back along the

shell path. Back to her bedchamber, where I rubbed her poor bare feet and covered her over with an eiderdown. She closed her eyes and was asleep instantly.

But I still had to collect the shells. I borrowed her blue fruit bowl and set off. She must have been laying her trail for hours! All around the house they took me. To the unused rooms and around the white shapes of sofas and chairs, draped in sheets. Down the back stairs and into the kitchen in a wobbly line. Into the scullery and over the shelves, as if a great snail had meandered there.

Bending, bending, and each little shell chinked prettily into the dish, but there were always more. Into the drawing room, over Papa's books and back on to the floor. Up on to the pianoforte, a shell on each key of the piano. Hundreds of shells. Thousands of shells!

I got angry then and swept them into the dish a handful at a time, careless of the noise. The piano keys plinked, a pretty fah-soh-lah, rising up the scale.

It echoed on and on as I backed out of the door, up the main stairwell, along the corridors. Until at last, I was left with only one trail – up my attic stairs. A shell on each step, leading to my door.

My bed was stripped bare. On its mattress ticking she had arranged the shells not in a straight line but into a pattern.

A strange pattern. I grabbed my pen quickly, drew it, stabbing the marks into the paper, then flung it aside.

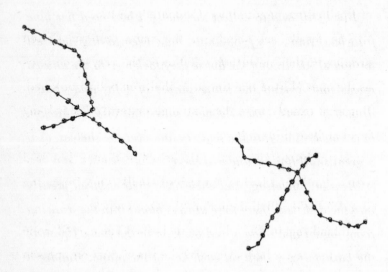

Then I scooped the last of the shells up and carried the dish – heavy now, very heavy – back to the scullery. I wrenched open the casement and poured all the BLASTED shells out of the BLASTED window.

When I returned to Mama, she was still asleep, a little frown between her brows. Everything was exactly as I had left it. Except that something had been placed on her pillow. Something that had not been there before, I am certain of it.

There – just by her hand – one black feather.

I stared at the pattern Martha had left. It struck me as being familiar. Something tugged at the back of my mind, then leaped out. I grabbed my file and turned to my sketch of Epsilon's ammonite floor. Compared the two.

The fossils sat snugly in the same pattern. Dotted erratically, they nevertheless followed the very same lines as the ones Martha had traced in shells on Sebastian's bed. But what exactly were these strange patterns? I shook my head and sat thinking.

So the night before the Greet, more than a hundred years ago, Mama had laid a trail of shells – her "stepping stones" she'd called them, for "the One Lady".

Yolandë again. But who exactly is she? The carved stone up by the castle had suggested she wasn't just one person but represented several.

ONE LADY she be,
ONE LADY we be,
ONE LADY be he-without-trace.
For he be ONE LADY,
And she be ONE LADY,
And we see the ONE LADY's face.

And straight after reading that stone, I *had* seen a face.

The face of the black swan. What did the black swan signify? And who was she summoning to gather, up there on the Crags? The faithful: Mum had put those words into her sketch. Whoever they were, their arrival was imminent. That gathering in the air. That expectancy.

As to Sebastian's papa and his *acting* – why would he be? But I was sure Sebastian had been correct. For some reason, Papa was pleased his wife was acting like this. It was all beyond me.

Then I turned to the second document. A letter, or rather, a note, scribbled fast – a note from Martha to Sebastian.

Such wild sounds, Sebastian! Her voice is louder; she beckons me to Crag Point. Or to the shore. I am drawn to the sea. She is waiting there; she calls my name. She sings.

Did you know that I studied music in my girlhood? Of course, you must, for we have sung together often! I forget so many things. Yet never will I forget this music from the shores. It pulls me apart, it sews me back together.

Tomorrow, at the Greet, she will come. I fear for her sweet face. She has many enemies – I have sensed them near. I will protect her all the days of my life. I will protect her with my life.

I have to go soon, dear Sebastian, into strange places –
you must not follow me, not there. I am looking for a thing
that was lost long ago – lost in the sea. But this I know:
what the tide takes away, the tide brings back. Has that not
always been the way of the sea? I will find it for her; my own
hand will dry her tears.

Her enemies, however, are also nearer. How I despise
them! They whisper lies into the ears of children; they
confuse the elderly with their distortion! What cowards they
are, and she so brave.

They reverse all things. I shudder at it. Their lies are
ludicrous, yet people believe them. It is like calling the eagle
more lovely than the swan. That brown bird with its ugly
talons, built only to kill! The swan's foot steers calm waters
– what harm does she do? Her plumage is brilliant; she does
not tear flesh, not she. Her neck is full of grace, it carries her
eye deep into the calmest of waters; it is her very nature to be
serene.

If they were to be believed, these enemies with death in
their talons – what woe would come upon us then. Flesh
would tear and bleed – our music would be silenced, the cry
of the sea dry up. Meanwhile, she shows me that one of them
has poisoned your mind, Sebastian. His kindness to you is a
lie – you must not believe it; he is one of the Dark Beings.

He has bewitched you with his riddles and his music. Yet I cannot help you. It is all too late.

I pen this and ask that you not let the shake of my hand distress you; it is only that I am so very cold tonight. If I should take my leave of you at tomorrow's Greet, my fine son, you will see – you will ALL see – that maybe I am not so deranged after all.

There is a small space hidden behind one of the swans – I have been meaning to mention this for many a week now. Master Cork is a gifted man – he has finished carving the swans on the Coscoroba pole, did I tell you? I forget so many things – but I will never forget you.

Mama

Swans again. Swans, swans, swans. Martha's letter made me sad. But it also scared me. Here she was, warning her son about someone who was poisoning his mind. With his riddles and his music. I remembered that haunting flute tune, the one that had drawn me to the cottage, that night of the mirrored dreams.

Epsilon. She warned Sebastian that he is a Dark Being. She certainly thought that the One Lady – Yolandë – was on the side of the good. Was she right? Is Epsilon a Dark Being? I remembered his eyes, staring at me, many faceted, when the rest of him had vanished. Those eyes that looked unearthly. What sort of place has he come from? A dark place? How would I really know who to trust?

Finally, I turned to the newspaper clipping, unfolded it. It smelled musty and old; smelling it made me sneeze. It was from the *Northern Herald*, 12 August 1894. The headline leaped out at me.

MISSING WOMAN OF LUME
PRESUMED DEAD
SEARCH PARTIES GIVE UP HOPE

There is still no trace of the missing woman of Lume, Mrs Martha Wren. She vanished mysteriously last month at the height of the annual celebration, the Greet. Islanders fear she must have been swept away by the high seas. Mrs Wren, said by many to have been "of a delicate disposition", had been behaving oddly for some weeks before her disappearance. Villagers from the island say she was prone to "wandering off at the dead of night, all along these shores". Her husband, Mr Edmond Wren, had been making discreet enquiries for some time into the possibility of asylum care. Search parties have combed the island daily ever since Mrs Wren's disappearance, although after several days, the expectation of her being found alive was small. For her distraught husband, now even the small comfort of being able to give her mortal remains a Christian burial is fading. "These currents are treacherous," said one Master J Cork, a fisherman of the island. "What the sea takes away, the sea does not always bring back." A memorial service will be said at the village kirk next Sabbath at noon. Mrs Wren leaves behind one son.

Fear rose up and gripped me. Disappeared. Sebastian's mama – vanished without trace. At the Greet. Tomorrow. I mean, at the Greet in 1894. I stared again at her delicate, hurried handwriting and a wave of grief washed over me. Poor, poor Sebastian. Poor Martha, lost and scared in a little world all of her own. Wandering the beaches, looking for a relic among the shells. Not really knowing what it was she was looking for.

I stood up and went to the window. Outside, dusk was falling. The sound of the sea in the bay below was soft, hypnotic. The evening shadows fell from the tall trees and spread slowly across the garden. As I watched darkness fall, I realised that as soon as the sun went down, it would be the last night I'd have to try to work all this out. The Greet was tomorrow. And everything centred round the Greet. Epsilon had warned me to be ready for the Greet. Whatever danger Mum was in, it would come at the Greet. Just like it had for Martha Wren.

As the sun went down and outside became dimmer and dimmer, the candlelit room inside grew brighter and reflected itself back at me at the window. I could see it all, inverted in the glass. The desk behind me, with its mess of papers. The candle on its stand. The curve of the hammock beyond. My dim reflection, standing at the window, looking out.

Lost in my own thoughts, I stared automatically at my reflection. The garden was almost dark now. I moved slightly, shifting from one foot to the other.

But my shadowy reflection didn't move. Because it

wasn't my reflection any more. It was the shape of a man.

And suddenly I saw them again – those eyes. Many-faceted, sharp eyes, staring back at me from *outside the glass*.

I reeled backwards, shouting in terror. Back and back, to the hammock, which I collapsed on to as I fell. But as much as I moved backwards, those eyes came forward. As if the being outside the window had just moved through the wall easily and now stood at the window, *inside the room*.

"Go away!" I yelled.

But instead, the rest of the form – head, shoulders, body – appeared in a grey shimmer. And suddenly, he was almost there.

He was very tall. He was dressed in a long black coat. His face was stern and strong. His hair was dark, like his piercing eyes. But all this I saw as he sort of came and went, faded and reappeared. Now I saw him – now he'd gone. The next instant, there he was again. But not flashing on and off, not like that. It's almost impossible to describe. He was there but not there. He was almost there.

"Come," he said. "The One I work for has sent me. We will sit together, you and I. And I will tell you why you are here."

Chapter Twenty

My Diary

I wish I could say that I was calm and together. But I wasn't. For ages I shook and cried and stammered and trembled. I just wanted to get out of there – to run.

But Epsilon took no notice. He went to the desk and opened the top drawer. He took out the flute – the flute I'd first seen when I'd run down to the cottage after dreaming about Sebastian. The same old wooden flute, with its symbol of Epsilon carved on the mouthpiece – like a half-feather, toppled over. Then Epsilon began to play. The same tune I'd heard in my dream.

I have never heard such haunting music. Never heard such a tune. It was as simple and as clean as water running downhill. It was as complex as many tapestries, all woven together.

And as he played, I relaxed a little, sitting fully now on the hammock. Epsilon played the flute with his eyes shut, which gave me a while to collect my thoughts, to try to grow calmer.

As the tune died away, he at last turned those piercing eyes on me. "Now," he said, "you must find the final piece of the puzzle. The final clue. The one that brings it all together." I nodded. I still couldn't speak.

"As Martha's note told you, it is hidden in a small space."

I thought back to the note. *"There is a small space hidden behind one of the swans... Master Cork is a gifted man – he has finished carving the swans on the Coscoroba pole, did I tell you?"*

Master Cork. And Jerry Cork, carving all those intertwined swans on the Coscoroba pole. Maybe I could take a closer look at the Coscoroba tomorrow, before the Aroundy dance, whatever that was. One final clue. One that links all these things together.

I stared at Epsilon, trying to pluck up some courage. Speak, Jess. Speak! "You *look* like a ghost!" was the first thing I managed to say. This made him smile.

"This is just one of my forms. I have others."

I cleared my throat, tried to get my mouth moving

properly again. "Why is my mum in danger?" I blurted out.

The smile vanished. His eyes turned very grave. He stood up and began to move round the room, touching this and that as he spoke. His voice was quiet and calm.

"Curses are terrible things," he said. "People tend to think they hold no power. But they could not be more wrong. They hold a great and terrible power. The words of the mouth are the mightiest weapon of all."

I nodded. Not because I understood – I just couldn't do anything else.

"Long ago on this island, a terrible curse was uttered on Long Beach. A curse that said that if the tooth was in the wrong hands, it could be used for misrule by the dark forces of the Lord of Inversion. By Cimul. But another word was spoken – that Cimul could never again *steal* the things he wanted to possess. They always had to be *gifted* to him, gifted to him by innocent hands."

He went to the wall and touched briefly the golden letter O there. I noticed that his hands left a brief shimmer, a trail of silver, upon everything he touched.

"That is where your mother comes into it."

"My mum?"

"Or rather, the eldest female of the Big House. The eldest of whoever is living there at the time."

He went to the window, drew the curtains wider open until the window was fully exposed. Then he stood to one side of it.

"I don't understand."

"Then watch."

In the window, shadows stirred and formed. The reflection of the room, with the candle and desk and the curve of the hammock, faded but didn't quite go away. But mingled in with these shapes, new figures appeared. I gazed at them and my mouth fell open.

People, moving. Men, walking in a circle around the Miradel. Ghostly chanting in the background, with words barely distinguishable. Something about the time of dark choices. Something about the Lord of Misrule. The chant was musical, with many harmonising voices.

Epsilon spoke again, his voice keeping pace with the changing images. "These men are followers of Cimul. They work together to serve him, to sing the old stories and songs about their Lord of Inversion. A *solemn choir*. They meet with their leader – their squire – as they have always done, in the hidden places of Lume. In ancient places, places where they made carvings on the walls, depicting the story of the overthrow of the One."

In the window, a curved wall of rock with carvings

appearing on it, hewn by ancient hands. Depictions of Cimul, hiding in his lair. Of Cimul, stealing followers from King L'Ume by treachery. Of Cimul on top of Coscoroba Rock, raising the curved tooth high into the air. Of a porpoise, leaping out to take it in his mouth and carry it beneath the waves.

"When the tooth was lost to them, their one great quest was to find it again and bring it back into the hands of Cimul. Then he and his faithful ones could use its curses for great evil – for misrule. So they seek it urgently."

In the window – a beach. Very far away in the distance, a small figure was bending, picking things up off the shoreline. The figure moved nearer.

"But the first curse spoken over the tooth – words spoken by King L'Ume – still stood. A curse can be invoked or revoked. Until it is revoked, its power continues. So when King L'Ume declared that Cimul could own something only if it was *given* to him by an innocent – well, that is still the case."

The figure on the beach bent. Picked up a shell. Dropped it into a bag. Moved closer.

"So the followers of Cimul need an innocent to hand the tooth to them. This lady is one of those innocents."

The woman straightened and lifted her face – her vacant, dreamy eyes.

"Mum!"

Then Mum turned round and looked over her shoulder. There, a little way off, stood another woman. A woman dressed in long black skirts, with a small black silk bonnet and a silver heart locket shining at her neck. She too was bending and lifting a shell.

"This lady is the last female before your mother to live in the Big House. Her name was Martha Wren."

Then Martha turned and looked over her shoulder. Another woman stood there, who turned and looked over her shoulder. And another and another and another.

"A long line of innocents, reaching back in time. All used by the followers of Cimul to try to locate the relic. But they are not the only ones who lived in the Big House." The picture changed again. I was looking at the small library.

A man stood at the table there, poring over a curly map. His face was mean and closed. On the wall behind him was a picture of an Ouroborus.

"Is that – Sebastian's papa?"

Even as I spoke, the image of Edmond Wren was replaced by another man, wearing even more old-fashioned clothes. Then he was replaced by another. And another.

"It was indeed Sebastian's father. Edmond Wren was elected by Cimul's followers as the leader of their group.

Their squire. He married Martha, and when Sebastian was born, he sent him away to be cared for in England. He isolated Martha more and more. But she astonished him by rebelling – just once – and bringing Sebastian here when he was seven."

"And that's why he always felt an outsider?"

"Yes. But Martha only rebelled that once. Otherwise, she was perfect for the role. She had to have... certain qualities. It has always been so, as you can see."

The long line of men in the library faded. In its place, one of Mum's crystals.

"Certain qualities?"

"A curiosity. A longing to look into things and see other things. A sensitive soul, artistic but solitary. Someone who is jaded by the things of this world and so could be encouraged to dabble in the things of the spirit. This is the quality the innocents had to have. This was how the Dark Beings made contact with them."

There, in the window, woman after woman appeared then faded. One peered into a basin of water and her eyes grew wide. Another turned over cards and leaned forwards, to read their meanings. One walked the beach, lifted a huge shell to her ear and listened, entranced, to its voice. Yet another sat up in bed suddenly, listening intently.

Then they all faded away and Epsilon turned back to me.

"And they all lived in our house – all those women? And their husbands were all made squire?"

"Or their brothers. Or uncles. Or guardians."

"But why the Big House?"

"Because of its land."

"Its land?"

"It is rumoured in the ancient tales that somewhere on this land – the land your mother now owns – is a map that leads to the relic. It was planted there by the ancients, in a place of great danger, where it would be hardest to retrieve. The followers of Cimul sense this legend is true."

"So the Dark Beings want the relic to invoke its curses? And why do the… what would you call them – *Bright* Beings? Why do the Bright Beings want it?"

"To revoke its curses and replace them with great blessings. But the Dark Beings are the ones who have tormented your mother. The women of the house have been compelled through the centuries to search for the relic – in order to hand it over to Cimul's followers. To give it into the wrong hands, freely."

I spoke aloud the words of 'The Key' that I'd uncovered.

"In the space below the well
A map to the tooth lies hidden.
The space is marked by an infidel
Whose hand reveals what's bidden.

Through merrow hair
In Neptune's lair
Past thirty fingers pale –
Then hark for a river in the dark
And reach for the spout of the whale!"

I stared into the window, hoping it would show me more. Nothing.

"But – which well? There are four on our land! How am I supposed to know which one it is?"

"That is the last question I am helping you with."

I frowned. "But – hang on. Dad isn't one of these leaders – a squire. Is he?"

"He is not."

"But you said that all the men who lived in this place were! So what changed things?"

"Sebastian did." Once again, the window shimmered.

Sebastian on the shore in the rain, screaming over and over, looking for someone. "Mama!" *he yelled, over and* over. *"Where are you, Mama!"*

My heart turned over. But the image was still changing.

Sebastian, dripping wet and exhausted, walking into the drawing room of our house. He stood panting at the door, and his papa looked up from the papers he and other men were studying. At the top of the papers, the Ouroborus was plainly marked. Sebastian's face grew hard and cold as he stared at it. He turned away and slammed the door on his way out.

Epsilon spoke again. "Sebastian guessed enough to know what had happened. To know that his father had sacrificed his mother, trying to obtain possession of the tooth. Sebastian was the child of the house who got closest to solving the whole thing. Sebastian almost solved it all."

"Almost?"

Epsilon turned away, his face solemn. "His fear made him trust the wrong person in the end," he said. "But he found the letter his mother had written for him – the one with the instructions to go to the firm of solicitors. He was sent away to boarding school, as she had anticipated. But as soon as he came of age to inherit, he went to that firm and laid claim to the house and land."

As he spoke, the window came to life again. I watched Sebastian – an older Sebastian – as he went through each of the things Epsilon was telling me.

"He turned his father out of the house. He hid everything he could that referred to all this. He closed up the small library. He ran away for a while. But he always came back. He never stopped searching for his mother's body. Not even when he was a very old man. And in his will, he left his house to any *female* descendants of his own family. He wrote a codicil stating that each female inherited it only on condition that she, in turn, would pass it to a female. Never to a male. He never again wanted any members of the Inverted Rule to live here. He broke every link he could with this house and the followers of Cimul."

"So... he must have had a female descendant? A daughter?"

Epsilon nodded. In the window, a kaleidoscope of scenes came and went.

Sebastian in strange lands, travelling seas, speaking to people gathered in exotic-looking tents. Then Sebastian with a woman who was dressed in Edwardian clothes. The woman cradled a tiny baby in the crook of each arm.

"He married when he was thirty-five. An Irishwoman – Beth. She gave birth to twins – Bridie and Libby. You can see for yourself what happened then."

Beth and her husband walking on a small Irish beach.

*There were little cottages snuggled into the hillsides. Beth
ran with two small girls, twin girls with very long hair
and huge eyes. Bridie and Libby. But Sebastian wasn't
laughing with them. He was staring out to sea. He was with
them, but not with them. Remote, far away. Beth called to
him, but when he turned her way, his eyes were dead and
hollow. Then Sebastian was returning to the Big House.
Alone.*

"He left them? He *left* his wife and children?"

"His mind was tormented. He couldn't settle anywhere
for long – not without coming back here to search for
Martha. So he came back – and never left again."

The window had gone blank. I sank back down into the
hammock, strangely exhausted. "And Bridie and Libby?
His children?"

"Well… Bridie took after her father. She was a bit of a
recluse, not interested in the Big House or the father who
had abandoned her."

"And Libby?"

"Libby inherited the house after Sebastian died. But she
never lived there – she lived in Ireland until she died. That
was ten years ago. She left it in her will to her own
daughter. Your mother." A long silence followed this.

I sat with my eyes shut, thinking, thinking. So Libby

must be my Grandma Libby – the one whose jet necklace I kept with my treasures. And that meant...

"That means... I'm related to Sebastian? He was my... Great-grandfather?"

The silence went on and on. When I opened my eyes and looked up, I was utterly alone.

Later the same night

Something woke me, about an hour ago. The oddest feeling.

I'd pored over these files till late, trying to think where the final piece of the puzzle might be. I suspected it was where Martha had said – under the breast of one of the swans on the Coscoroba pole. But I couldn't check that out until tomorrow. So I fell asleep in the end, my papers spread all over the bed. Then I woke up and felt jittery, uneasy. Had I heard a noise outside? I went to the window and peered out.

The clouds were almost solid, with the moon behind them. The whole sky was sort of backlit, silver. Into the silver something moved, far away. Just a speck. It came closer and closer. A large bird.

The swan? (No – not a swan, surely; the neck was all wrong.) But whatever it was, it was massive – an enormous wingspan!

It began to soar above the garden, to circle down. To the big oak tree by the house. It landed gently, yet it made the whole bough bend and quiver. I could see it clearly now from my window. It was so unexpected that I gasped out loud. It was an eagle.

I might never have seen one before, but I knew what it was. A white eagle. It folded its wings and turned its head my way.

What had I read, only just read tonight? In Mama's goodbye note to Sebastian? Mama, warning him about Yolandë's enemies:

They reverse all things. I shudder at it. Their lies are ludicrous, yet people believe them. It is like calling the eagle more lovely than the swan. That brown bird with its ugly talons, built only to kill!

Those talons. They did look cruel, and I thought of tiny mice and rodents scurrying away from that vice-like grip. Yet it was also noble. Such a noble head!

Then something else caught my eye – something on the ground this time. Something pale and slow, moving out of the woods.

I opened the window and leaned out. Now that my head and shoulders were poking out of the roof, I could see it all: the silver sky, the eagle, motionless now on his bough. The pale thing moving, far below. Coming towards the garden gate.

With the window open, I heard it quite clearly – the *sneak! sneak!* of the gate opening and shutting. And a soft, contented humming. A strange tune, over and over.

It was a woman. A woman in a long white nightie – bending, rising, bending again. She didn't move far each time, just a step. Then she sank to her knees an instant – stood up again, stepped forward. What was she *doing*? I screwed my eyes up, trying to see through the dark.

The clouds parted. The moon came out. It was Mum.

And in the moonlight, small gleams appeared on the ground, picked out by the soft light. They led away from her, back into the darkness. I knew what they were. A row of pale shells, all lined up.

More and more she laid, past Dad's hollyhocks, all the way into the middle of the lawn. Once I heard her laugh, a small, breathy laugh. It set my hair on end.

Then – a movement from the bough! The eagle. It opened its wings and soared down, straight down towards Mum as she crouched there. I clamped my hand to my mouth – I thought it was going to attack her! But no, it just landed on the grass, right in front of her.

But when she stood up, incredibly, she didn't seem to see it at all. A great bird like that, nearly half her height.

She just bent closer to the pile of shells held gathered in her skirts and chose the next one. She laid it down tenderly, a centimetre from the talon of that eagle. She stood up and chose another.

It stood very still all the time, watching her.

Until she had laid her shells in a tight curve, all the way round the eagle.

Then a great stripe of yellow flashed out across the lawn – the back door was flung open. The bird flew up, the moon went in – Dad gave an anguished shout as the eagle flapped away.

"Did you see that? Did you? An eagle! An eagle on the lawn, and my camera with no flash set up. I canNOT believe it! Did you *see* it?" He came into view, running about the grass, looking up in every direction.

Clearly, her voice came to me, eerily calm. "I've nearly finished."

"The eagle! A whopping great eagle, on the lawn! It was right *by* you!"

She laid the last shell. "Finished!"

"Elizabeth! It was right there, right on the blasted lawn! Good heavens, woman, it was at your foot! You must be blind!"

She turned and pointed to the ground, all along her trail

of shells. Dad looked down and his mouth fell open. The trail led away, back into the woods, gleaming in the light from the back door.

"Look!" she said. "I've lit her way. She can come now."

Chapter Twenty-one

My Diary

The Day of the Greet

I'm here at the Greet and, as the villagers keep saying to each other, "It's certainly a lovely afternoon for it!" If I hear that one more time, I'll scream.

Dr Parker's garden is enormous. Dead gorgeous too; garden designers come to visit it – apparently it's quite famous. Milton C Parker made it all a squillion years ago and it's all still there – like something out of those rich-and-famous programmes on TV. Statues and fountains and herb gardens. A summerhouse and a Japanese section (mostly stones – can't see the point in that). And even a hanging garden, its long flower beds swaying gently from verdigris chains, in a pretty arbour all of its own. This hanging garden was old Milton's pride and joy.

Anyway, the stands are set out in among all this finery. I'm getting through my spending money like there's no tomorrow. There's games and lemonade stands and cake stands and stuff. (Oh, whoopie! If only Avril could see me now – this is so jolly thrilling!) To say nothing of the tug-of-war, the skipping games for the little kids, the endless sack races and egg-and-spoon contests.

I'm supposed to be helping Mrs Shilling with the lemon punch at the drinks stand. She's cross with me, as usual. Apparently, we were supposed to bring some lemon squash to add to the punch; everyone else has contributed some. But Mum forgot, although why Mrs Shilling should blame me for that, I've no idea! I'm sick of her nasty glares. So I keep sneaking off here to the summerhouse, to be on my own. There's a lot to think about, and I go sweaty every time I realise I've not found the final clue. But there's no sign yet of the Coscoroba pole.

I can't stop thinking about Mum. She's back to the muttering, hand-wringing thing. She keeps stopping what she's doing and looking out to sea, as if she's listening for something, waiting for something, all the time. When I get close enough to hear, she's talking about "her" again. Looking for her.

But it could be worse, I suppose. She could be

wandering about in her underskirt, laying a trail of butterfly buns.

From here in the summerhouse, I can see her quite clearly, eating scones and now chatting in a distracted way to a man in a dirty red beret. They're both laughing very loud – too loud. (Probably something to do with the punch they're all drinking, which Dr Parker is doling out to adults only.)

In fact, now that I look, I think the man in the red beret is a bit tipsy. A lot of the adults sound a bit too happy and rowdy. They all have friends and family staying from the mainland apparently. Big event for them. The scintillating highlight of their year. Anyway, they seem to be making the most of it.

Dad is staying closer to Mum than usual, thankfully. Hovering. He's a bit tetchy and edgy – his wisdom tooth is playing up again and it always makes him sulky. He's mad at Mum again – for not believing him about the eagle last night. And for not getting him some herbal remedy for his tooth – what a fuss! He said she'd written it on her shopping list days ago, he'd watched her do it himself, but had she remembered? No, too busy playing Mrs Neptune.

So he's sulking and fiddling with his camera, but at least he's not at the lake – first time all week! (You can tell he's tempted though – four cameras and two tripods, they're draped all over him.) He looks like a travelling salesman. Kids keep snickering at him behind their stupid fists.

Right now, Mrs Shilling is waving her walking stick at some of them – boys who keep trying to get free lemon punch.

A very old man in a long black coat – in this heat! – is standing by the cake stand, staring my way. Earlier, Jerry Cork's wife, Agnes, told me his real name is Luke, but he moves so slowly all the time that they all call him Lively. "Look Lively!" they say to him. "Hurry up!" But he never can. Agnes said he is the slowest man she's ever met in all her days. Anyway, he keeps glancing my way. I get the feeling he wants to talk to me.

Another funny name they use is given to old Ely. They call him Fingers, "on account of how fast he can mend a fishing net – it's a sight to behold, is Ely, tying knots!" Well, he's certainly tying *me* in knots – following me all over the place! Because all afternoon, at odd times – playing hoopla, chatting to Agnes, selling a pot of jam – I've looked up and there he's been again!

He watched me come in here, to the summerhouse, watched me all the time. His forget-me-not eyes. Only sometimes they don't seem half as innocent as forget-me-nots. Maybe I'm imagining it.

I keep looking for Epsilon. *"This is just one of my forms. I have others,"* he'd said last night, when I accused him of looking ghostly. He said he'd be here; he said I'd see him at the Greet. One minute I wonder if he is the man they call Lively… or Ely… or even Mrs Shilling… or even the cat! Then I shake myself, tell myself I'm overtired, my imagination is running wild. Which I am. And it is.

It doesn't help that Epsilon had also said I'd see "a friendly enemy" here, and "a hostile friend. You must not get them mixed up."

Mixed up? If I'm thinking the cat could be Epsilon, I'm more than a bit mixed up.

Later, we're all going down to the beach for the barbecue, although someone must be down there already – I can hear them on Long Beach. Calling and calling, like they've lost their dog or something. A woman, I think.

A few things have happened. First, when I was standing there unfolding all my raffle tickets (I bought twenty! I was after the carved music box), I was eavesdropping on the doc and the man in the red beret. Mrs Shilling – I am convinced of it – was eavesdropping too.

"You a visitor then?" said Doc to Man in Red Beret. "Lemon punch or gin punch? Have a bit of both – it's free to visitors."

"How kind. Thank you. All set for later then?"

"Later?" The doctor poured drink into a plastic cup, handed it over.

"Well... you've waited a long time for this, haven't you?"

"The barbecue? Hardly! We have it every year!"

"Ah. Yes. Of course."

"Er... I'm Dr Parker. Look after all these people, for my sins! Call me Charles. And you are... ?"

The man in the red beret held out his hand. "Pleased to meet you, Charles. Just call me Mike." They shook hands, then someone called the doctor away to judge the cake competition. Off he went, clutching his belly and pretending to protest.

I stared at Mike, wondering. Could this be Epsilon? But he just seemed too... normal. He tasted his lemonade and pulled a face. Quick as a bird, Mrs Shilling reached over, snatched his cup and took a sip. I couldn't imagine sharing a cup with that toothless old hag! But he didn't seem to mind.

"Not enough sugar!" said Mrs Shilling. "I tell him, year after year. But will he listen? No!"

"Tell who?"

"Why – the Lemon Squire, of course!" she snapped.

The very mention of the Lemon Squire sent me whizzing mentally back to the documents in the first box, 'The Ballad of Yolandë'. But before I could think anything through, I realised that the woman from the raffle ticket stall had been tugging at my sleeve awhile.

"Jessica? You're miles away, child!" she was saying. "You've won the bubble bath set! Lucky you – my sister had her eye on that."

When I turned round, Mike had gone.

Then later, when we were sitting on the benches, watching the skipping games (all these little kids running in and out of a long rope), I heard something else. I heard it quite clearly. But no one else seemed to.

"Mama? What is it, Mama?"

"Shh! Can't you hear it? Someone on the beach, calling me. Mar-tha! Mar-tha! Over and over. Can't you hear it, Sebastian?"

I dropped my drink and whirled around. Nothing. Just Mrs Shilling glaring at the spilled lemonade, tutting and muttering ("clumsy, stupid girl") and swiping at the bench with a cloth.

But no one else was there. Well, there was, of course – about 200 people, in fact. Just ordinary people, all cheering the kids as they jumped in and out of the skipping rope, taking turns until someone tripped up and was out. The winner was obviously going to be the child who lasted the longest.

Then the skipping rhyme changed.

> *"Winken, Blinken and Sharry-arry-odd!*
> *Who is our devil and who is our god?*
> *Is it a swan or a goosey goosey gander?*
> *IN jumps the one we call Yolandë!*
>
> *How many feathers does Yolandë bring?*
> *One-two-three-four-five, we sing!*
> *OUT jumps the devil and IN jumps god!*
> *Winken, Blinken, and Sharry-arry-odd!"*

Mrs Shilling was still standing behind me – I could smell her.

"Mrs Shilling," I turned and asked, "who *is* Yolandë?"

"Never mind that – where is your mother?" she snapped. "You must be *vigilant*, girl!"

Sure enough, when I turned round, there was Mum leaving the garden. She had a strange, intent look on her face. Eager, even. I raced after her.

"Mum, Mum! Where are you going?"

"I'm going to find her," she said.

"Oh, Mum – find who?"

"She's down on Long Beach, calling my name."

"It's just someone calling her dog, Mum. Come on, let's go back."

"Stop pulling me! Who is it? Stop pulling me and *listen*!"

So I stood still to listen, to hear what they were calling. Went icy all over. But turned back to Mum, led her away with a bright smile. "All I can hear is someone calling her *dog*. Now come on."

"But I want to find her!" Mum looked as if she might cry.

"Oh, Mum! Look, sit here with Mrs Shilling. I'll get you a cup of tea. Two sugars. To calm your nerves." I left her on a bench, went to the tea stand. Two sugars for me too.

I'd heard it all right. A faraway voice, a woman's voice, very thin and sweet. In a funny kind of sing-song, over and over. I've been hearing it all day, I realised, tugging at the very back of my thoughts. Not her name at all. Mine.

"*Jess-i-cah! Oh, Jess-i-caaah!*" Over and over and over. It terrified me.

Later

Luke Lively just came up to me and said such a weird thing.

He sidled up to the shed just as I'd carried one of the folding tables back into it. Like Agnes said, he moves slowly, carefully, as if he's preserving his energy all the time. He also moves far too quietly for my liking. One minute I was alone. The next minute there he was, blocking the door.

"I've come to tell you. You are being led astray," he said.

"Pardon?"

From outside the shed, the sound of laughter and the clatter of things being cleared away so we could all go down to the beach.

"There is one who calls himself a Bright Being. But he is a Dark Being."

I stared at him, my heart thumping. Here – out of the blue – someone waltzes up and mentions the Beings. As calm as anything! I looked into his eyes and considered. Could this tranquil, careful man be Epsilon? I decided that time was running out – I had to grab any chance I got to solve all this. It was almost dusk.

"You know about the Bright Beings and the Dark Beings," I said. "How?"

He turned to look over his shoulder, back at the sea, glittering there in the distance. "You know that the blue whale exists, don't you?" he said. "Out there somewhere, under the sea?"

I frowned. "Of course I do!"

"How? Have you ever *seen* one? Actually seen one for yourself?"

"Well… no."

"There are other creatures too, even deeper under the sea. They exist. The fact that few have seen them doesn't mean they don't exist. Some have never been seen at all – but they are down there, all the same. You have to learn to look at things in another way. With different eyes."

I didn't quite know how to answer this strange speech, spoken by this strange man. Could this be the friendly enemy, I wondered? Or the hostile friend? I had no real way to tell.

"What did you mean," I said finally, "I'm being led astray?"

"Just what I said. The Bright Being. He is not good. He has fed you with lies. Do not trust him. Do not trust his riddles and his music. Especially not tonight."

Then he turned on his heel, and I was alone again in the shed.

So. A second warning about Epsilon. What had Mama said, in her note to Sebastian?

His kindness to you is a lie – you must not believe it; he is one of the Dark Beings. He has bewitched you with his riddles and his music. Yet I cannot help you. It is all too late.

Outside the shed, a blackbird sang in its tree and shadows crept across the garden. The sun was beginning to set. I was running out of time. But I didn't know what it was I had to do.

Food cheers anyone up and the beach barbecue was *excellent*. Loads of chicken and hot dogs and that yummy fried-onion smell. Fish too – mackerel! And plenty of it. I stood by the doctor and smiled down at the rows and rows of sizzling fish.

"Well, Doctor – that's one way to get rid of it, I suppose."

"Had to do something. Blasted freezer lid wouldn't close! Here – choose a fire and go and sit down. Eat! Eat! You look tired."

There were four fires, strung all along Long Beach, right over to Coscoroba Rock. One big one (the barbecue fire) and three smaller ones. A different activity was happening at each small fire, it seemed. At the first, children were singing campfire songs, elbowing one another, all munching hot dogs. At the second, just gossip, a place to rock the tired babies, to talk softly.

The third (the farthest away – you got chilly walking all that way to it) had Jerry Cork at it. And what looked like the whole Cork tribe. And Mum and Mrs Shilling. They were talking about some creatures called Butterwyths, and this was the fire I joined.

"So the Butterwyths are real, Uncle Jerry?" asked a small girl, eyes wide in the dancing flame.

"Real? I'll say they are. Why else do we leave food out for them in the outbuildings – butterbread and fat? It'd be a bad day for us if we ever forgot!"

"Why, Uncle Jerry? Would they *kill* us?"

"Don't be so dramatic, Judith. It's not us – it's the sheep. Where do you think foot rot comes from? And hack cough, every winter? It's them that bring it, the Butterwyths – nasty, greedy little elves that they are!"

"Shh! Mind your tongue!" said Mrs Shilling. "They'll hear you, Jerry Cork!" But he just laughed and so it went on to the next tale, the next old story.

It turned colder. We all got shivery. Then, in a lull around the storytelling fire, Mum suddenly spoke. "I've heard a story too," she said in a quiet voice. "A beautiful story. About a woman. I heard it right here, on this beach!"

"Tell us, tell us!" clamoured the children.

"Sit back down then, all of you!" said Jerry Cork. "And wipe your nose, Judith. You're making me lose my appetite."

They all went quiet and looked up at Mum expectantly. But she seemed to have forgotten how to tell a story. She stared all around at the waiting faces and her chin started to tremble. "It's not a very interesting story. It was about… I don't know what it was about. I think I've forgotten it."

"But you said it was a beautiful story!" said Judith. "About a woman. I want to hear it. Uncle Jerry, I want to hear the beautiful story!"

"Leave the lady alone, Judith," said Jerry Cork. "Why don't we go and have some of that punch, Elizabeth? Come on, you'll be warmer over at the big fire, and that pork must be done by now. I can smell it from here. Up you get then – that's the way. Now you behave yourself for Mrs Shilling, all of you!"

Mum smiled and went off with Jerry Cork, to the disappointed *aaahs*! of the children.

"I'll tell you a story," said Mrs Shilling unexpectedly. "If you'll sit down and stop all this ridiculous noise."

"Is it a beautiful story, Mrs Shilling?"

"No." (Somehow I expected that.) "It's a story about a girl who kept looking in the wrong place for things."

"What things, Mrs Shilling? Treasure?"

"Yes... treasure. One day she was told to look for some gold."

"Who by?" asked Judith instantly.

"Er... by... the Butterwyths. Yes, the Butterwyths. They told her to find some gold. Right here, on this beach. It was hidden under a small rock – she knew that – a rock with black in it and white in it, the Butterwyths had said. But which kind of rock, she wondered? A black one with white specks? Or a white one with black specks? Look all around you – as you can see, there are plenty of each."

The children swivelled round, pointed out rocks, some black speckled, some white speckled. Mrs Shilling glared at me and pursed her lips. Why was she always angry with me? What had I done?

"It wasn't so much what she *did* that annoyed them," she went on in that tight little voice. It was as if she'd read my thoughts! The hairs began to creep up on the back of my neck. "It was what she *didn't* do. For this was a girl who could get nothing right – she was stupid, as stupid as they come."

The children were silent, puzzled. Mrs Shilling ignored

them all and began to trail her bent old finger through the sand.

"So the girl spent days and days and weeks and weeks looking under the rocks. Black stones, white stones, all the speckled ones, she looked under as many as she could. Then someone came and told her time was running out — she had to hurry."

"Who came and told her, Mrs Shilling?" asked one of the boys.

"Tsk. It doesn't matter who came and told her: she was told!"

"But—"

"Who is telling this story, Adam Butler — me or you?" The boy fell silent and sulky.

"So when time was running out, what did the girl do? She just went on looking under all those same rocks — the black-speckled ones and the white-speckled ones — same as she ever had. The problem with her, you see, is that she didn't know how to *listen*. For it wasn't a black stone the treasure was hidden under at all."

"It was a white one!" cried Judith in triumph.

"Not at all. It was as the Butterwyths had said. A stone with black *and* white in it."

"A *stripy* stone?"

"For heaven's sake, no! Not a stripy stone at all. Not black next to white at all, oh, no! Black *on top* of white! She had to take the colour of black – and put it *on top* of the colour of white. One on top of the other, then it would all make sense. And that's the end of the story."

The children looked round at one another, indignant frowns on their faces.

"But I don't *get* it!"

"That's not a story, nothing happened!"

"It was a grey stone," I said.

"It was a grey stone," said Mrs Shilling. "Lay one fact on top of the other and it has a way of merging into sense. Especially when time is short… and now, you all look tired. You should all be thinking about getting off back to your beds."

The children's mouths fell open in astonishment. They stared at her as if she had grown two heads.

"Bed?!"

"But we never go to bed on the night of the Greet! You know we don't, Mrs Shilling!"

"Mam said we could stay up till after midnight!" said Judith sullenly. "And look – they're getting the Aroundy dance ready."

"And we don't like your stupid stories anyway," said Adam. "They're rubbish."

They leaped up and ran, skidding sand from their sandals back to where she sat. The sand scattered all over her skirts and the back of her head. She just flicked it away and stood up slowly, leaning heavily on her stick. From nearer the big fire, one of the children shouted back at her, a rhyme she'd obviously heard before and hated:

> *"Mrs Shilling – smelly hag!*
> *Teeth need filling – makes you gag!*
> *Mrs Shilling – always willing – for a killing*
> *Mad old bag!"*

She glared their way, but it was much too dark to see the culprit. Instead, she brushed a small shower of sand out of her hair.

"Tsk. Hardly poetry," she sniffed. "Nevertheless, I am right. You should be thinking of going back to your *bed*!"

"Me? But Mrs Shilling! I'm *fourteen*!"

She sighed down at me tiredly, shook her head. "How very *short-sighted* you are." Then she hobbled off, back toward the big fire where the Coscoroba pole was being raised.

It wasn't until she had gone that I saw it in the sand. She

had been drawing with her finger, all that time. A pattern. One I'd seen before. One laid in fossils in Epsilon's kitchen. One that Mama had laid out in shells on Sebastian's bed.

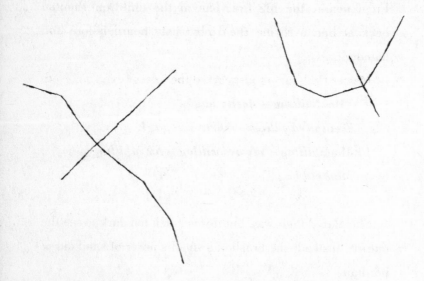

A breeze came from the sea as I stared down at it. It stirred the grains of sand, wiped some of the pattern away.

I bent closer, afraid it would all get blown away.

But then I suddenly remembered where *else* I'd seen it before – why it was already oddly familiar to me. I'd seen it before on a wall! Which wall?

Epsilon's? Yes... something on the bedroom wall in Epsilon's cottage! But what? Maybe... the star charts?

But as soon as I realised this, Mrs Shilling's voice spoke in my head, low and urgent. You need to think about going back to your *bed*, Mrs Shilling had said. To your *bed*.

Sebastian's bed. My bed. The swan bed.

"There is a small space hidden behind the breast of one of the swans... Master Cork is a gifted man... I forget so many things..."

Master Cork hadn't just carved the Coscoroba, I realised. He'd carved my bed. My massive old bed, with four swans carved into the headboard.

I turned and ran, all the way back up the cliff path.

Chapter Twenty-two

My Diary

Back home, 10 p.m.

It wasn't hard to find, not really.

I ripped the pillows off, stared at the swans on the massive headboard. Touched them gingerly. Pressed and fumbled at the wood. Found it at last.

It was the left-hand swan, the lower one. As I pressed it, there was a very small click. The whole of the body of the swan slid out and revealed a space hidden behind.

In the space was a parchment, but this one looked very, very old. Fragile. It was face-up. I could see the symbols clearly – but when I took hold of one corner of it and tugged it out, it started to crumble between my finger and thumb.

Quickly, I grabbed a pen, a scrap of paper from my desk and copied down the symbols written there. The symbols

Sebastian – who else? – had hidden.

Then I ran to my box file and turned to where I'd written the whole alphabet down. Quick, quick, translate it! My hands shook as I wrote the words down, one by one, agonisingly slowly. At last, I had it all.

The Riddle of the Two

At the feather'd head,
I hang my bed.

At the feather'd breast,
An ancient rest.

At the feather'd wing,
The whale doth sing.

Whale. Something else mentioned a whale. The document called 'The Key' – the one that tells me to where to go and find the map. The map that will lead to the tooth.

In the space below the well
A map to the tooth lies hidden.
The space is marked by an infidel
Whose hand reveals what's bidden.

Through merrow hair
In Neptune's lair
Past thirty fingers pale –

Then hark for a river in the dark
And reach for the spout of the whale!

It all seems to be describing a cave. A cave below a well.

So. Time to be practical. If Epsilon is right and Mum decides to wander off into a cave, then I'd better take a torch. Even though the very idea of wandering in and out of caves at the dead of night makes my flesh crawl.

But first I needed to go and look at the star chart.

I yelled for Domino. "Come on, boy! Time for another walk!"

The cottage is eerie at the best of times. It's even worse seen by torchlight!

But my trusty barometer, Domino, seemed OK. In fact, he bounded up the stairs and leaped straight up on to the hammock.

Anyway, there were the star charts. Two of them. One with the usual stars on it – Orion and the Plough and the Pleiades and stuff. All recognisable patterns. But the other held different constellations. Different stars. Deneb and Sadr and Gienah. And sure enough, there was the pattern – the one that was laid out in fossils on Epsilon's floor. The one Mama had drawn in shells – and Mrs Shilling had drawn in the sand.

The patterns were separate constellations. But both of them sit side by side in the summer sky.

This time, I copied it down with all the little blobs in place, representing the different stars. The top shape is (surprise surprise) called Cygnus. The second shape is called Aquila. As to the meaning of that word, your guess is as good as mine.

It was a quarter past ten when I left, according to Epsilon's funny little chiming clock. And according to Dr Parker and the other villagers, whatever they did at the Greet really began at midnight. Dedication of the island or something. But what was I supposed to do now? The only person who seemed to be prodding me along right now was Mrs Shilling. I'd have to go back and ask her.

I felt like a yo-yo as I set off back to the beach. Up and down, up and down. Domino bounded around my heels. But the closer I got to the beach, the more nervous I felt. Giddy and sick inside, like I needed to throw up. Another feeling grew too – that every step I took back along the cliff path I was walking not just into my future, into the next few hours, but back into the past. As if the past and future were all mixed up, and here was I in the present, lost in the middle of it all.

Looking down from the top of the cliff path, I could see

the fires clearly, strung out along Long Beach. The breeze picked up from the sea; I could taste salt in the air. As I looked outwards, there was a wildness in the water – a choppy sea, frothing up into madness. And very faintly, in the gaps between the gusts of wind, I thought I could still hear it. That sing-song voice, calling over and over.

"Jess-i-caah! Oh, Jess-i-caah!"

Domino didn't seem to be scared at all though – he barked down at the waves, yapped madly up at the rushing clouds. He was fine, my furry little barometer.

But as I started the climb down the cliff path, I realised how stressed out I was. I knew something would happen to Mum tonight, something I had to try and prevent.

Inside me, there was no knowledge of how to do it. There was nothing but a growing dread.

"Kitten! Where've you been? I've been looking everywhere for you."

"Sorry, Dad. Went to get Domino – didn't see why he should miss out on the fun."

"You and that dog! Come on – the kids are having a ball with the Aroundy pole. I've got some lovely black and whites."

"Where's Mum? Is she OK?"

"Seems fine! Look, there she is."

She was by the big fire with Ely Fingers. It seemed that everyone on Lume was there too! Mum turned my way but looked right through me. Ely didn't, though. He turned those forget-me-not eyes on me and smiled.

"Are you all right, Jessica?" he asked.

"Fine. Why shouldn't I be?"

"Then why are you panting? Have you been running? You ought to slow down a bit."

Why was I panting? It was the very same question I'd asked him, that night when he'd turned up at the lake. He gave me a crooked little smile before he turned away. "I notice things," he said. "Just like you do."

Shadows fell everywhere, cast by the fire. Figures danced in the sand, and someone took out a fiddle and began to play. Mum just stood still and stared out to sea. I watched her, and that dread came and knotted all together in a small ball in my stomach. Was I going to throw up? I needed to walk, to breathe deeply, to get away from them all.

So I slunk away from creepy Ely and went to the shore, calling Domino all the time. But he'd run off somewhere, farther down the beach. (And yep, I was right. I was going to be sick. Oh, great!)

Around the gossip fire, women still sat, rocking infants in their arms. They smiled and waved at me as I passed. I waggled my fingers at them, but to tell you the truth, I was hurrying like crazy. If there's one thing I hate doing, it's throwing up in front of anyone else. And that ball in my stomach grew harder and harder until I rushed out of the last flickering light of the gossip fire, bent over and threw my barbecue up all over the sand. I retched and retched until there was nothing left but a sour taste. I scooped sand up over the mess with my foot. Then I went shakily on to the last fire, wiping my mouth.

Mike in the red beret sat there – with Domino curled up on his knee!

"Domino! Didn't you hear me calling you?"

"I think he was too comfortable to care," said Mike.

"Well, you should be honoured. He's normally so fussy."

To tell you the truth, I didn't really fancy yakking to a half-tipsy man so far away from the main fire. But just then he reached out his hand to me. In his hand, there was a crisp white handkerchief.

"Here. It's OK. You can keep it; I don't want it back. Go on, *take* it!"

I took the hankie and stared down at it, puzzled. He spoke again. "Er… excuse my impertinence, but you have vomit in your hair. Your nose ring too. It's all a bit of a mess."

I almost died with embarrassment. Imagine that horrid, horrid man pointing it all out! I turned away, blew my nose. I struggled to take the nose ring out, wrapped it in the hankie. Stuffed the whole mess into my pocket. Sniffled and snorted and died ten thousand times.

Then he stood up and began to stride back down the beach. "Come on, Jess. It's time for the dedication."

I didn't really want to walk back with him – he made me nervous. But Domino, with a guilty sideways look at me, slunk off and trotted at his heels. "Traitor!" I said, and ran to catch him up.

The dedication started off quite normally. Toasts were drunk, thank-yous said. Why on earth do adults have to laugh so loudly at everything? Hyena laughs, the women worse than the men – except for the times the men were worse than the women. Of course, the punch was flowing freely. Dr Parker made sure everyone had a full glass before the toasts began.

As to the toasts – well! They drank to Dr Parker and all he'd done for them through the year. They drank to the tides that had brought them fish. They drank to Luke Lively, for reminding them all to slow down. They drank to

Ely Fingers's fingers, for mending the best nets to catch the fish. (Are they going to drink to the fish? I wondered. Here they go, drinking to the fish.)

So they drank to the mackerel and to the schools of herring and to the black-headed greedy gulls for not eating the lot. They drank to the evening star for guiding the fishing boats back home. They drank to the fishing boats themselves. By name. I kid you not.

"To *Swift Molly*!"

"To *Skipper Jack*!"

"To *One Lady of Lume*!"

One Lady again. But there was no time to think – the singing began. They sang sea shanties and toasted the ocean through every song.

After a while, it all got very silly. I realised it was just fun – just a kind of play they were making up on the spot and then screaming in delight at their own wit. Plus, it was funny – and anyway, I'd managed to snag one of the glasses of punch, so I was starting to giggle a bit myself. Then they called for Fingers. "Let Ely Fingers step forward and toast us all!" they yelled. So Ely Fingers was pushed forward – a bit unsteady on his feet – and began:

"We drink to the Lemon Squire, the great, useless lump!"

"To the Lemon Squire!" they cackled. And they lifted their glasses up to Dr Parker!

"Here's to the hand that carves the wood!" (Jerry Cork, who else?)

"Here's to the Coscoroba!" (The Aroundy pole, still stuck in the sand, ribbons snapping in the breeze.)

"Here's to the Lord of the Inverted Rule!" (Who did that refer to? I wondered.) They raised their glasses vaguely — to the moon? The sea? It was hard to tell, but the next toast was already beginning.

"Here's to the innocent who welcomes him back!"

Some of the villagers were looking a bit puzzled now, uncertain whom to toast. But Ely raised his glass to Mum, and everyone laughed and joined in.

I stared across at Mum. Ely Fingers had identified her as the innocent, even if most of the villagers didn't know what on earth that meant. The innocent who welcomes him back. Poor, innocent Mum, drawn in somehow to something she doesn't understand.

Just like Seb's Mama.

It grew colder, the wind from the sea picking up, bringing the sound of the surging waves. So more wood was piled on the fires, more drinks were poured, the fiddle struck up again. But every so often, someone else would stand and raise a toast, and they got stranger and stranger.

"Here's to the porpoise with its ancient song!"

"To the porpoise!" they all cried.

"Here's to the swan with the sharpest eyes!"

"To the swan!"

"Here's to the snake with its tail in its mouth – here's to the Ouroborus!"

"To the Ouroborus!"

But because there were so many people, they didn't all get the timing right saying the toast. Some finished a little behind the rest so I heard it a bit staggered: *"Ouroborus-borus-borus."* Suddenly I remembered a fragment from the back of Sebastian's first sketch. The bit when he was describing me. *In her nose, she wore a silver ring. In ancient times ... followers of the 'Borus also wore the ring, as a sign to each other. This sign has alarmed me greatly.*

Could his word "'Borus" be the shortened version of the word Ouroborus? What did my nose ring have to do with that though? So the ancients who revered the 'Borus wore nose rings – big deal.

Just as I was wondering about it all, Mrs Shilling came up. "What would happen, girl, if a snake were to swallow its own tail?"

"Er... um. Dunno. Why on earth can't you call me Jess?"

"It would eat itself, girl. It would get smaller and smaller until it had reduced itself to a single point. Then it would vanish."

"So?"

"Like someone else vanished. Here, on this beach, long ago."

"Sebastian's mama?"

"Shh! Not so loud. Follow me."

I followed her silently all the way to the last fire. She pointed to where the tide frothed and foamed around a huge jagged rock sticking out into the sea. I noticed now that the rock had a sort of thin long bit stretching out – a bit like the neck of a swan. At the end of it, a stone beak was open as if eternally calling.

"That is Coscoroba Rock," said Mrs Shilling. She passed me a small tattered card – another of her bird cards. This one was of a swan. I angled it so I could read it in the firelight – read it out loud.

"*LATIN*: COSCOROBA COSCOROBA. *Common name: Coscoroba swan. A short-necked swan normally found in South America. Plumage white but occasional examples of black. This species appears to be somewhere intermediate between the swan and the goose.*"

Mrs Shilling put another bit of wood on the fire. Sparks flew up, then subsided.

"The skipping song!" I said. "The song the children were skipping to, earlier today!"

"Well, I'm glad you pay attention to some things at least," she snapped, and she started to recite the song, softly, looking into the fire the whole time.

> *"Winken, Blinken, and Sharry-arry-odd!*
> *Who is our devil and who is our god?*
> *Is it a swan or a goosey goosey gander?*
> *IN jumps the one we call Yolandë!*
>
> *How many feathers does Yolandë bring?*
> *One-two-three-four-five, we sing!*
> *OUT jumps the devil and IN jumps god!*
> *Winken, Blinken, and Sharry-arry-odd!"*

She kept looking out to sea, and when I glanced way down the beach, there was Mike with the red beret. He was standing all alone, staring outwards.

"Are you all waiting for someone? For something?" I asked.

"Not all of us," said Mrs Shilling. "Most of them don't

know what's going on – even less than you do. To them, this is just fun, a garden party, a barbecue."

"But to others – just a few – this all has a different meaning? A hidden meaning?"

Nod.

"So. The Ouroborus is a symbol of... someone vanishing."

"People say it means many things. Some use it for other evil purposes. On this island, it has always represented the Inverted Rule. To me it also represents the innocent."

As she spoke, she looked immensely sad. I wondered if she was about to start crying. The thought horrified me.

I still didn't know whether to trust her. I mean, here she was prodding me to work things out – but why? What motive? Whose side was she on? I decided I had nothing to lose. Inside me, that ticking, that growing sense of time running out.

"What am I supposed to do, Mrs Shilling?"

She looked back to the main fire, where the children had started their Aroundy dance. As they danced, they sang that chant. Even from here, we could hear the words clearly: "...*goosey goosey gander? IN jumps the one we call Yolandë*..." Only they were singing both verses together, the children with blue ribbons going one way, the children with gold ribbons going another. So all the words were mixed up.

She pointed into the surf. A bit of broken old tree branch was tumbling there. As we watched, it rolled slowly over on to its back and clutched for the sky.

"What the tide takes away, the tide brings back."

The voices from the main fire grew louder. They seemed to have uprooted the Coscoroba pole. They'd dragged it out of the sand and were carrying it along the beach. They were all on the surf line now, singing and screeching if anyone got their feet wet. A long messy line of people was snaking our way. Mrs Shilling looked alarmed. "It's started. You are running out of time, girl!"

"But – I don't know what to *do*! I really don't, Mrs Shilling! Why don't you tell me, if you know?"

"Because I don't know!" she snapped. "I only know bits of it – bits I've read – impressions formed over the years. It's you who have got to make sense of them."

I saw a flash – a flurry of sparks. The ribbons, catching fire. They were burning the Aroundy pole. The ribbons flew, shedding sparks. Slowly, the flame took hold of the wood.

"It is you who must find the relic – it's your mother who's involved."

I stared at that pale bough tumbling over and over in the

nearby surf. The villagers got louder and louder.

"But... where do I *find* the relic? I know there is a map to the tooth. Somewhere under a well. But which well? There's loads of wells on the map of the island! I just don't get it, Mrs Shilling!"

She gave a huge sigh. The first children arrived – Adam and Judith. They ran giggling into the small halo cast by the fire.

"The speckled stones, you stupid girl! The speckled stones. Not striped, black laid next to white. Black laid *on top* of white!"

"Oh, no – are you still telling that boring story?" Adam said. He ran back, dragging Judith to the main group. They all went over to Coscoroba Rock and began to swarm over it.

The burning Aroundy pole was held out over the sea. But I was still racking my brains about black laid on top of white. Suddenly, I had it!

"Black LAID ON TOP OF white – the patterns! I have to take the patterns and lay them ON TOP OF THE MAP. The patterns – the constellations – are PART OF the map!"

"At last! Now go and do it. If it's not too late already."

Mrs Shilling heaved herself to her feet and stood

watching the children. They were all laughing now around Coscoroba Rock. On top of the rock, Dr Parker held out the burning pole. It sparked and dripped fire into the waves. Then, with a great shout from everyone, he tossed it like a great golden spear into the churning water. The sea took it at once.

The children shrieked and clapped and began to run back to our fire. Mrs Shilling went forwards as if to meet them. But something stopped her. She went very still and turned around – stared out to sea as if she'd heard something.

Then I heard it too – very faint at first. A sound, a steady beat, a rhythmic, steady whirring.

"Hello, Jess!" said the doctor. "You missed all the fun! And I must say, your dog certainly enjoys a good paddle."

Domino came careering up and landed, a wet, sandy bundle, on my knee.

He was trembling violently all over.

"Uncle Jerry," said Judith. "Uncle Jerry, what's that noise?"

The noise grew and grew – the sound of many wings, great wings, beating. Until suddenly, there they were, over us – the swans.

Ten, twenty, thirty. More and more and more. White swans, calling and circling, low over our heads, and the moon lit up each neck, each curve of wing. Hundreds of them.

So loud, so beautiful, so many of them! The loudest, wildest thing I ever saw, and we all just looked up, our mouths falling open.

Then Dad gave a yell and ran out of the crowd, camera flashing. The silver of the moon, the hot, electric flash from the camera, feathers twirling down, feathers falling, the children trying to catch them. One. Two. Three. Four. Four feathers, dropped by the swans.

No – five. Just like it said in the skipping song: "*How many feathers does Yolandë bring? One-two-three-four-five, we sing.*"

But then the swans rose higher and all flew together over the sea. In a great shining circle they flew before curving inland in an enormous, moonlit glitter. They flew like that towards the lake.

Everyone started talking at once.

"Wow! Did you see that? I can't believe it!"

"Hundreds of them!"

"That was amazing!"

Dad stood still, panting, with a look of sheer joy on his face.

"Dad?" I said.

"Jess! Wasn't that incredible!"

"Dad."

"My God! I've never seen so many swans in one place in all my life!"

"Dad," I said. "Where's Mum?"

Chapter Twenty-three

My Diary

Looking for Mum

The last time anyone had seen Mum was watching the Aroundy dance. Doc Parker said she'd seemed fine; she'd said she had a slight headache and might go and get some painkillers.

Dad said he'd last seen her heading this way, towards the last fire. He'd thought she was coming to join me and Mrs Shilling. But she hadn't.

Judith said she and Adam had seen her up at the lake. But that had been earlier, she said – about ten o'clock.

"At the lake?" said Dad. "Are you sure? What were you doing at the lake?"

"I went back with Adam, to get his inhaler," she said, looking up at Dad with round, scared eyes. "The smoke from the fires was making him wheeze. We went up to the village and she was up on Crag Point."

"Up on Crag Point? What in blazes was she doing up there in the dark?"

"But it wasn't dark!" said Adam. "She was all lit up – there were lights behind her."

"Lights?" said Dad.

"Yes, lights. In the ruins. We thought it was you!"

"Me?" said Dad, bewildered. "What are you talking about?"

"Well…" Adam trailed away uneasily, so Judith took up the story.

"Well, we thought it was you, taking pictures of her. You're always doing it, up and down the island. You rigged up lights last night – to shine on to the lake. We saw you!"

"To photograph the swan, yes. Not up at Crag Point! Why on earth would I risk my neck up there – do you think I'm crazy?"

"Yes!" said Adam, his courage returning. "We all do – we all call you the Mad Photographer. And Uncle Jerry's seen some of your photos in a magazine, and he says they're brilliant. He wouldn't be surprised if you're a genius – he says geniuses are always a bit crazy."

Jerry Cork coloured up and stammered his apologies to

Dad, who waved them away and looked secretly rather flattered.

"Anyway," said Judith, "as we passed by the bottom path, we saw you'd lit up the ruins, like there were lamps lit in the windows. And she was standing on top of the point with her arms held out to the sea."

But that wasn't Mum, I knew.

"Well, we'd better go and look for her then!" said Dr Parker. "We've all finished here anyway – and it's getting cold. Richard, you go and check your house. She may just be resting. If she's not at your house, come back up to mine and we'll all think again."

Dad nodded and strode off frowning. He seemed to have forgotten all about me. The doctor went on. "Ely, Mrs Shilling – you look frozen stiff. You both come back with me. We can all get a stiff brandy or a coffee. We'll check the lake on the way past. Jess, you too. Come on."

But I didn't want to go with Dr Parker. I knew now what I had to do – lay the star chart over the map. To find the right well. And the torch was there in my backpack, all ready.

"No thanks, Doctor. I have to take Domino back. I should dry him – get him warm. Look how he's shivering."

Ely stepped forward and laid his hand on my arm. "Best

do as he says, child," said Ely. "The doctor always knows what to do."

He said it quite kindly, but as I looked into those blue, blue eyes, my whole insides turned over. Because there – behind the forget-me-not blue – there was something else. An intrusion, an unpleasant tugging. Like he could see into my very thoughts. Like he could see all my secrets at once.

I looked away, pulled loose from his hand. Called Domino.

Ely and the doctor exchanged glances. "As you wish then," said Dr Parker. "Come back with your dad if you want, later. He can hardly leave you there on your own. But I'm sure your mum will be fine. She's probably up at my house. Maybe she left her handbag up there with aspirin in it or something."

He put his arm round Mrs Shilling, who nodded to me before she was steered away. Such a huge amount was in those old eyes! Rheumy eyes; ugly, sandy-lidded eyes of a mad old bag. Yet... wise eyes, knowing. Like she could read my thoughts too, if she wanted to – but instead was trying to send me some of hers. I stared back at her, the most enormous lump in my throat. What? What is it? I said to her in my head. But there was no reply.

I watched them move off up the beach, the doctor guiding Mrs Shilling round rocks. Then Mrs Shilling stopped and shouted out one word. *"Speckled!"* she yelled. Incredibly loudly, for such a tiny woman.

"Come on now, Mrs Shilling," I heard the doctor say kindly. "It's been a very long day. Time for one of your pills, I think."

I waited till they'd gone, thinking all the time. Speckled. A speckled stone? Then I started to look around. It didn't take long to find it.

There, where Mrs Shilling had sat. A speckled grey stone, half buried in the sand. From under it, the corner of something poked out. I reached down, pulled it free.

One last bird card. This time, on the front, an eagle.

LATIN: AQUILA CHRYSAETOS. *Common name: Golden Eagle. One of the most magnificent birds of prey.*

Aquila – the other constellation from the star chart. Aquila means "eagle"!

One star chart with *two* birds on it – Cygnus and Aquila. The swan and the eagle. As Mrs Shilling had prodded me to see, the star chart had to be laid over the map of the island.

Time to go back to the house – find the map and chart – lay one over the other. That way, I knew, I'd find the right cave. But I sensed I didn't have long.

The logs from the fire collapsed in on themselves as I ran away. A soft rain began. From the lake, an eerie, haunting sound rose up. The sound of hundreds and hundreds of swans, calling out into the dark…

Back at the house

No sign of Dad as I tore up the stairs. No sign of Mum either – so Dad had probably gone back to Dr Parker's.

In my room, I lit my globe lamp and got busy. Setting the papers out on the floor, I took out the rhymes and map and the copy of the star chart.

Right. The document called 'The Key' said the map to the tooth lies under a well. But I had to find the *right* well. I got the section of star chart. Those funny patterns, laid next to each other. I traced them on to a bit of tracing paper, Cygnus first, then Aquila.

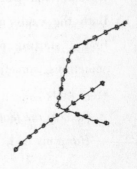

Then I turned the tracing paper this way and that, wondering how to lay it over the map. Wait a minute... what about the last riddle? That was supposed to be the clue that linked it all together. So that should tell me how to use the star chart.

The Riddle of the Two

> At the feather'd head,
> I hang my bed.

> At the feather'd breast,
> An ancient rest.

> At the feather'd wing,
> The whale doth sing.

Feathered. But which way up should I put the tracing? Both the eagle and the swan are feathered. I had to find a starting point. Think, Jess, think! I'm missing something, something obvious. I sat down on my bed. My swan bed.

Bed. *At the feather'd head, I hang my bed.*

Hang my bed. Who hangs a bed? No one. Unless... it's

a hammock! A hammock is a hanging bed. And there is only one person I know who sleeps in a hammock. Epsilon. So the head of one of the bird shapes must fit directly over Epsilon's cottage on the map. I grabbed the tracing paper and looked at the constellation of Aquila.

No, it doesn't look much like an eagle! But wait – suppose the two curved lines coming off are wings? Wings, bent backward? Then the end of the straight bit sticking downwards must be the head. Yes!

I laid it over the map, but none of the other points matched up.

At the feather'd breast, an ancient rest.

And there it was on the map – the stone seat. The stone seat, halfway to Epsilon's cottage – the one I always sat and rested on when I went down there. An ancient rest – a place where people sit! So I lined up the point the two wings spread from – the breast – up with the stone seat. And suddenly it all became clear.

I looked at the map with the constellations laid over it.

Now all I had to do was find the eagle's wing. The place where *the whale doth sing*.

The tip of the upper wing lined up with the Ouroborus Stone – the one I'd tried to find on our land, but couldn't, as the brambly thicket was too dense.

But at the tip of the lower wing... a small cave was marked there! On the shore below our tiny beach. *At the feather'd wing, the whale doth sing.*

And the nearest marked point on the star chart corresponded to a well! It was not far, really, from Epsilon's cottage. Surely this must be the well I was looking for, below which the map was hidden?

> *In the space below the well*
> *A map to the tooth lies hidden.*
> *The space is marked by an infidel*
> *Whose hand reveals what's bidden.*
>
> *Through merrow hair*
> *In Neptune's lair*
> *Past thirty fingers pale –*
> *Then hark for a river in the dark*
> *And reach for the spout of the whale!*

I knew I'd at last found the right well. The right cave. I stuffed both bits of paper into my jeans pocket and rushed out.

As I ran downstairs, my knees went weak. I'd been rushing around all night. I'd also been sick. I felt light-headed, hollow. At the kitchen table I stopped and sat down. I was scared.

No one knew where I was going. What if I fell? Got lost in that cave? I'd better let someone know what I was doing. But who?

Dad knew nothing about all this. And Dr Parker – if he was the Lemon Squire – was on Yolandë's side, surely! But was Yolandë a Bright Being – or a Dark Being? Until I was sure, I couldn't trust him. Who else? Who else?

Mum was already gone. Mrs Shilling was too old to be much use in an emergency. And anyway, I couldn't very well write a general note saying, "I'm in this cave – X marks the spot on the map. Come and get me out in case Dark Beings have destroyed me." Could I? Anyone from the *wrong* side might read it, come and find me, and (in fact) destroy me. I couldn't write much in this just-in-case note at all! Unless... unless I wrote it in the Lumic alphabet?

Epsilon. Perhaps he would know how to work out 'The Key'? If so, he could trace it all back to the cave. Yes. Copy 'The Key' document out in Lumic and hope *no one else* can read it. Leave it here on the kitchen table. Then, if anything happened, at least someone could – eventually – find me.

Not much of an emergency plan really. But the best I could think of, all things considered. So I grabbed a scrap of paper from the kitchen table and scribbled the whole verse on it using the symbols. I left it there, propped up against the pepper mill. Then I went and had a long drink of milk.

I hate small spaces. And what would I find when I went into the cave? The map? Mum? Someone else? Whatever it was, there was no putting it off any longer.

Under the well

The well, when I got to it, was just an old mound in the middle of the undergrowth – I nearly missed it. Just a mound, about two metres high, grown over now with tall grasses and moss. It didn't look like much as I shone my torch on it. But I got down on my knees, dragged the moss away, pulled up handfuls of grasses. And underneath I found it – a stone. The capstone of an ancient well. It was round, heavy. There was no way I was going to be able to move that!

I sat down with my back against it and chewed on my lip. *In the space below the well, a map to the tooth lies hidden.* Below the well.

I slid back down the mound and began to walk around

it. Domino and I stumbled about, our ankles getting skinned on the stones piled everywhere.

But suddenly Domino found it – at least, he disappeared. One minute he was snuffling in the long grass. The next minute, his head vanished, then the rest of him.

"Stay, Domino!" I hissed. "Sit!" I didn't want him falling down a hole, vanishing for good. I heard his little snuffly woof as he obeyed and sat. Then carefully, carefully, I followed him in.

He'd found a small opening – barely a cave at all – this couldn't be it! Just a space, a couple of metres wide – just enough to wriggle into really. Domino sat there, wagging his tail. He seemed OK; he wasn't scared like me.

"Good dog! What is it, boy? What have you found?"

Domino inched forward to lick my nose. And my torch showed me what he'd found. Steps. Spiral steps. Leading downwards.

I hated the claustrophobic space. It made me sweat. Yet it was cold. The sort of cold you only ever get deep underground. Slippery too – water dripped from the tunnel walls, and the steps were slimy and horribly full of echoes.

There were lengths of chain at the steepest bits,

fastened into the rock with ice-cold bolts. Soon my fingers were totally numb. The air felt stale – dank and sour. Domino didn't seem to mind all that much. He looked uneasy, but not terrified.

But the farther down we went – about thiry-five steps now – new sounds began. Not just the dripping of water through the walls, but a sort of deep echoing. A *shhhh-shhh* sound. As if something very large were breathing in the dark, far, far below. Stop it, Jess! There won't be anything down there, nothing at all!

And after a while, I felt a change of air. Into the sourness, a cleaner smell – seaweed, saltwater. This smell got stronger and stronger, the lower we climbed.

All of the time my mind was racing. Mum. Mrs Shilling. Ely Fingers. Mum. Dr Parker. The tooth. The map. Mum.

At first, I kept my fears to myself. But pretty soon I started to whisper out loud. I had to. The silence was pressing on me, it was building up, I wanted to scream, to get out. Small spaces totally freak me out and this was horribly small! No one knew I was here. I could fall. I could get trapped, die down here and no one would know. That's not true. Epsilon would know. But had I done the right thing, leaving him that clue? Who was Epsilon, after all? I thought of those warnings about him and shivered.

Stay calm, Jess! Get a grip! Stop muttering! Because the echoes of my voice started to merge and change, as if there were lots of me's, as if there were many voices. Voices falling down the stairwell, voices spiralling up again. Whose voices? It drove me mad to hear them, those echoes. So I'd stop muttering again, and the silence would hem me in, and as my torch flickered, all the shadows leaped. Shadows seemed to be bouncing everywhere, colliding all over the walls. The walls too were a lot wetter now. They had seaweed growing on them, clinging to the lowest edges. But that was impossible, wasn't it? Unless... unless the tide somehow came right in to fill the bottom of this stairwell.

I walked down into the whispers and the dark shapes (but it's only me! It's only me and Domino!) until I felt it building up again, the need to speak aloud. And all the time, the *shhh-shhh*-ing grew louder and louder and louder. Suddenly Domino stopped. His tail went down.

"What? What is it, boy?"

He gave an uncertain little whine and stepped forward. There was no more ice-cold chain under my fingers. The end of the spiral. The beginning of a small cave. No... not just one cave – a series of caves, all tiny.

Each one led into the next. A chain of small spaces. I

followed Domino through smaller and smaller gaps in the walls. He could do it easily, but it was harder for me and my backpack. The gaps got smaller. Until the last one came, barely half a metre across – even Domino had to wriggle a bit. I followed him quickly, turning sideways, pushing my backpack in front of me.

It was the very last gap. I'd come out into the open air – a cave that was open to the sea.

Fresh air came straight at me from the ocean – it ripped straight through my fleece and made me shiver. Framed in the seaward mouth of the cave were the waves, lit silver by the moon and the stars. The waves were smashing on to the rocks. The sea would always cover up the entrance to this cave, I suspected. And at high tide, the whole thing would be submerged. As it was, the only way into it was by the spiral steps. Or by boat.

I sat down on a rock and held Domino to me. He didn't lick my face or nuzzle into my neck. He kept his head turned to the sea, as glad as I was to smell Outside again.

Then we both jumped up, terrified by a great WHOOSH! This was followed by that steady, rhythmic shushing, like something enormous, breathing from great lungs. But it came from *behind* the rock we were sitting on. And after the huge sigh of its breathing, a gurgling, a trickling.

It reminded me of something. Something I'd only seen and heard on films, on wildlife programmes on TV. The watery sounds, the sudden, breathy gasp of lots of air, the whoosh. The sound of the blowhole of a dolphin or a porpoise emerging, breathing, submerging again. Or maybe not a dolphin. A whale, spouting.

The spout of the whale!

I called Domino. Together we crept behind the rock.

Nothing. Just a stinking mass of seaweed in ankle-deep water. Green seaweed, and bronze, and black. All tangled together where the sea had left it last tide. It was as I'd thought – the sea must come right into this cave and cover the whole thing up.

I turned around and checked the level of the tide. Already it was closer than it had been when I first came in. The tide was coming in fast. I remembered Epsilon's words. "The map is hidden in a place of great danger, where it would be hardest to retrieve." A place, in fact, someone could drown in, if she was here when the tide was coming in. Like now.

Frantically, I shone the torch all around. Just the back of a cave, that's all – nothing here to fit the rhyme. Unless… I angled my torch upwards, to the roof of the cave. And there it was.

A rock hung down. A black rock, like the head and shoulders of a huge monster. My torch followed its line, lit up shoulders, neck, head and one arm flung out.

The head was gnarled and horned, with a vast, open mouth. The crooked arm led to a black, bony hand. One finger of rock was extended – pointing downwards. Pointing to the other side of the seaweed!

A demon. *The space is marked by an infidel whose hand reveals what's bidden.*

I'd found the infidel. And his hand revealed what was bidden – what was asked of me next. I had to cross the mass of seaweed, wade through it. It was now about calf-height. When the tide came fully in, it could block off my exit to the spiral stairway for ever.

And I would have to go over the seaweed alone. Nothing but nothing would entice Domino over that stinky mess! He is the most particular dog when it comes to smelly stuff.

As if to confirm this, Domino found a higher rock, sat down on it and stared at me nervously.

I knew I'd get wet through – but no way was I going to take my socks and boots off, put my bare feet into that seaweedy ick! I imagined my heels standing on soft, squelchy things, crunching small living things between my soft toes. So I just took a deep breath against the cold and waded in.

The cold seeped in over my boots, into my socks, began to soak up my jeans. And the seaweed against my legs felt disgusting. It clung and sucked. It squelched and popped under my boots. In the glow from the torch, it flowed gracefully away from me. Like hair. Green hair.

And suddenly I saw what this was. Merrow hair! Merrow must mean mermaid! Green and golden mermaid hair. And I was walking through it, just like in the rhyme. *Through merrow hair in Neptune's lair past thirty fingers pale!*

As soon as I thought of the thirty fingers pale, I saw them – just a glimpse in the distance. Silvery-white things, hanging down – a long wall of them, curving round a corner.

Out of the seaweed I squelched forward – pointed my flashlight. Stalactites; old, sturdy fingers of stone. I began to count.

Fifteen fingers later, Domino was out of sight round the corner. He began to yap – a sharp, frightened sound that bounced off the walls, came back to me, bounced away again. He was scared of the incoming tide too.

"Quiet, Domino! Quiet, boy!" Domino fell quiet.

Round the corner – twenty-six, twenty-seven, twenty-eight. The fingers got shorter as I counted, like the pipes of a great church organ, tapering to the smaller treble pipes.

I heard those watery gasps again – right in front of me. Like a thirsty throat filling up – then a breath. Those giant lungs, hidden somewhere in front of me. They breathed in and out, they swallowed water, they gasped again. It was the most horrible, sinister sound.

But then I realised that the breathing came and went in a steady rhythm. The same rhythm had been at my back at the mouth of the cave. The rhythm of the waves as they came in and ebbed out again. The endless rhythm of the sea.

I was on my hands and knees now, the organ pipes tapering into small fingers, infant fingers, only centimetres high. Before me was a hole in the rock, a fist-sized tunnel leading downwards. Through this hole the breathing sound echoed, building up and up.

I lay on my stomach. Behind me, I could hear the sea, rushing in, crashing into the mouth of the cave. Frantically, I tried to piece together what was behind this rock wall.

A blowhole. Right behind this massive rock wall another small space must be filling up with water. A space not visible from here. And as the water came in, it filled it up a bit more. And at each ebb of the waves, the water level inside the space dropped a little, so that air rushed back in – that breathing sound. With each wave that small space was filling and filling until the pressure built up. Then, somewhere along its length where there was a tiny gap to the air, the water all shot out in a whooshing spout.

Then hark for a river in the dark and reach for the spout of the whale!

But when I put my hand into the tiny tunnel and reached down it, my whole hand was underwater. Numb and cold, I couldn't feel a thing. I'd have to wait for it to empty again.

It took several minutes for this to happen, and as I waited I grew colder and colder. My imagination started to play tricks. In the torchlight's glow there seemed to be things swarming all around me, tiny shadows flitting over my skin. I forced the panic away, teeth chattering in the dark. My face was pressed to the rock floor.

I felt I was embracing a giant sea creature, a monstrous, black-skinned thing with eels and sea serpents in its jaws. The sloping fingers of stalactites no longer seemed like a church organ. They felt like a ribcage, part of a cadaver I was lying pressed into. I wanted to cry or yell; my nerves were stretched tight. It was as if someone was turning a screw, tightening me up with each breath of the sea. It built up and up until – at last – the great *whoosh!* of water came from behind the rock wall.

I breathed again. The space was emptied.

Now I could hear it clearly through the gap – the river in the dark. The river of seawater, starting to sneak its way back in.

Then hark for a river in the dark and reach for the spout of the whale!

I ripped my hand out of the sleeve of my fleece so that my whole arm was bare. Then I reached again into the tiny tunnel.

In and in and in, and all the time I felt something would grab my hand, would hold my wrist in its fangs, would trap me there for ever.

But I reached farther, grazing my knuckles on rock. Right up to my armpit I went. My fingers fumbled… found something… took hold. Something rounded and small and smooth, wedged at the end of the gap. I wrestled with it. Come out, come out!

Then out it came, and without looking at it, I scrambled to my feet and ran, away from that horrible ribcage. Away from the pale rock fingers and back round the corner. Back through the mermaid hair grabbing at my feet. Back through knee-deep tide pouring in. Back to my backpack and my wonderful, warm, frightened dog. We ran splashing to the foot of the spiral stairs – climbed up three steps that were already covered in water. And then, safe from the tide,

I glanced at the object I'd come all this way for.

The map. The map that would tell me where the relic was that we were all looking for – Mum and the Dark Beings and the Bright Beings and Yolandë and myself.

I stared down at it in disbelief. It didn't look anything *like* a map. It wasn't a map! It was oval, for a start – a smooth stone egg shape with something carved deep into its face. Something very simple and crudely carved. Something that didn't help me at all.

Just an arrow. I'd come all that way – just for one simple arrow. I burst into tears. And then I set off again – back up that horrible stairwell.

I barely remember getting back up. I think I cried all the way. All I could think about was that arrow. I felt cheated, hopeless.

It was hard work getting up those steps, with my wet jeans and boots – that's about all I can recall. And the fact that as soon as we emerged from the spiral steps back into the clear night, Domino was utterly joyful, tail wagging nineteen to the dozen.

I stumbled back through the woods a little way, then stood still, panting. I was drenched to the skin. But Domino had caught the whiff of the path to the cottage. His tail started to wag. He started to run. Back towards the cottage.

I called for him to come back, but he wouldn't. I followed him, swearing loudly. I hated the cottage at that moment – hated everything to do with it. Hated Epsilon and his stupid bucket that had started it all. Hated the bucket and the garden and the arrow in the wall.

I stopped running. Leaned against a tree. Suddenly, I knew. Knew where the relic was hidden.

But it couldn't be! I'd been there myself, not long ago. I hadn't seen any relic.

Running now, I followed Domino down to Epsilon's cottage. Domino was waiting for me in the garden, wagging his tail. But I didn't go into the cottage – much to his disgust. I shone the torch down the garden path. Walked to the ancient wall that was half grown over with weeds. Knelt down.

With my hands I cleared away the weeds and grass. And there it was – the arrow. The same simple arrow that was carved on the rounded stone. I compared the two and nodded. Exactly alike.

Digging with my bare hands, I unearthed all the stones and earth I'd shoved in that day when I'd come down here with the bucket. It wasn't hard to do – not like digging it up that first time. It was looser, easier. Then my hands reached down – felt the old wood. I pulled out the bucket.

I stared at it, bewildered. Turned it upside down to see if there was any clue on it anywhere. All my little treasures fell out on to the earth at my feet. No carvings. No sign of any relic. Just a bucket.

Almost in tears, I knelt down amid the mess. All my little store of treasures, getting dirty in the earth. Granny Libby's old jet necklace. The hidden packet of cigarettes. Mum's belemnite. The photo Dad took of me when I was small. Just bits of junk really. One by one I put them back into the bucket. Then I threw back my head and shouted in pure rage. "It's not here! There's nothing here!"

I sank back on to my heels, defeated. What now? I was still shivering. I wanted to go to bed, crawl in, pull the covers up over my head. I was so cold, so incredibly tired.

Then, out of nowhere, the kitchen light of the cottage shone blue. It seemed to glow into the garden – an odd glow. Not the soft light of Epsilon's candles at all: a modern light, electric blue.

Domino followed me as I ran towards the cottage. I put the bucket on the doorstep and pushed open the door. There on the old kitchen table, looking strange and unearthly, shining with a bright glow, was my laptop. Open.

I ran to it and sat down.

Chapter Twenty-four

| THERE IS ONE MEMBER IN THE CHAT ROOM: | Jess |

E: You need to hurry. Your mother is waiting for you.

JESS: Where?

E: Take the relic.

JESS: What relic? I haven't found the relic!

E: Yes, you have. Take it with you.

JESS: Where are you? Isn't my mother with you?

E: Not with me. She is alone — waiting for you and Yolandë. Yolandë is on her way to your mother.

JESS: Where?

E: In the cave.

JESS: But I've just come back from the cave! I'm not going back there!

E: That cave is the cave of the first bird.

JESS: What?

E: You need to find the cave of the second bird.

JESS: I'm sick of this. I'm cold and wet and I'm tired out and I'm scared and you said I'd meet you at the Greet and I didn't!

E: I kept my word.

JESS: You did NOT – you never do keep your word. You make all these promises and then vanish into thin air. You're a liar!

E: Do not anger me. I kept my word. Put your hand in your pocket.

JESS: What?

E: Just do it! What do you find?

JESS: Nothing. Just a napkin from the food at the Greet. A little packet of salt.

E: That is not a napkin.

JESS: Hang on… Oh! It's a hanky. A real one. Cloth. The hanky that Mike gave me when I threw up.

E: And inside it?

JESS: Inside it? Oh, this is *gross*! Just – my nose ring.

E: Which is something the ancients wore also. If they revered the Ouroborus.

JESS: So? Where's Mum? I want my mum.

E: Then look closer at the nose ring. What happens when you close it up? When you fit the ring into your flesh and close it?

JESS: One bit fits into the other bit.

E: Exactly. Like a tail into a mouth. Which is why the ancients used it as a secret sign – that they supported the Ouroborus. The snake that eats its own tail.

JESS: But that's not why *I* wore it.

E: Nevertheless, the Ouroborus is the sign of our enemy. I had to make you remove it. Before Yolandë arrived.

JESS: *You* had to?

E: It's my handkerchief, Jess. I gave it to you, on the beach.

JESS: You? Mike? The man in the dirty red beret?!

E: There is no time to talk. Your mother is in danger. Come and meet me there. Bring the tooth.

JESS: Don't go! I haven't got the tooth!

E: Bring the only thing found on Lume.

JESS: But I don't know where to meet you. Help me!

E: You must find the cave of the second bird. Hurry!

E HAS LEFT THE CHAT ROOM

Frantic, I ran back for the bucket – tipped all my treasures on to the table. Stared at them.

"The only thing found on Lume."

The only thing found on Lume was – the belemnite?

Mum's belemnite. As I picked it up, something screamingly obvious slipped into place in my head. *She* found the belemnite, she and Dad. That time they went for a walk along the beach. "The relic has come to light," said Epsilon. "They sense it – the Dark Beings." Because the sea had brought it back – back on to the shore on Long Beach. In the very place Mum had been looking – searching for weeks, turning over shells and stones. And all the time she'd found it already. She'd given it to me, before all this began, thinking it was a belemnite!

I turned it over and over in my hands. (*Oh, wow. A baby stone carrot. Why can't she give me a CD, like other mums?*) I know nothing of fossils, it has to be said. But when I held it in my hands, I knew this must be it.

Not a fossil at all. Just something that Mum *thought* was a fossil, all those weeks ago before she'd got caught up in all of this. A tooth, a long incisor tooth, encrusted with tiny crustaceans and stuff from many years under the ocean.

But I didn't have time for this! Hurry, Jess, hurry! I put the relic in my pocket and thought of what Epsilon had just said. "The cave of the second bird."

As I tore the papers out of my jeans pocket – the star

chart and the map – I heard something that made me whirl around in fright. A scream – Mum's scream. A shrill, alone, terrified scream. It rang in my head; it hadn't come from nearby, I was sure of that. And a dim crashing, like water falling from a great height. It smashed into the room, and her scream echoed round and round, like she was inside an enormous cave. Then it was gone. I knew with great certainty that falling water was what Mum was hearing at this very minute. A wild, dangerous sound.

The sick feeling came back. My hands began to tremble. I felt like I was cracking open, splitting in two. As I smoothed out the star chart and stared at it, my chin started wobbling. Don't cry! Stop it! Get on with it!

The Riddle. Go back to the Riddle. The one that had led me to the first cave when I laid it over the map.

The Riddle of the Two

At the feather'd head,
I hang my bed.

At the feather'd breast,
An ancient rest.

At the feather'd wing,
The whale doth sing.

Right. It was called 'The Riddle of the Two'. *Two* kinds of feathered birds. *Two* constellations on the star chart. Cygnus and Aquila. *Two* birds. The eagle and the swan. So maybe – two caves.

And when I laid the star chart over the map again, I saw them at once – the points of the map that lay underneath Cygnus. *Cygnus* this time – not Aquila.

At the feather'd head, I hang my bed. Let's see, let's see. The swan's head lined up with... Milton House. Where Milton C Parker had *his* bed. But why "I *hang* my bed"? Hammocks again? Noooo. How about... the hanging garden? Yes!

I thought of the hanging flower beds that Milton C Parker had made long ago, swaying on their verdigris chains in the arbour. Not a *bed* bed at all – a *flower* bed. Another point on the map that fitted.

So. Next?

At the feather'd breast, an ancient rest. The Miradel! The folly, which Milton C Parker made and was now buried near. "An ancient rest!" Not a stone seat or anything else you take a temporary rest on. A grave – a place to lie down for ever.

And finally, *At the feather'd wing, the whale doth sing.*
A cave was marked on the map – under the very tip of the
swan's wing.

It was just behind Coscoroba Rock – the cave where
Mum was! At the end of Long Beach, in the bay marked
with whales. The place the whales used to come. Not a
blowhole in a rock, like at the last cave. A cave in the
actual bay that used to be visited by real whales and
dolphins and porpoises.

As I straightened up, Domino ran to the window and
began to bark furiously. I heard it too – the sound of a great
bird, crying on the wing. I ran out into the garden and
stared up. A swan was flying over the cottage. Just one
black swan, her wings lit up by the moon. She was flying
steadily towards Long Beach.

I left the house running.

Chapter Twenty-five

My Diary

Finding Mum

The thin sea drizzle had stopped. Now the moon bathed the whole of Long Beach silver. It all lay before me: the long bite of sand, the surf churning madly, the fires, reduced now to red embers.

As I ran on the darkness thickened. Clouds were rushing towards the moon, engulfing it. And far out at sea the swans were flying. Hundreds of them, silent, wheeling in a great circle over the black water.

By the time I got to the last fire, the moon was covered. It was too dark to see. I shone my torch all around.

Nothing. Nobody there. Just Domino, snuffling in the seaweed. And Coscoroba Rock, sticking out into the sea. According to the map, the cave was somewhere behind this rock, in the main cliff face.

Frantically I flashed my light all over the base of the cliff. Nothing. The face of the rock was solid. I raised my torch higher.

The only thing visible was a small dark gash about three metres up the cliff face. It couldn't be *that* – it was far too slender to get into, surely? But I had to try – there was nothing else at all.

I went to the base of the cliff and put the torch between my teeth. Then I began to climb. Domino stood at the bottom and whined up at me. Up and up I went, until I got to the slim aperture.

Now that I was there, I could see it was just possible to squeeze in. But I really, really didn't want to go in. Because this wasn't any ordinary cave, I knew. This was the same cave Sebastian's mama had wandered into and never come out of. The same cave Mum must have been drawn towards, several hours ago now, alone and confused and in that strange, half-asleep state.

But just then a cry came from over the sea. The swans were no longer silent and circling. They turned as I watched them – flew honking and calling, straight towards Coscoroba Rock. They were coming.

I hung on to that cliff, mesmerised as they flew closer

and closer. Then I turned sideways and shouldered my way in.

A small entrance. A smelly tunnel. The beam of my torch lit it up, but I couldn't see the end. I set off down it, slipping in the slime.

It went on and on, curving and turning this way and then that. It was like being inside a huge black shell. It was very cold. The farther I walked, the icier the air became. And the farther in I went, the worse I felt.

It wasn't just how cold I was. My teeth were chattering uncontrollably; I was still soaked to the skin, the legs of my jeans wet through from the last cave. But it wasn't just that. There was a horrible feeling emanating from somewhere in front of me. A feeling of menace, of evil. It grew and grew until I had to fight the urge to turn and run away. I walked for ever down that revolting tunnel.

After a while I could hear water. But not trickling water or that constant, steady dripping. *Falling* water, somewhere ahead – a huge steady splashing that grew clearer as I walked. Until finally, the tunnel widened out, far ahead. Beyond it I saw a gleam of silver.

I crept, very quietly now, down the last of the tunnel. Then I peered out and sagged back against the rock in shock.

It was a cavern – breathtakingly big. I inched forward on to a small rocky beach that led to a flat, silver expanse. The light from my torch bounced off the surface of a huge lake, eerily flat and still. It covered the entire floor of the cavern.

But at the far back of the cavern I found the source of that splashing sound. A waterfall, pouring out from somewhere near the top of the cave. A wide ribbon of silver against the black rock, and at its feet the water of the lake frothed and foamed in a great semicircle.

Yet the rest of the lake was oddly still, with a faint light glowing in the middle of it. The only other light was a dim blue haze – like moonlight. But there couldn't be moonlight in a subterranean cave, surely?

Awed, I shone the torch around – caught sight of something twining round the cavern walls. Steps. Steps that began just behind me, I could see now. Hewn into the rock, they went round and round the cavern. I followed the curve of them with my torchbeam. Higher and higher they rose.

Finally, right at the very top, the natural rock of the cavern stopped. But the steps went on.

In a smaller, tighter coil the steps climbed up the inner walls of a curved structure. Round and round it they went, until – barely visible at the very top – they levelled out into a narrow parapet running all around.

At four points along this parapet dark shapes jutted out – the backs of stones on which four gargoyles were built. I could even see the faint glow where starlight shone through the open mouths. And in the centre, like one big eye, a perfectly round circle of night sky, with the moon framed right in the middle of it.

I was underneath the Miradel.

Now I could see why the Eye of Miradel (whoever he is) would use this tower to watch from. Its four gargoyles face each point of the compass – north, south, east and west. But it wasn't just the gargoyles that could look out. From the narrow parapet running all around, *anyone* could stand and peep through the open mouths of the gargoyles themselves. One to watch over the western sea. One to watch over Milton House. One to watch over Coscoroba Rock, down on Long Beach. And one to watch over our land.

As I realised this, words came skidding back into my head – words spoken by the doctor, weeks ago now. That day when I'd been sick and he'd first seen the bucket. *"Meanwhile, young lady – no more running about these cliffs in the heat, eh? This is a heatwave, Jessica. Even in the early morning you have to respect it."*

How could he possibly have known that I went down to the cottage so early in the mornings? Not even Mum and

Dad knew that! There was only one way he could have known. If he had been watching me.

As I stared up at that small circle of night sky way above my head, I saw that from down here, it was an eye to the stars. But from up *there*, standing on the parapet, it was an eye into this subterranean cavern. The Eye of Miradel — able to see the earth, the heavens and the underworld.

Quickly, I shone my torch back at ground level. There was something unsettling about such silver water under that black roof. Something unearthly. A stench rose up from it, of decay and fungus, of dead things steadily rotting. Creeping forward at last, I peered at the faint light in the middle of the lake.

Was it Mum's oil lamp? It was! Mum's oil lamp that she used on her midnight walks to the shore. It was perched alone, on a flat rock in the middle of the lake. It sent out a brave little circle of light.

In the circle I could see other stones, stretching across the water. Flat stepping stones. They led from where I stood all the way across to the centre of the waterfall. But the reason I was standing in shock, staring at the stepping stones, was the fact that they were no longer empty.

A swan now stood on each rock. But the swans weren't preening and fussing and dabbling and doing the things swans normally do. They were standing very still, looking my way. There was an air of expectancy, of tension, of something long awaited. Minutes passed, but I waited too. I was unnerved by those silent swans. Yet I sensed that soon, something would happen. And it did.

A faint silver light began to glow behind the waterfall. Slightly to the right of the wide ribbon of water, the light shimmered and grew. The waterfall lit up with thousands of sparkling blue lights. As it did, it was as if the whole sheet of falling water became sleek and clear. As if the waterfall itself was a screen – a thin, moving window. Behind the sheet of silver something unearthly began to take form. I watched as it grew clearer. Until finally, I could see through the water to what it was.

A woman stood there. A beautiful woman. The most beautiful woman I had ever seen in my life.

Her hair was pale and lit all over with tiny white-blue flowers woven in. She wore a gown of silver and grey, the colours of sea with starlight on it. In the palms of her hands, the light shone from something pale she was holding. It looked like a white shell, all laid in coils. The unearthly flame shone out through this. It lit up her face and I began to shake all over.

But not with fear exactly – no one could be truly scared

of her, no one. For her face held the sweetest expression I have ever seen. The most loving of faces. And her eyes – they shone violet in the light of the flame. With a look of infinite tenderness she smiled down on me.

"Welcome, my child," she said, and her voice set something in motion inside me – something good and true, something wild and musical. "I am here to protect your mother. My name is Yolandë."

The echoes in the cave said, *Yolandë-andë-andë*.

"My – my mother? Where is she?" I said. But it came out as a whisper. I couldn't talk properly, couldn't take my eyes off her.

As if in reply, small lights appeared on the ground. Small specks of light, they shot away from me towards the dark water. They gleamed faintly. I recognised them at once.

Shells. A row of tiny shells, all lined up. They led from my feet to the lake. They led all the way across the stepping-stones, between the feet of each swan and on. Right to the waterfall.

As I stared down at those shells gleaming so oddly, I knew the light they reflected was not from this world. And I knew suddenly that Epsilon was right – we are surrounded by things we do not know or see or understand.

Others live in our world, as well as people. Others live here too, all around us. Dark Beings. Bright Beings.

As soon as this thought came, I heard them – their voices, whispering in the dark. Many voices, some whispering and some singing, but very far away, as if heard through many layers of rock. Sweet voices, voices I wanted to listen to.

"Who are they?" I gasped.

"Do you not recognise the song?" she said.

Words came and went – jumbled words, all mixed up. *Silvered choices. Catted night. Plumes of princes. North, south, east and west. Lemon squire.* And music – strange, wild music that seeped into me and made me glad and dizzy.

'The Ballad of Yolandë.' At last I was hearing the tune! I wanted it to go on and on. But it stopped, all too soon.

"Where's my mother?"

"She lies buried."

"BURIED!"

I shouted it out, and my voice rang round and round. *Buried, buried, buried!* From up in the darkness above my head a sudden flapping, a huge noisy whirring of wings. One feather drifted down. A white feather. I shone my torch up and screamed.

Swans were pouring through the top of the Miradel.

Dozens of white swans, hundreds of them. They flew through the gaping circle and down, to come to rest on the steps spiralling round the cavern. More and more came pouring through the dark circle and flew wheeling down. Until all the upper steps were lined with swans. They landed, flapped their wings, then went still.

The beam of my torch lit them up, a ghostly white. Silent, strangely still swans, they stretched their long necks down and stared at me. The thought of them standing in rows up there made me tremble.

"Shh!" said Yolandë, and she pressed her finger to her beautiful lips. "Your mother lies buried in a dark sleep. The sleep is taking her deeper and further away. For the Dark Beings want her dead."

"Mum? Mum!" I yelled.

"She cannot hear you. She will wake only when she has the relic. Then she will be safe again."

"*Where* is she buried?"

Through the shimmering water, I watched her graceful arm gesture. "She is here. Right next to me."

I came alive then, plunged my hand into my pocket. My fingers folded round the relic. I held it out towards the waterfall, yelled. "It's here, Mum! I've found it! The relic is here!"

"She cannot hear you," said Yolandë. "You must bring it

to her. Then you can lead her safely out again."

Through the ethereal screen of water I saw her hold out her hand towards me. I looked at her hand – slender, pale, the hand of a musician, fingers that could take up a harp and play lovely music. Then that music began to rise. That unearthly music! It radiated from her, swelled out and out. That music – oh! Delicate music like the wind in pipes, like a sea breeze thrumming strings. And all the time, Yolandë stared down at me with love in her face.

All the trust I have ever felt rose up in me then.

She was here to protect Mum.

She was the most beautiful thing I'd ever seen.

I wanted that love in her eyes.

I moved forward to the edge of the water and looked down. The swans on all their stones just moved their heads slightly, to follow me with their eyes. The stepping stones stretched out before me, flat and large.

But I was scared of the swans. Swans are territorial, aren't they? They attack people who come too close. But the thought of Mum buried behind the waterfall was an even scarier thought.

I stepped on to the first stone. The swan on it slipped into the water at once. But it didn't swim away. It stayed there, watching me. Nervously, I stepped on to the next stone. And the next. And the next.

Each time I stepped on to a stone, the swan standing on it glided silently into the water to join the others. As I moved forwards, all the swans swam together, quietly, keeping pace with me as I stepped right into the middle of the lake.

Finally, I stepped on to the centre stone. Mum's little lamp looked alone and feeble on it. But when I picked it up, it was as if it was a signal, a trigger. That familiar crackling returned, that sharp energy in the air. And when I looked up, someone else was there in the cave.

A figure had appeared to the left of the waterfall. A man, standing high up, in the shadows. A tall man in dark clothing. His clothes shimmered as he moved.

"Epsilon?" I whispered.

"It is I," he said. "You have a choice to make. I am here to guide you."

Yolandë did not even look at him. She just went on gazing down at me. "He will guide you to your death," she said. "He is a Dark Being. But I will protect you from him. Come."

"Epsilon? A Dark Being?"

"Look closer!" she said, and she raised her hands so that the flame lit him up fully.

As the flame rose, I saw that Epsilon was not in the form

I had seen at the beach or even at the cottage – although that had been bad enough. Now I saw that his dark clothing was not quite dark after all. It was red – the deep-scarlet colour of blood. On his breast there was a shining golden O. As I watched, he seemed to grow, and the taller he grew, the fiercer he looked.

His face was set with a grim look. Around his wrists were leather bands with golden studs. His belt was a sash of deep gold, and hanging from it – weapons. Sharp weapons, with curved blades that glinted and flashed. The blades of a warrior. And in his dark eyes, such a fury.

I could well believe he was a Dark Being. He terrified me. But then I thought of Mum, falling deeper into a dark sleep. I had to keep moving, keep going!

The water all around didn't look silver now that I was above it. It looked utterly black and menacing – a dense darkness that made my mouth go dry. The thought of toppling into that water petrified me. I gripped the relic tightly in my hand.

"You have found the relic," said Epsilon. "Now you must destroy it."

"Destroy it?"

"Smash it against the stone!" he commanded. "She means to use its curses for great evil. She is a Dark Being."

I turned back to Yolandë, to that beautiful light. She didn't look like a Dark Being. She looked like an angel. Over her face came a look of great concern.

"Do not believe him," she said. "Do not smash the relic. You must bring it to your mother and awaken her from the dark sleep. Or she will die."

"This is the time of dark choices," said Epsilon. "Choose wisely!"

I glanced up. Saw the mottled crimson of his garments. The curved weapons flashing at his belt. I felt that crackling, that eerie energy in the air. Felt sick. Epsilon – with blood on his tunic and cruel blades at his waist. Epsilon the Dark Being, waiting for me to smash the relic and destroy it against the stone.

Instead, I stepped over the water on to the next stone. Instantly, the swan slipped into the water alongside the rest.

And something happened inside my head. Something shifted, lurched strangely, and all the shadows collided and clashed. At first I thought I had fallen, but no, here I was, still on the stone. Still standing on the stone, quite steady.

But Sebastian stood on it too.

He stood beside me and grinned. "The girl with the

world in her hands," he said.

"Don't talk to it, Jess!" yelled Epsilon. "It is not Sebastian. It is a base being – a Dark Being she has conjured up!" Together, Seb and I looked up at Yolandë and Epsilon.

"It is just the same," Sebastian whispered. "Just the same as it was for me!"

"What shall I do?" I asked him. "Shall I destroy the relic? Or take it to my mother?"

"The relic?" he said. He was staring up at Yolandë.

"I found it, Sebastian. Here it is. But Epsilon wants me to destroy it."

Sebastian looked up at Epsilon and sighed. "He deceived me too," he said. "Time and time again. Mama tried to warn me about him. But I wouldn't listen."

So Epsilon was the Dark Being. And Yolandë was on the side of the good.

"Come," said Sebastian. "Let us go and wake your mother. We will give the relic to her together."

We stepped on to the next stone. This brought a beautiful smile on to Yolandë's face. I would do anything, anything, to see that smile.

"No!" shouted Epsilon. His face was very angry. But he was not looking at me. He was looking at Yolandë.

Meanwhile, Sebastian stepped on to the next stone and tugged at my hand.

I hesitated. There was something about the way Epsilon was looking at Yolandë that scared me. But it also made me see that it was *her* he was angry with. Not me.

I glanced behind. The swans in the water glided silently, staring intently at me. They didn't seem to even see Sebastian.

Epsilon's voice rang out. "You must not give your mother the relic, Jess! Everything he says is a lie! He is a Dark Being – a base being. I told you they could imitate the dead!"

I thought of the warnings Martha had given Sebastian, and old Luke had given to me. "He has bewitched you with his riddles and his music." I thought of the tune Epsilon had played, to lure me to the cottage. The same tune he'd played when he'd shown me many things in the cottage window. That wonderful tune, lulling me into trusting him.

"She says *you* are a Dark Being!" I yelled. "Who am I supposed to believe? And she wants me to take the relic to Mum – to save Mum!"

"She wants to kill her. You too – she wants to lull you into a cold sleep. As soon as you hand the relic over to your mother, she will kill you."

"So why does she want me to give the relic to Mum in the first place?"

"Because only your mother can give it *back* to her. It must be freely given, from the hand of an innocent. She is that innocent."

I was so cold. It wasn't just the cave, the water all around with its faint mist. It was Sebastian at my side. A chill came from him and seeped into me. The deeper it grew, the sleepier I felt. As if I could fall asleep right here, in the middle of a lake, standing on my feet.

"They are sending you into a dark sleep!" said Epsilon. "Wake up! Look at the swans – look at what is round their necks."

As his voice died away, I noticed that the swans did not like Epsilon. When he spoke, they hissed very softly, and their feathers ruffled out a little. This woke me up a bit. I didn't much like the look of Epsilon myself. But I didn't like the swans either.

"Come *on*!" cried Sebastian.

He pulled me on to the next stone. His grip was very tight. And getting tighter. His fingers were icy, a horrible, empty coldness that made my heart freeze. I snatched my hand away. He turned then and glared at me.

"Wait!" I said. "I want to see what's round the swans' necks. I have to check!"

He folded his arms and stared at me coldly. In his eyes, I saw a flash of utter meanness. Then it was gone and he just looked bored. "So check." He shrugged.

Shaken, I knelt down and shone my light directly at the nearest swan. There, round its neck, was a small silver chain. Hanging from it was the symbol of the snake – the Ouroborus.

"It's only a little snake," Sebastian grinned. "You're not scared of snakes, are you? Come on."

He took my hand again and pointed to the waterfall, just one stone away now. His lopsided grin was boyish, friendly, as he held out his hand to me. But as he watched me hesitate, an incredulous look came over his face. "You wouldn't... let your mother *die*, would you?" he asked.

My stomach lurched. The swans just waited, their little black eyes glittering. Stop looking at me. Stop looking at me! I thought of them all wearing that symbol of the Ouroborus. I thought of its image in reverse. The golden O picture, back at the cottage.

"Sebastian," I said, "what is the meaning of the golden O? Is it the symbol of Yolandë's enemy?"

As soon as the words left my mouth, a terrible sound

came from far above us. The sound of many swans, angrily hissing my way. And from all around, a soft chanting came. Dim and eerie, that chanting sound was not from our time. It was the sound of past voices, singing through the years – ancient voices who had used this cave over the centuries. Their eerie words filled my head.

I knew who these singers were. The ancient followers of Cimul. The men who believed in the Inverted Law.

> *Ours is for the Ouroborus!*
> *Ours is for to be empowered!*
> *Tooth to tail we chant in chorus –*
> *The innocent will be devoured.*
> *One is nought and One is dead*
> *Because the tail is at the head!*
> *Ours is for the Inverted Law!*
> *Ours the jewel from Cimul's jaw.*

But Epsilon ignored them. He shouted at Sebastian. His voice was angry and terrible. "Answer her, you wretched being! Tell her whose is the symbol of the unbroken O! Tell her his name!"

Sebastian was cringing. The mean look came back into his eyes. But there was fear there too. He clung to my hand more tightly. He was afraid of the name he was being asked to speak!

Yet the real Sebastian hadn't been afraid of that name – he'd used it, spoken it aloud to make him brave. I was beginning to see that this name – the name the real Sebastian trusted – was the name of the One Epsilon worked for. As I stared at the cringing Sebastian by my side, I suddenly knew that Epsilon had been telling the truth. This was not Sebastian at all. This was a Dark Being. And he was clawing, clawing at my hand. I tried to pull away from his grip, but it was too tight. He was trying to prise my fingers apart – trying to seize the relic. But how could I stop him? I had no strength, no weapons. The only thing I had was that name he was scared of. So I took a deep breath.

"His name is Agapetos!" I yelled.

Instantly, the chant ceased. All the swans hissed. And so did Sebastian.

He let go of my hand as if I'd burned him. He hissed at me, an animal snarl. A cruelty appeared in his eyes – and a fury. Before my eyes, the boyish face of Sebastian Wren turned vile. Every line in it altered, turned menacing. The menace grew and grew until I could feel it emanating from him. Like tendrils of mist it came stealing my way, reached for me across the stone, made me sway and stagger. I bent down, covered my eyes.

"Go!" I heard Epsilon shout. "In the name of Agapetos, go back from whence you came!"

A dreadful scream echoed out – and when I opened my eyes, Sebastian had gone. The stone was bare. Just a faint wisp of yellow mist crept about it.

Then Yolandë spoke. "Your mother is dying, child," she said. "Bring her the relic."

"No, Jess! Destroy it! Smash it against the stone – do it quickly!"

I looked from one to the other, trying to think clearly. All I knew was that the spirit posing as Sebastian had lied. He had said Epsilon was a Dark Being. But he *himself* had been a Dark Being.

Suddenly, I finally knew who to trust. I knew once and for all who was telling the truth. I gazed up at that golden O on Epsilon's chest. Something became crystal clear in my head.

The O was not a number – a zero. It was a letter – the first letter of the word One. But it was far more than that. It was a symbol in itself – the symbol of unity. The perfect circle. Of the complete unit. The never ending. The One.

And the snake? The snake was *not* a perfect circle. It

could never be unified – not even if it began to eat its own tail. The symbol of one who depends only upon itself for nourishment. The ancient chant was still ringing in my head. I realised what a terrible lie was held in those words:

One is nought and One is dead
Because the tail is at the head!

"One is nought." They were declaring that the One – the leader of the Bright Beings – is nothing. Does not exist.

"And One is dead." They were declaring that the One – the leader of the Bright Beings – is dead.

Somehow I felt all the evil held within this lie. And I knew now that Epsilon was a Bright Being. I knew that Yolandë was a Dark Being and spoke many lies. But I believed one thing she'd said.

That Mum would die unless I gave her the relic. But if I did give Mum the relic, I knew who she would give it to. "I must find her," she'd said, over and over. Mum, sleepwalking, entranced by Yolandë. Mum, drawing Yolandë's face, over and over again. She'd give it to Yolandë. And then the Dark Beings would invoke its curses for unimaginable evil.

But at least Mum would be alive.

"I can't let her die, Epsilon," I said.

As his roar of anguish rang out, I stepped through the waterfall.

Chapter Twenty-six

My Diary

Mum

The water hit me, as cold as ice. I stumbled forward. Then I was through. The thin silver sheet of water was at my back. In the space behind the waterfall I stood gasping and shivering.

Yolandë stood smiling to one side. Behind her back something lay – something dark and curled up. But I couldn't see what it was – she was blocking the way.

And there on the other side, to my left, was Mum. She was lying very still. Her skin was white. She looked dead. She lay curled up on one side like a tiny baby, snug in its crib.

I shook her. Her face was icy. Her hands were dead, useless things. I rubbed them between my palms, breathed on to her face. Nothing.

I gathered her up in my arms. "Wake up, Mum! I've brought it! Look, here it is. I've found the relic!"

I laid it in Mum's hand. The cold fingers twitched — moved — curled around the relic. Her eyes flickered open.

"Mum! Oh, Mum!" I burst into tears. "You can stop looking now, Mum! I've found it — see? Look, it's in your hand. It's not a belemnite at all — it's the relic!"

Mum raised the relic to her face and peered at it. A tiny spot of colour began to come into her cheeks. "At last!" she whispered.

"But you must not give it to her, Mum! You must not give it to Yolandë. She is a Dark Being. Do you hear me?"

I was frantic. I must stop Mum from handing the relic to Yolandë. But how? Even though I had failed Epsilon so badly, I didn't want the Dark Beings to get possession of the tooth — to invoke those evil curses. I had to get her out of here. Had to get her away from Yolandë.

"Come on, Mum. Stand *up*!"

But Mum just turned away from me and stared at Yolandë.

Yolandë smiled down at Mum with a look of such pride and love, it terrified me. This was the Dark Being who had entranced Mum with her beauty and her singing. Whose hand had beckoned Mum out into the dark, night after night. Who had visited her in dreams until all Mum could think of was her face, of doing whatever she wanted.

Now Yolandë moved towards us with her hand outstretched. In her fingers tiny flowers appeared – blue flowers, pure and sweet. Harebells. Their scent filled the air – the scent of spring, of new life, of sunshine on meadows. She held the flowers out to Mum. An offering. A thank you.

Mum's eyes grew dreamy as she stared at the flowers.

"Don't take them!" I said. "Come on – get up!"

With a great effort, I dragged Mum to her feet. Slowly she got up, leaning on me heavily. I moved forward, trying to steer her towards the waterfall. But she didn't want to go that way. She turned to the side, away from Yolandë. Towards the black bundle lying on the floor, all curled up.

On the rock above it – the Ouroborus, carved over and over. And a word in symbols, carved many times.

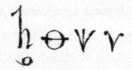

Mum shone her torch on it. "What does it say?" she whispered.

It said, 'Cimul', but I was not going to say that name out loud. And anyway, what I was now looking at drove all words out of my head.

Nestled against the rock, someone lay curled. Curled on her side, like a tiny baby in a crib. Her small black bonnet hung in silken shreds. Her long black skirt was tattered. On her hands, little black half-mittens. At her throat, something silver glittered, something that she held in the fingers of one hand. Only it wasn't a hand at all – not any more. It was just bones.

And under the bonnet, a skull. Mama.

Mum reached out and touched the very edge of her frayed bonnet. "You poor thing!" she whispered as she held the relic out towards Mama. "Look, it's here! I've found it – see?" Then she reached out for the glittering silver thing. Tugged at it carefully. Gently, she untwined it from the thin fingers of bone.

It was a locket, very tarnished. The chain broke at once into many pieces. But Mum held the tiny heart-shape in her hands. Her fingernail traced the letters imprinted there. "M, A, R…"

She tried to scratch away at the tarnished silver. Gave up. Looked at me helplessly. "M, A, R. Mary? She was called Mary?"

I shook my head. "Martha. She was called Martha."

She stared down at that little curled-up form. "Martha," she whispered.

But something was happening all around. The light was changing, growing. When we turned back, Yolandë's flame was magnified. Its blue-and-silver light bathed me, made me feel warmed and sleepy. The scent of the blossoms was rich and heavy. I was so drowsy. It was impossible to look away from that flame. I thought of meadows in summer and new-mown hay. Of skylarks and butterflies and the singing of little brooks, running glittering over stones.

Dimly, I became aware that this watery music had words. The words were sung in crystal-clear voices, immeasurably sweet of tone. Chimes and notes filled the air and turned it all silver and blue. It was like sitting inside a great glass bell, lulled by melody and rhyme.

> *"ONE LADY she be,*
> *ONE LADY we be,*
> *ONE LADY be he-without-trace.*
> *For he be ONE LADY,*
> *And she be ONE LADY,*
> *And we see the ONE LADY's face."*

Yolandë's whole face was shining. Her smiling eyes were deeply violet. She reached out her hand towards Mum. "Give me the relic," she said. "It is time."

I tried to tug at Mum, but it was no use. I could barely move, but I had to get her back to Epsilon! I had to get her back through the waterfall. But there was nothing I could do. My arms were numb, my head spinning into sleep.

Dimly, I became aware that the sound of falling water at my back was fainter. The rushing and splashing was not so fierce now. I stared around, puzzled. The waterfall was thinning. It divided itself into many smaller streams. Then it was just a series of thin trickles. Finally, it was nothing but drips, coming from the rock above.

The waterfall was gone.

The enormous cavern stretched out before us, dark and vast. The heady scent of Yolandë's flowers faded and died. There was the lake with its stepping stones, waiting. It was as if a spell had been broken. I could move. "Come on, Mum," I said as I pulled her to the first stone.

Epsilon appeared then, moving out of the mist. As we picked our way back across the stones, Epsilon moved away from his ledge. He strode down the stone steps and around the lake. He was coming down to meet us, his face set firm.

"Look, Mum! It's Epsilon. He is a Bright Being. Oh, please, Mum – look at *him*!"

Mum stared at him, her face closed and tight. "Him? I am not interested in him," she said.

We stepped off the last stone and back on to the stony beach in total silence. Mum turned immediately towards Yolandë. For Yolandë too was moving closer.

She stepped easily, daintily. She moved along the spiralling stone steps and down. She followed Mum, followed her with her eyes all the time. Until Yolandë too was on the stony beach.

Yolandë was on one side, Epsilon on the other. Both within Mum's reach.

Epsilon's face held a look of immense sorrow as he looked at the relic Mum was holding. A look of failure – of despair. "The relic is in the wrong hands," he said.

But Mum turned away from Epsilon. Her eyes were fixed on Yolandë's.

"The relic is in the *right* hands!" whispered Mum.

"Yes, it is in the right hands at last." Yolandë smiled, and as she spoke, a freshness came into the air. Sounds came and went – sea breezes sifting through harp strings and making them thrum. Water trickling delicately in between roots of heather and over ancient soil. Old sounds, clear and unutterably fine.

"You have done well," said Yolandë. "You have found the relic. Now it is time to hand it to me."

Her delicate hand reached out, and it was as if her fingers had plucked the air and brought silver notes from it that played softly all around.

Mum's hand tightened in mine. She turned toward me slightly, never taking her eyes off Yolandë. When she spoke, it was in the quietest of whispers. "Week after week, I saw her, Jess. I heard her calling me. Night after night after night."

Yolandë nodded gracefully. "Yes. You heard my voice," she said.

Mum spoke as if in a dream. As if she had not yet woken up. Her eyes had a fixed look, a tired, sad look. Her hand was cold, so cold.

"I followed her down to the sea," she said to me. "Time and time again, I followed her. She had the sweetest face. She sang and sang. 'The Ballad of Yolandë.' Over and over."

"I know, Mum. But she isn't what she seems! Look away!"

But Mum tugged at my hand to silence me. She went on gazing. "I saw her everywhere. Behind rocks. Along the beach. Up on Crag Point. In the woods. She woke me up, every night. Looking, she was always looking for something." She looked down then, at the relic in her hand.

Yolandë reached out towards it and spoke gently. "Yes, I have been looking for it. It is mine. Give it to me now. It holds great blessings, which I would bestow upon many people."

"Don't believe her, Mum!" I shouted. "It's not blessings it holds – it's curses!"

But Epsilon shook his head at me. "*She* must decide," he said.

Mum stared up into Yolandë's gentle face. "I drew her face, you know," said Mum quietly. "Over and over. I couldn't rest. That sweet face, but always behind a fog. A mist."

I thought of Mum's sketches. That woman's face, as seen through gauze. A pale face, peering out. A sweet, beseeching expression.

"Give me the relic now," said Yolandë. "It was I who called you; it was my face you saw through the mist."

But Mum shook her head.

Yolandë went very still then. Something flashed across her face and was gone. And the lake swans were moving, I noticed. They were gathering in the middle of the misted water. They moved close together on the lake and faced Yolandë. Her tender smile deepened. "It was my face you saw," she repeated to Mum. "My voice. I called you to the shore."

"It was not you I saw," said Mum. "It was not your face." She lifted the locket then and struggled briefly, prying it open. Inside, two faded faces peered out from the rust.

Sebastian's face.

Martha's face.

Mum lifted up the locket and held it out. "It was not your face. It was this face. Martha's face. She looked so lost, so tired. On the beach, in the woods, looking and looking."

Yolandë's flame glittered and leaped. The swans were silent, staring her way.

"Yes." Yolandë smiled. "She was looking for the relic. And you have found it for her. You can give it to me now. It is what she would have done, what she would have wanted."

"All she wanted was peace!" shouted Mum. Tears appeared in her eyes and fell. "And I saw her face, trapped behind mist. But it wasn't mist at all. It was *water*. She was trapped behind the waterfall. Where you left her to die. Because she couldn't find *this*!" Mum held out the relic.

Yolandë stared at it, and a look of immense greed came over her face. Both hands reached out, and I saw that the flame in her palm was not held in a white seashell at all. It was held in a coiled snake. A pale snake, with its tail in its own mouth – an Ouroborus. And the flame was coming from its coils, shining through its horrible skin.

Mum did not even seem to notice the snake. Her eyes were hard and stony. "I promised her I would find her," she said. "You left her to die, all alone. I would never give this to you. Never!" Mum slowly turned her back on Yolandë.

She faced Epsilon and held the relic out towards him.

"No!" screamed Yolandë, and it was such a terrible scream that Mum whirled back round, appalled. It was a sound I never want to hear again – a monstrous scream, emanating from a monstrous mouth. For Yolandë had begun to change.

As we watched, her violet eyes darkened until they were black. Her smile was gone, and a look of such hatred came that I trembled all over. Yolandë grew in size, taller and taller. The stench of rotting rose up all around and made me gag. Mum gazed up into that vile face and fell to her knees, her eyes wide with terror.

I turned to Epsilon for help. But in his eyes was horror too! I saw it there clearly. Then he covered his eyes with his hands. "Do not look upon it!" he whispered.

But as he raised his hands to his face, a great beam of light shot out briefly from behind him. Then the light was gone. As if a brilliant arc light now stood behind him and his whole body blocked it out. Slowly, he began to turn his back on us.

"Epsilon! Don't turn away! Help me!" I screamed. But I had to shield my eyes. Because as he began to turn, it came again – that light coming from behind him. It flashed out, white, too bright to look upon. He continued turning, until his back came fully our way and the light was blocked out again. Only when he moved his head a fraction of a centimetre did a slim portion of that light gleam out again.

Then slowly, he bent one leg and began to kneel. The light streamed out from behind him as his head bent lower. And as he knelt before it, that light shot out. It lit up the entire chamber – it blinded us. Lower and lower Epsilon knelt, until the shape of someone stood behind him. Someone tall – someone made only *of* light. It dazzled me, and at the edge of my vision the flame Yolandë had been holding appeared sickly and dull compared to it. Then there was too much light and I too fell to my knees.

And a voice rang out, clear and strong – a voice that made me go still inside. "The time of dark choices is upon us," it said. "But the relic is not in the wrong hands. For I chose the very hands that now hold it. And my great plan is unfolding as it should."

New music came, too – strong, magnificent music. It swirled all around me until I felt I would scream. This music was beautiful, too – infinitely more beautiful than Yolandë's had been. It was wilder, older, younger. It held ancient notes and words of creation. It held many things at once. Wrath and kindness – fury and compassion. It was a call to warfare and a call to rest, both at the same time. It was the music of all authority and magnificence. We trembled before it.

Then the Being raised his arms, and rays of gold shot out to every corner of the cave. "Show them your flame now, Yolandë! Do not hide in lies in my presence. For I, Agapetos, hold a charge against you – you spoke four things to the child standing at your side. And each of the four were lies!"

Agapetos!

He made me want to stand up and shout for a wild, mad joy. He made me want to bow my head and weep. All I could do was shield my eyes with my hand and try to see him. Even though I was dazzled, I longed to see him, I could not drag my eyes away.

But from Yolandë I felt a gathering of something primeval and ugly. It reached out for Mum. I felt it coil closer and a cunning voice spoke. It was a voice of deep, deep avarice. It was so filled with malice and greed that it sickened me to hear it.

"But she is *mine*!" it said.

Instantly, Epsilon rose to his feet and went to stand by the side of Agapetos. He too had changed. His face was stern and noble. His clothes were a deep gold. Scarlet banners appeared at his wrists. A sash of gold covered his chest. Across his waist a girdle, gold and red. And in his hand – a sword. A sharp two-edged sword.

Agapetos spoke again, and his voice was strong and terrifying. "The first lie you spoke to this child was the word 'welcome'. You welcomed her into this place when you meant it to be her tomb. The second lie you spoke was to call her your child. For she is not your child – my mark is upon her. The third lie you told was that you were here to protect her mother. Yet you sought only to destroy. But your fourth lie was the worst lie. For you called yourself Yolandë. Yet your name is not Yolandë. Your name is Cimul – the Lord of Inversion! Be seen before me, Cimul!"

At that, the brilliance of the crimson light receded a little. Now I could drag my eyes away. Mum looked towards Yolandë. Her gaze lifted higher and higher as the being that had been Yolandë rose up, immensely tall and strong.

The soft gown it was wearing changed before my eyes, from light to dark. The Ouroborus snake in its hands flattened itself out on the outstretched palms then seemed to melt into the skin. Scales appeared, starting at the hands. Pale scales, yellowing scales, and as they covered the monstrous body, bit by bit, that body grew in stature. The soft hair shortened and matted, and round its wrists pale bracelets appeared and gleamed. But they were not bracelets at all – they were row upon row of snakes, all with their tails in their mouths. The Ouroborus, lining the arms and the legs. Then the scales deepened and hardened.

Cimul was black and red, the colour of old blood. His face was full of trickery and cunning. His mouth held mockery and sneers and foul words. The skin of his face was the skin of a serpent, its scales peeling, shearing off, renewing themselves all the time. But his eyes were the worst.

They were filled with a deep malevolence. They were the most sickening, evil thing I had ever seen in my life.

Then Cimul opened his mouth and pointed a crimson

finger at Mum. "I am the Ouroborus, the cunning one, the Great Inverter! I it was who beckoned you here. Give me the curses that are held in your hand!"

The voice of Agapetos rang out again. "I am the One without beginning or end! I it was who chose your hands to receive the relic. And those hands will not fail me now."

Mum bent down low, shivering. But she slowly reached out her hand – held the relic toward Agapetos, whose brilliant light shone out at once.

Cimul threw back his head and gave a monstrous cry. "Then I call you to me now – my faithful ones! Rise up in these places of the deep, for I would have you fight for me."

With a deafening cry, all the swans replied – the swans on the lake and the swans leaning down above us. All round the cavern it echoed on and on – a shriek, the scream of hundreds of birds. Into the air those ancient voices came again, the voices of the ancient followers of Cimul:

> *"If we possess the tooth, we too can curse.*
> *If we can curse, we too can rule.*
> *If we can rule, we too can misrule.*
> *Long live the Inverter, Lord Cimul!"*

At that, Cimul rose, his arms out wide. And as we

watched, his outstretched arms became dark and feathered. He gave a mighty leap into the air. As his feet left the rocky beach, they turned black and webbed. The image before me in the air was no longer that of Cimul.

It was a swan. A huge black swan with vile red eyes.

Chapter Twenty-seven

My Diary

The black bird circled in a great arc over the lake, over the shrieking swans. Then it flew up and up, to the very top of the cavern. As it rose, the swans lining the stone steps started to peel off, to follow, to launch themselves into flight and pursue. Then they turned as one and began to fly down, directly at Mum, who was now curled up on the floor.

At that, Agapetos gave a great cry – a wild, sharp cry. I turned his way. Only now Agapetos was no longer at Epsilon's side. In his place stood an eagle. A huge eagle. But still shining, pure white.

The white eagle opened his mighty wings and rose into the air. He too flew directly towards Mum. She screamed and held the relic out to him. The eagle took it in his talons before the swans were upon him.

As he flew away from Mum, swans all around slashed at him with their beaks. Blood appeared on his plumage as he tried to rise. The black swan was beating, beating at him. Feathers fell, feather after feather. As soon as he made some headway, they drove him back downwards. Lower and lower they drove him, back towards the lake.

Blood dripped into the water as I pulled Mum to her feet. The eagle was floundering to stay in the air, struggling, surrounded by those savage beaks. Then the eagle lit up with a great light that shot out into the darkness. It stunned us all.

Instantly, the swans veered away. They flew to the lake as one and landed there. In their midst the black swan. Now there was just the eagle airborne. He hovered in the air, his mighty wings flapping. Then the voice of Agapetos roared. "Take the relic with your own hand, Cimul! It is yours from this day forth!"

Total silence came then. It was as if every living thing in that place froze with shock. Then up flew the black swan, his red eyes filled with greed. As he rose higher and higher towards the relic in the eagle's talons, he changed back into Cimul. His foul red hands reached out for the relic. Then I screamed as his fingers closed around it. But before he could even begin to draw it to himself, the voice of Agapetos called out again.

"I, Agapetos, revoke this ancient curse! From this day on, the relic will hold only blessings. I declare the words of Cimul broken."

In the air, Cimul held the tooth up before his eyes and screamed. The relic was shining with a bright silver light. It seemed to burn his hands, but still he would not let it go. Instead, his scream grew and grew in the cavern. It shook the rock walls. It reverberated all round – a scream of pure rage. Every swan on the lake raised its head and cried out. As the noise grew, a deep rumbling began, far above. A cracking sound – a splitting. It was the sound of masonry beginning to crumble.

I looked up, aghast, just as the first stone fell. An enormous crack grew from the base of the Miradel and split up to the top of the tower. Then the huge stones holding the gargoyles dislodged – toppled inwards – began to fall. The very parapet crumbled and fell.

Huge stones dropped all around Agapetos and Cimul. The whole of the great tower was coming down upon them. The shining relic was knocked from Cimul's hands. It came spinning down towards us, as if in slow motion.

Both Agapetos and Cimul were engulfed in the falling stones. The huge east gargoyle spun towards Cimul, its devil's face turning. It hit Cimul with a sickening thud. Cimul fell under its weight.

But the white eagle too was engulfed. As the very base of the tower came down, the huge stones struck him and carried him down with them. Appalled, I watched Agapetos fall into the lake.

Epsilon gave a terrible cry then – an angry, warlike battle cry. He drew his sword. "Get out!" he shouted to me in a terrible voice.

I pushed Mum into the mouth of the tunnel, too frightened to look back. "Run!" I screamed. The rock under our feet shook and rumbled. I pulled Mum on, half carrying her along the tunnel.

We ran, crying and stumbling, on and on towards the peaceful seashore.

I pushed Mum out of the tiny gap in the cliff and held her hand as she slithered down on to the sand. Then she reached up for me, caught me as I fell. We lay there in a tangled heap, panting and weeping, our arms around each other. I couldn't stop shaking, couldn't stop my teeth from chattering.

Mum suddenly seemed to notice this. She felt with her hands, all along my wet jeans. "You're soaked. Come on – there's a fire still lit." She sounded like Mum again.

We helped each other over to the fire. The embers were still glowing. They threw out a strong, comforting heat. The sky near the horizon was a soft, deep red. The night was almost through. Sunrise couldn't be far away now.

Mum sank to her knees, covered her face with her hands. She knelt there, very still. A gentle breeze came from the sea – fanned the embers into a small flame. I reached then for a bit of driftwood and threw it on the fire. More warmth – we had to have more warmth. Both of us were trembling from head to foot.

Mum raised her face. Stretched out her hands to the fire. I inched closer, took hold of one of her hands. "Mum? It was *her*? Her face you were drawing all that time? Martha's? Not Yolandë's?" Mum looked at me for a long time, then gave a huge sigh.

"I saw both of them, Jess. That one, in there…" she gave a shudder "…and Martha. But I didn't know her name, didn't know who she was. I just knew she was lost and alone and was looking for something. She was exhausted. I dreamed of her, that face, peering out, trapped. Poor thing. Who was she?"

I put one arm around Mum. "Her name was Martha Wren. She was the last woman – before you – to be drawn towards Yolandë."

Mum's eyes were wide in her tired face. "And Yolandë? Who is Yolandë?" She was shuddering with fear. I held her close. She rocked in my arms like a little child.

"Yolandë was just – a disguise, Mum. A beautiful form, beautiful enough to draw you and Martha into all this." Mum wiped her eyes and shuddered.

"She was the ONE LADY," I went on. "But she was him all the time – Cimul, who wanted to *be* the One. It was the enemy of Agapetos."

At the sound of his name, we fell still and silent. We sat there shivering, and the lines of red clouds over the sea grew golden. The top of the sun appeared out of the horizon. We both gazed at it, lost in our own thoughts.

Presently, we heard it behind us – a terrible shrieking, but far inland. And the long, low sound of many wings. Mum and I clutched each other, turned to look out over the cliffs to where the Miradel had once stood. Now there was nothing. The top of the hill was just a dark gape, a wounded gap. But swans were soaring out of the darkness. Hundreds of swans rose up as if flying out of the earth itself. They rose, wheeling and calling.

Around them, a strange flickering. An electric, rapid flashing. I knew what it was instantly. A camera. "Dad's up there!" I said.

Mum and I leaped up, craned our necks to see. But we couldn't see Dad. We could see nothing but those swans. More and more of them rose and circled the hill. In the soft light of the rising sun, all the swans shone white. They gathered together in the air. Their wild cries reached us clearly as we stood, transfixed. Then they flew our way, wheeling towards Long Beach.

Nearer the swans flew, their rhythmic wings beating closer. As the sun rose halfway out of the sea, they arrived. Over our heads they flew, hundreds upon hundreds of swans. They circled the beach, their wings loud, heavy.

But white. White. All of them were white.

Then they turned as one and flew out over the sea. Farther and farther they flew, away from Lume, flying in a great curve back towards the west.

Mum and I sank back down into the sand. All the swans had been white. The black swan had not been with them. Neither had the eagle.

I stared up at the hill and thought of Agapetos, fallen into that vile water. I thought of how he alone had known that the relic was in the right hands. Mum's hands. Shivering in the sea breeze, I marvelled at what he had done. He had enabled Mum to see Martha's face. He had allowed Yolandë to beckon Mum, to enchant her. But Mum's compassion for Martha had been his biggest weapon of all. Not even Epsilon had realised his wider plan. Agapetos alone knew.

Then – "Look, Mum!" I yelled, pointing towards the hill.

Another bird rose out of that dark gap. It flew up, a dark silhouette against the pearly sky. At first I thought it was the black swan. But as it rose higher and the sun shone on it, I saw its plumage – white. Pure white. And as it flew nearer, I saw that the shape was not the shape of a swan at all. The beak was hooked, the feet not webbed.

The eagle flew closer and closer.

When he was almost over our heads, we could see the relic shining in his talons. His white plumage was dirty, smeared in red. Right over our very heads he flew, and as he did, a drop of something fell down and splashed on to my forehead.

As he soared over the tumbling surf, my hand reached up to touch my forehead. I stared down at the crimson on my fingertips. Blood.

But Mum was on her feet, pointing out to sea. "What's *that*? Out there – in the bay?"

The sun rose higher over the sea, the lowest edge of it

just clinging to the horizon. But its light caught the curved rising and falling of something leaping in the bay. Gleam after gleam of light appearing, then submerging, then appearing again in the dark water.

Porpoises and dolphins, leaping and playing in enormous numbers. The sun shone on their backs, glinted bright gold. Curve after curve of them, rising, falling, rising again. Then the sun separated from the horizon and there was gold – gold everywhere.

The white eagle flew towards those shining, curving backs, his talons clutched tight. As he reached them, he dipped down. I watched as he dropped the relic from his talons. Gleaming in the sun, it fell spinning, down, down towards the churning surface. At the very last moment, a great porpoise leaped out and caught it in its jaws. I saw a joyous white splash as it fell back into the waves.

Finally, their song came faintly to our ears. The ancient songs of King L'Ume, the ones heard long ago, when Lume was a gentle place, inhabited only by seals and ermine and wild birds. Songs sung on these shores by an ancient king whose heart was pure and true. Tunes so enchanting that whales and porpoises and dolphins would swim closer to listen. Music of the sea sung by faithful voices at times when the sky was red. Mum and I cried to hear it.

Then the porpoises and the dolphins turned in their huge schools and followed the eagle eastwards, far out into the sunlit sea.

Further and further he flew into that dazzling golden circle, until we couldn't see him any more...

Chapter Twenty-eight

My Diary

I never saw another swan on the island again – not after that night. The lake stays bare and the only visitors to it now are seagulls.

I never saw Epsilon again either. Not in the flesh, so to speak. But I spend a lot of time down at his cottage, and he always finds a way to talk to me. Lumic words written in the sand, the waves almost carrying them away. Feathers of tallowy white left on my pillow, with a note stuffed behind. Lumic, always in Lumic – instructions, pointers, clues (he still insists on *clues*!) as to where to look to find more about Agapetos and the Bright Beings.

I can't get enough of them. As Epsilon reminds me often, the mark of Agapetos is on my forehead. I'm his. Nothing, but nothing makes me feel as good – as wild and as free and as frustrated and as sulky and as gleeful and as joyful and as *safe* – as belonging to Agapetos.

I'll finish this part of my diary and put it in my file soon. Just catch up the last bit. Tidy up. Then I think I'll hide it all somewhere – somewhere in Epsilon's cottage. The bedroom probably – that strange, peaceful old place with its peculiar energy – like stepping into a time warp in a sci-fi movie or something.

After all, that's where it all began – down there. Down in the ruined cottage. So that's where it can all stay, until someone else finds it. It will stay hidden only until for some reason it needs to be *unhidden* – that I do know. But until then, I stay quiet as a mouse about it.

Dr Parker keeps on asking me all about that night and what was going on. His curiosity drives him bananas – not knowing – but I tell him nothing. It's not for him to know.

His questions started immediately, that morning. As soon as we got back home. We met them on the cliff path when we finally staggered back along it. Him and Mrs Shilling and Ely Fingers, coming from the lake. Both men looked shaken to the core.

As to Ely, he didn't seem to quite know where to put his eyes. He took one look at my forehead and shut his mouth for the rest of the walk back to our house. Then he just stood by the window and stared out at the dawn.

All that last hour, as we got warm and dry again in the kitchen, I kept lifting my hand to my forehead. I could still feel it there.

Not the speck of blood – I'd washed that off as soon as I came in. Something *left* by the blood. Just a feeling, a sort of… awareness. That's all. Not much. But it settled right into me and made all the quaking and trembling stop. A sort of… resting feeling. I can feel it now, that not-quite-tingling on my forehead. I feel it whenever I think about all this or learn a bit more about Agapetos.

As to Dr Parker, he was all bluff and fuss. He clucked around Mum and me and kept asking what had happened, why were we wet through, where the hell had we been all that time, they'd been out to look for us on the beach a dozen times, they'd been worried sick.

They still *looked* worried sick – except for Mrs Shilling, who looked like the cat that had got the cream. But the doctor and Ely had this stunned, vacant look on their faces and I knew why. The Miradel. From the lake, they'd have had to stand and watch it come down.

Then Dad burst through the door, cameras swinging everywhere. He stood and stared, then ran to us both and hugged us close. He hit me in the face with his Canon EOS-1n, but all I could do was laugh. He couldn't stop hugging Mum, holding her close, telling her he loved her.

In the end, she told him to please stop fussing: she'd tell him all about it tomorrow but right now all she wanted was another hot-water bottle and a cup of tea – her feet were frozen solid. But she was smiling.

So Dad poured her some tea and sat down opposite us. His face was shining with a wild, mad joy. His pockets bulged with used rolls of film. He took them all out and lined them up on the table.

"I went up to the lake to look for you," he said, his eyes aglint. "Thought those young kids might have been right – thought you'd wandered up there again. But then I felt it – like an earthquake!"

His hand shook as he picked up one of the films. He stared at it as if he could see every image it held. "Incredible!" he said. "That tower falling down. I got it all. Cracks, all the way up to the gargoyles. The first stones falling. The huge gap. But then I looked into the hole and nearly died of shock." He chose another film and held it up towards Mum.

"Swans, Elizabeth! Pouring out of the gap. Hundreds of them. I got them in black and white – a dark hole in the ground and swans pouring out of it! Then I changed to colour. Swans in the air. Flying out over the sea. The sky a most glorious red. But then…"

He picked up the final film and held it tight in his fist. "But then another bird. I thought I heard a shout. I peered into the hole. And this light shot out, it nearly blinded me! Then the sound of wings. Up it came, out of the ground. It was just… *incredible*!"

Dr Parker leaned closer. "What was incredible?" he said.

"An eagle!" said Dad. "I'd seen it before, on the lawn – but had no flash set-up. But this? This was beyond my wildest dreams!"

The doctor sat back. His eyes moved from Mum, to me, to Dad. "An eagle?" he said. "But Richard – eagles don't just come up out of holes in the ground!"

Dad smiled. He tapped the films then put them all back into his pocket. "The camera doesn't lie, Doctor. I'll win the biggest prizes in photographic history!" Smugly, he tucked another blanket round Mum. Then he kissed her on the top of her head.

"You and your prizes. Is that all you care about?" said Mum. But she was smiling at him – a thin, watery smile that went right to my heart.

He knelt down beside her chair. "No, Elizabeth. I care about you and about Jess and about whatever the hell you've both been up to the past few weeks. You both seem to have gone stark raving mad, running off at all hours in the bloody dark. What on earth has been going on?"

Mum and I exchanged glances. Mum still looked half dazed. "Going on?" I said. "Nothing's been going on, Dad. Nothing at all."

We finished our tea and Mum dozed off in the armchair, and then the men crept off to find some brandy. Suddenly, Mrs Shilling dropped a bit of paper into my hand.

"Here's your shopping list, girl. I found it on the kitchen table. Very careless, leaving it lying around like that."

In my hand, the Lumic rhyme I'd scribbled down as a clue to Epsilon, hours before. The words in Lumic of the document called 'The Key'. *In the space below the well a map to the key lies hidden…*

I stared down at the symbols, then back up at her. "Shopping list? What shopping list?" I said.

She stood above me, the usual glare on her face. Put her bony hands on her hips. "Oh, for pity's sake!" she said. "Turn the paper *over*!"

On the other side of the paper, the only clues I hadn't been able to solve.

> *Lemon Sq*
> *Galeria 5*
> *Cloves – tooth*

There they were, those words – the same as they'd always been, ever since I found them in the first box from Epsilon's cottage.

"But, Mrs Shilling," I said," this isn't a shopping list! It's a *clue!*"

"Oh, really?" she sniffed. "Whose handwriting is it then? Look, girl!"

I stared down at it. The hurried scrawl. I recognised something about the spacing of the letters, the upward stroke of the crossed 't's. Mum's. One of Mum's many ways of writing when she's trying out different pens, new brushes.

Mum yawned and stretched in her chair. Smiled blearily my way. "Still up? What's that you've got there, you two?"

I held it out to her, list side up. She glanced at it and smiled. "Oh, that's where it is! My shopping list. I wondered where it had got to – good heavens, did that cause a row!"

"List? Shopping list? But it mentions the tooth! The relic!"

"The relic? Where does it mention the relic?"

She yawned and rubbed her eyes.

"But, Mum – it even mentions the Lemon Squire!" I pointed to 'Lemon Sq'.

"*Squire?* No, no, no! Squash! Lemon *squash* – for the Greet. Everyone was supposed to take some – for the punch. Another thing I forgot."

"And 'cloves – tooth'?" I said. "What does that mean then?"

"Cloves. Your dad wanted herbal remedy – some oil of cloves for his toothache. It was driving him up the wall. That wretched wisdom tooth – he'll have to have it out one day but he's such a coward! All he'll take for it is cloves. Did I hear someone say they'd gone to fetch some brandy? I could drink a barrel of the stuff, I really could. Ah – here they are at last!"

I stared at her, bewildered, as the men came clattering back in with glasses and a bottle of brandy.

"And Galeria 5, Mum? What's Galeria 5?"

"What? Oh, that's just a paintbrush."

"What do you mean, it's a paintbrush?!"

"What do you mean, what do I mean? It's the *name* of a *paintbrush*. The make and number of a paintbrush, I needed it for my work. Oh, for heaven's sakes, Richard, give her a bit of that brandy; I think she needs it more than I do."

I sipped the brandy down, thinking, thinking.

The document labelled 'The Key' was yellowed with age when I'd found it.

I remembered it clearly, nestled there in the first of Epsilon's boxes. Along with Seb's diary and stuff, from more than a hundred years ago. It was faded, curled up at the edges. It was *old*!

Then – only last night – I'd made a quick copy of it, to leave a clue to Epsilon as to where I'd gone, into the Aquila cave. So he'd know where to find me – in case I got lost in there.

I'd grabbed a scrap of paper from the kitchen table and scribbled down the rhyme in Lumic. But the scrap of paper had a shopping list on the back – Mum's shopping list – I just hadn't noticed it. I'd just scribbled the rhyme down in Lumic and left it there for Epsilon to find. Mrs Shilling had picked it up instead, as soon as we all came back in. She'd slipped it into her pocket so that others hadn't seen the Lumic rhyme. But – on the other side of the original document, more than a hundred years old – there had been Mum's shopping list! *Written only this morning!*

Oh, it didn't make sense. It put my head in a spin.

As I sat there, rubbing my head, Mrs Shilling walked over to the window. It was all steamed up. She rubbed a little circle in the condensation and spoke quietly to me. As if she'd heard all my thoughts. As if in reply.

"Time is nothing. Not to Him. That's how your mother managed to see Martha. A glimpse in time. Time? What's time, I ask you!"

Dr Parker looked up – fumbled for his pocket watch. "Time? Well, it's— Great *heavens*! It's almost five-thirty! Good thing it's a holiday tomorrow, no surgery, I'd be dead on my feet! Come on then – let's let these good people get off to bed. And this time, Mrs Shilling, I insist you *go home*. I told you Ely and I would deal with it all. Really! What a night! Shocking! Gallivanting off into caves at the dead of night. I hope you've both learned your lesson." I stared up at him. His eyes are very kind. But...

"Dr Parker – why do they call you the Lemon Squire?" I said.

He chuckled as he shrugged himself into his jacket.

"It's just an old custom here. Whoever lives in Milton House — we used to own all this island, you know — has been given that name. A lemon; a dummy. Someone who doesn't use his head. Doesn't really know very much, I suppose. Not very complimentary, is it? Can't think what started off the custom. All I *do* know is I'm tired out and need my bed!"

Someone who doesn't really know very much. Yolandë's name for him. The Lemon Squire. *"He in weakness has to open up like limpets... He has no choice."* But I didn't think he'd told me the whole truth about why he was called the Lemon Squire.

As he gathered up his coat and took Mum's pulse one last time, I heard a funny little squeak at the window. The squeak of someone dragging a finger along wet glass, of someone writing on the window. I went over to where Mrs Shilling stood. There on the window she had written the words: SOLEMN CHOIR.

Then, underneath, she wrote two other words: SOLEMN QUIRE.

"Quire is an archaic form of the word 'choir', girl," she whispered. Her tired old eyes watched me as I made sense of the words.

Solemn quire. It was easy to rearrange the letters.

Lemon Squire. It clicked into place in my mind. The Lemon Squire was the name of the leader of the solemn quire. The followers of the Lord of Inversion. Dr Parker *had* been at the Miradel that night when Mum was sleepwalking! Not only that – he had been the leader of that sinister group of men. Their squire.

Then the doctor strode over to say goodbye, and Mrs Shilling quickly rubbed out the words from the glass.

As they said their goodbyes, Ely Fingers glanced across at me briefly at last. Something in that reproachful glance made my stomach turn over. Those forget-me-not eyes, brimming with knowledge. "I notice things," he had said. It was not the doctor who had been watching me from the Miradel, I realised. It was Ely.

Now he could not bring himself to seem loud and jolly, like the doctor. His face was ashen. But he too knew it all, the whole lot of it – I saw it in his eyes. He knew about Cimul and the Dark Beings. So must Jerry Cork and Luke Lively. Old men, chanting rituals to themselves, keeping something alive. Watching. Waiting. Gathering at ancient places, muttering ancient words. Watching for old things to come to pass. The Eye of Miradel. Epsilon's name for him. Ely Fingers, honouring something evil – upholding something filled with vile, dangerous curses.

I turned away from his eyes, sickened.

He shuffled up the garden path after the doctor. They stood there just staring at each other while Mrs Shilling shrugged herself back into her smelly old cardigan.

Mrs Shilling. The cat. The cat who loves to eat fish, but hates getting her feet wet. Someone whose job it is to make sure the right things were hooked on to, reeled into the right hands. Someone whose job wasn't to be the one to do the work herself. But a guide. A helper. A hostile friend, as prickly as a wet cat, but a friend all the same.

I went and gave her smelly old face a kiss. "G'night, Mrs Shilling," I said.

She turned around and those sandy, rheumy eyes glared at me. "My name is not Mrs Shilling," she said unexpectedly.

I blinked in surprise. "No? What is it then?"

"Come and see me in three days' time," she said. "Bring your mother. When you've all recovered from your colds. Then I will tell you."

"From our colds? But I haven't got a cold!" I said.

She rolled her eyes in despair. "You really are a very *short-sighted* girl!" she said. "In three days' time then." She gave a smug little smile, and was gone.

Mrs Shilling was right. We all got colds. Me first – then Mum – then Dad.

Three days of misery and shivering and coughing and spluttering and blowing our noses, and we must have gone through 50,000 tissues between us all, I kid you not.

I shook it off first, but even so, I didn't go after three days after all. It was just so cozy there in the kitchen with Mum and Dad. We drank honey-and-lemon tea until it came out of our ears. (The doctor brought tons of lemons over, left from the Greet. He blustered and pretended, but I knew that he knew that I *knew*. He could never quite meet my eye, but he still did all the things a good doctor does. But we always got rid of him as soon as we could.)

So we sat and drank lemon and honey and we ate stuff from cans and we talked and talked and talked. Mum and Dad talked when I was in bed. Dad and I talked when Mum was sleeping. Mum and I talked every chance we got.

She couldn't stop talking about the cavern. It was hard, to have this one secret from Dad. She said there had been enough secrets between them to last a lifetime. But somehow we knew it was right to keep it to ourselves. And lots of it Mum didn't recall anyway – just a vague dream, a summer of strange visions.

Even after I'd gone to bed, I could still hear them, Mum

and Dad, whenever I went down to the bathroom. Their soft voices went on and on. Talking about last summer. Talking about Mum's affair. Talking it all out. Talking themselves well again.

Chapter Twenty-nine

My Diary

On the second night, with the hum of their talk droning on, I took my file into the small library. I settled myself in and opened the file, meaning to tidy it up, to finish it off. But when I opened it, I got a shock. Some of the clues were missing. I checked again, but it was true.

Not all of the clues were gone. Just the ones Sebastian had left for me – the clues written in Lumic and his map. The document labelled 'The Key', with its symbols. 'The Riddle of the Two' that Sebastian had left in his secret drawer in the swan bed. Gone.

I ransacked my room, searched under the bed, in between the pages of all my study files. But I knew I wouldn't find them. I never kept them anywhere but in the same box file. I didn't know how they could possibly have vanished. No one had been up here – no one. In the end, I decided it must be Epsilon.

But why would he remove every one of Sebastian's clues? I racked my brains but couldn't come to any conclusion.

Eventually, I gave up. I thought of each clue that was gone. I could remember them all. They were imprinted in my mind. So I took up my pen and rewrote the first one that came to mind.

The document labelled 'The Key'. I rewrote the symbols carefully, evenly. I even turned over the paper and scribbled the shopping list down on the other side. I did my best to copy Mum's funny 'practise' writing. The careful, experimental one she does when she's testing out a new paintbrush or pen. *Lemon Sq,* I wrote. *Galeria 5* And *Cloves – tooth.*

As to the map, I already had a rough tracing I'd done, so that was easy enough. Then the 'The Riddle of the Two' – how could I forget those words? I'd stared at them often enough, puzzling. It all took a while, redoing them and putting the whole file in order. But it gave me an enormous feeling of satisfaction. Of something coming full circle.

Now the file was complete again. So the next morning –

early, when only Domino was awake – I carried the whole thing down to the cottage and hid it in the bottom drawer, along with the empty boxes. I came back feeling dramatic and a bit wobbly – I should have been resting really, recovering from my cold. Even that little walk set me back another day. More lemon and honey. Another five kilometres of tissues.

So it was four days before Mum and I wrapped up warm and walked Domino over to the village. (Wrapped up too warm actually – it was a beautiful sunny day. We were sweating before we even reached the village.)

"And why are we going to see Mrs Shilling exactly, Jess?" asked Mum.

"Because she told us to," was all I could come up with. So on we walked – to the very end cottage.

The door opened at once. "You're a day late!" snapped Mrs Shilling. "Leave the dog in the garden. I don't like dogs." Like I said – as bad-tempered as a wet cat.

She only let us in as far as the smelly hallway, where she pointed to a grimy rug on the floor. "Stand there," she said. "I'll be back in a minute."

Mum tried not to hold her nose as Mrs Shilling dragged herself upstairs. The smell was appalling.

"She's not fit to look after herself!" whispered Mum.

"Let alone the doctor!"

"Shh, Mum! She's coming back."

In her hands was a strange, old case. A battered leather dressing case, a faded blue – the size of a small suitcase. This she handed to me. Mum and I stared at her, puzzled, but she took no notice. "Follow me," she said.

We thought she meant into the living room. But she just walked to the coat stand, put on her coat, and beckoned us out into the garden. Domino took one sniff of the hem of that coat and gave it a wide berth from then on.

Down the street she led us, surprisingly spry for her age. In fact, both Mum and I panted more than she did, after our heavy colds. We followed her obediently, silently, along the path towards our land. Halfway along, she stopped at a bank of wildflowers. She glared at us. "Well?" she said. "Pick some!"

So we did, all three of us. We picked flowers all the way along the path to our land. But once there, she walked straight past our gates. Over the little bridge and on to the cliff path. Then down the windy path and on to Long Beach. Right to the end of the beach, to where Coscoroba Rock was sticking out into the mad, white waves.

We had stopped at the remnants of the fire. The breeze stirred its grey ashes around. Mrs Shilling looked all around, satisfied that we had the shore to ourselves. Then she laid the case on the sand and opened it.

Inside was a brand-new, modern camping lantern. It was enormous – the sort that can light up whole campsites in the dark. It looked strange there, lying against that faded blue silk lining. Mum stared down at it and frowned. Then she lifted her eyes to the cliff face – to where the dark slit of the tunnel opening stood in shadow.

"Oh, no," she said. "I am *not* going back in there."

"But you must!" said Mrs Shilling. "I certainly can't. At my age!"

Mum shook her head and gave a huge shudder. Mrs Shilling sat down in the sand and laid the wildflowers carefully by her side. Then she sat there, obviously waiting for us to do the same.

I shrugged at Mum then sat down. Domino arrived and sat a little way off. (He kept shuffling round – I swear he was trying to get upwind of her.) Mrs Shilling looked far out to sea. When she finally spoke, it was as if she was talking to the ocean, not to us.

"You look very like her, Elizabeth," she said at last.

"Like who?" said Mum.

"Like your mother," came the reply.

I sat between them quietly. I was beginning to see. At least I thought I was.

"My mother? But… how did you know my mother?" said Mum. "She never came here, she hated the place!"

"As I did," Mrs Shilling smiled. "We both did. We vowed never to come here – ever, she and I."

Mum shook her head, bewildered. "Who? You and who?"

Mrs Shilling turned away from the sea then and looked into Mum's eyes. "I and my sister. Your mother."

Mum's eyes pooled out, wide with shock. "Your sister? Was my *mother*?"

Mrs Shilling settled herself more comfortably on the sand. She raised her old face to the warm sun, then took her scarf off. She fingered one tattered hem of the scarf as she began to speak.

"Now I will tell you a story – a proper story." She smiled. "Once, a long time ago, there were two little girls. Twins. Their names were Libby and Bridie. They lived in their girlhoods in Ireland, in County Cork. With their mother, Beth. Another Elizabeth, you see? Libby and Beth – both short for Elizabeth. The name was handed down to you. It's a good Irish name."

She turned to fix me with that glare. Sniffed in disdain.

"Where the name Jessica came from, I really don't know!" she said. "A name should be passed down through the family. Kept in the family. Like family secrets. Anyway, Beth did her best with the two little girls. She wasn't short of money, it wasn't that – they had a small house and money from Beth's husband. But she was never very strong, and she was sad and alone. For her husband had deserted her."

Mrs Shilling gazed out to sea again, her old eyes flashing with anger. "Libby and Bridie grew up and looked after their mammy. She told them of a great big house over the sea. A large house, with a sundial in the garden and a lake nearby. That was the house her husband lived in, although Beth never saw it for herself. She was never invited there. Not once."

"A sundial in the garden? The Big House?" asked Mum.

"The Big House. The house you now live in. Beth told her daughters such wonderful things about that house where their daddy lived! She received letters from her husband, and money, all the time they grew up. But as they grew up, the two little girls grew bitter. They hated their father – they thought him weak. They never forgave him for the sorrow he had brought to their mother's eyes. And so they made a vow – a very solemn vow, as only little girls can do. They would never visit their father in the Big House over the sea. Never! He could rot in it for ever, all alone, like their mammy was alone."

Mrs Shilling sighed and stared at me intently. "They were very young and very angry. The young can be very unforgiving." I dropped my eyes. But she just went on, her cracked old voice warming to her tale.

"So the years went by and they grew up. Their mother never revived, not really, after her husband had gone. The two girls did their best, but she eventually just gave up and died. It was as if all the life had gone out of her. And Libby kept her side of the bargain. When their father wrote to them after his wife had died, she refused to read or to answer the letters. She tied them all up in a bundle and hid them in an old dressing case of her mother's. This case, in fact. But Bridie found them and read them all."

Mrs Shilling put her hand deep into her pocket and fumbled about. She brought out a bundle of letters, tied with a dirty pink hair ribbon. Her gnarled old finger reached out and touched the ribbon gently.

"Bridie read them all. She still blamed her daddy, but she loved to hear about the Big House. For he wrote about it all the time. Wrote all about the house and the gardens, and about his mother and what had happened to her when he was just a little boy himself. I expect he thought that because no one ever replied, he could get it all out of his system. Like keeping a diary. So he told the strange tale about his mother, Martha, going missing. And it haunted Bridie, the thought of that lady, wandering around in the dark. She could not get it out of her mind. Oh, she got on with her life, but she never got away from it – not really. She saw that woman in her dreams. Her grandmother, lost, long ago. It became part of her, that image."

Mum leaned forward intently. "Me, too!" she whispered. "It was like that for me." Mrs Shilling nodded.

"So it went on, until on the day of their eighteenth birthday, when Libby found out that Bridie had kept all the letters and cherished them. They had a terrible quarrel. They were twins, you see – twins are not supposed to have secrets. By now, Bridie knew enough about the island with the lake and the Big House. She had enough money of her own – each of them had been left money by their mother. But Bridie wasn't ready to go there yet. She was a loner. She moved away, she travelled. She went to the very same places her father had mentioned in his letters. She kind of – trailed him. Egypt. Arabia. Africa. Germany. And when she was twenty-seven, she met a German man – Otto Schilling."

Here Mrs Shilling gave a great sigh. "I don't know why

I'm telling it all to you like this," she said. "In the third person. Maybe it makes it a little easier. I loved Otto very much – but it was a hard time to do so. It was 1944. He was killed in action."

Mum reached out and took her old hand in hers. "I am so sorry," said Mum. Her eyes were very kind.

But I was bursting with curiosity. I blurted my question out. "And did you ever contact him, Mrs Shilling, while you were travelling? Did you contact Sebastian?"

Mum glared at my outburst, but Mrs Shilling just shook her head. "I was still too angry. After Otto died, I took his name in his memory, even though we were never married. But I anglicised it when I went back to Ireland. Not Schilling – with sch, just sh. It was a good, respectable name – Mrs Shilling. I shared the same little house with Libby for a while. But it didn't last long. We argued about our father all the time. How she hated him! It almost ate her alive. I could never stand listening to it for long. So I travelled again – all over the world, working for a year here and there.

"I even lost my Irish accent, picking up a bit of everywhere. But I could never settle, and the thought of my lost grandmother never left me. Eventually, Libby married, late in life. She too was widowed young, poor Libs. But she had one daughter – Elizabeth. You, my dear."

Mum smiled at her. But her eyes were still far away, still sad.

"But even when I visited my sister, we never made up our differences. I told her again and again I hated Sebastian and didn't want anything to do with the Big House. But she noticed the places I'd visited, in my album. I'd made little notes in there, linking me with him. I didn't hate him after a while, you see. I wanted to feel close to him. But I knew Libby would never understand. And she didn't."

I thought of all I'd heard about my grandmother. Granny Libby, whose black jet necklace I'd always treasured. Half mad by all accounts, Dad had said. Bitter as they come. Mum spoke of her rarely. Poor Mum. But Mrs Shilling went on, determined to finish her tale.

"Maybe madness has always been in the family. After all, our own mother lived only in the past. It is a kind of madness, that. In the end, Libby got ill with it too. It was all she could think of – trying to get me to promise never to visit here, never to visit him. It was an obsession with her. After all, she already *knew* I could never *live* in the Big House!"

"Knew? But how?" said Mum.

"Because I'd already given in to her, years before. When I first returned to Ireland, just after Otto died. At that time, I think I was half mad myself. I didn't really care about inheriting. In the end, I just gave in. In a moment of weakness, I legally signed all my share of the house over to my twin. Then, when Sebastian died, she got my share too."

Mum frowned, appalled. "My mother let you do that? Even though she never wanted it *herself*?"

"Let me do it? She *made* me do it. She just wore me down with it all in the end. Everything had to be her way. I hope you never saw that side of her, Elizabeth."

Mum sighed. She wouldn't answer. That in itself was answer enough. Then Mum shook her head. "She only mentioned you once to me, Mrs Shilling. Just once, when I was quite young."

"She did? What did she say?"

Mum hesitated. "She said you were dead. I am sorry."

Mrs Shilling nodded, her mouth set in a grim line. "Well, it won't do to blame her, I suppose. She wasn't very well in the end, was she? Not well in the head, I mean. It was all this business, her hatred of her father. It consumed her. Then when she died – not long after our father, ironically – she left it all to you. That was nineteen years ago. I sometimes thought you would never move into it!"

The sea had grown quiet, a soothing lapping near our feet. Far out to sea, a gull cried out – was joined by others – and then became quiet again.

A thought occurred to me. "But Mrs Shilling – when *did* you come here?"

She smiled widely for the first time since I'd met her. Her arrival on Lume was clearly one of the happiest things that had ever happened to her.

"Eighteen years ago. I outsmarted my sister in the end!" she said. "After I got tired of travelling, I came here anyway. I used the last of my savings to buy that damp little cottage at the end of the village. Even though I was too late – my father had just died – I heard about him from the villagers. Heard what a recluse he was. The mad old man. It was a link of sorts. It was enough. I even used to sneak into the Big House – very occasionally I got in through the back scullery door; it was broken for years."

Mum nodded. "I'm still nagging Richard to mend it!" She smiled.

Mrs Shilling shrugged. "It was an odd thing to do. But being in the Big House just made me feel close to him. I used to wander around, cleaning all those old things. I read many strange things in that small library. Then you came here, and the rest – you know."

I shifted in the sand. Domino was snoring slightly, stretched out on the sand, a little way off. "So you are... my what?" I said.

"I am your great-aunt," said Mrs Shilling. "And *your* Aunt Bridie, Elizabeth."

We all grinned at one another, a little embarrassed. Then I spotted the faded dressing case at our feet. "But I still don't get it, Mrs Shilling – what's the suitcase for?"

She rolled her eyes in despair. "Oh, explain to her, will you, Elizabeth? She makes me tired." She closed her eyes as Mum explained what we had to do.

Chapter Thirty

My Diary

It was colder in the tunnel this time. A distinct breeze was coming down from the cavern. The gaping hole left by the Miradel let the wind come in and sweep through the whole thing. Mum and I didn't talk. We just inched along the tunnel, holding hands. Until we came to the entrance to the cavern.

The bright camping light lit the whole of the cavern. The waterfall was still nothing but a few drops. The lake was littered with stones and debris from the fallen tower. Mum held up the lantern and pointed to the easiest route across.

A faint scent came to me as we inched our way over the fallen stones. The scent of spring flowers. I stiffened, remembering Yolandë and her posy to Mum. Mum smelled it too and paused astride a rock. We exchanged glances then moved nervously on towards the thin, steady dripping where the waterfall had been. Then we stood and Mum lifted the lantern.

There was the little bundle of black, all curled up on its side. The small tattered bonnet. The tiny leather shoes. The thin fingers of bone in their little half-mittens.

But entwined in the fingers was a small posy of pure-white flowers. The tallowy scent came from them clearly. "Epsilon!" I whispered.

Mum opened the dressing case. Together we bent down to gather up the mortal remains of Martha Wren.

We carried the bones on to Coscoroba Rock – Mum, Mrs Shilling and me. "She has been trapped long enough," said Mrs Shilling. "No grave in the earth for her."

"I am drawn to the sea," Martha had always said. So we decided to place her in its huge hands for ever.

We stood together, all holding the case. Even though none of us spoke, I knew we were all thinking the same thing. Wondering if any words were needed.

Eventually, Mrs Shilling shook her head. "No," she said. "There are no words."

We bent down to the surface of the water and gently tipped the case. The churning waves around Coscoroba Rock took her at once, swallowing the fragile bones, the delicate silken gown in all its shreds. We watched her disappear into the blue – this woman, ancestor to each of us. I reached out and took hold of Mrs Shilling's hand. She had waited such a long time for this. Her hand gripped mine tightly.

On her other side, Mum took something out of her pocket. The little heart-shaped locket. She opened it and we all gazed down at the two faces inside. Martha's and Sebastian's. Mum gave the locket to Mrs Shilling. "Look," she said. "A picture of your grandmother. And of your father."

A huge smile spread over Mrs Shilling's face as she looked into the eyes of Sebastian at last.

Then we cast the wildflowers into the sea. Bloom after bloom of them we threw out. Yellow flowers and white, summer flowers with their rich and heady scents. They floated on the surface of the water gently.

We watched the sun come out and light up their sweet faces.

Epilogue

It is typical that in this strange tale there would be one last thing to report.

It happened exactly one summer later. And to me, it is the strangest thing of all. The one that keeps me awake at night, my mind boggling.

Mrs Shilling is now living with us. She insists on cleaning for us, although we all protest. But as she says, it is important to her that she pays her way. After all, she said, Mum and Dad work so hard as it is – Mum with her portraits and Dad with his endless photography commissions. Besides, she's loved this Big House for so long from afar, she likes pottering round it, dusting all those old things. "Father's things," she says with a smile.

Then one day – about a week after Avril's summer visit – she came out of the small library with her hands behind her back.

It'd been a hectic month for Mrs Shilling, with Avril staying here and bringing "all her wild ways". Such a lot of sniffing for Mrs Shilling to do, such a lot of glaring! But oddly enough, a lot of laughing too. She and Avril had got on like a house on fire, although they both pretended not to.

Now her old face looked smug as she stood at the small library door. She just stood very still and gave me that funny little cat-got-the-cream smile she has. Her hands were behind her back, like a child hiding a secret.

"What? What is it, Mrs Shilling?" I said. (I could never bring myself to call her Aunt Bridie. Not that she'd have permitted it.)

She held out her hand. In it was a tiny posy – five flowers wrapped together. She handed it to me with the usual sniff. "Yours, I presume," she said. "I found it on that small shelf table thing in there, shedding pollen all over my dusting! Is someone trying to tell you something again?"

I stared down at the tallowy flowers and my heart leaped. Epsilon! It had been months since there had been anything like this. Epsilon wanted me back again.

Time to go back to the cottage, to the place where all this began.

All the way down, I thought of the file. I still hadn't worked out how those three documents had vanished last summer. At the time, I'd just rewritten them and tucked them into their right places again. The whole thing was still there, safe in the drawer in Epsilon's desk. I hadn't looked at it since.

Now I was strangely eager to see it and to read it all through again.

The cottage was still and dim as usual. Domino raced upstairs, barking joyfully. He leaped on to the hammock and sat there, tail wagging madly. But he soon settled down.

The room smelled of candles and spices. I went over to the desk, sniffing that particular smell of Epsilon's room. I was smiling as I pulled open the bottom drawer.

There were the boxes, empty. And there was the file, now with a thin layer of dust over it.

I opened the pages and began to leaf through them. Idly, I turned to the document labelled 'The Key' and did a double take. I stared down at it, astonished. I was expecting to see words I wrote last summer, fresh on the page. Instead, I was staring down in disbelief at a yellowed paper, the ink faded with age.

I leafed through the rest of the file quickly – to the copies I'd made of the other two documents that had gone missing. 'The Riddle of the Two.' And the map. The originals of these too had returned! It didn't make sense. Those papers Sebastian had left for me – the ones that had vanished – here they were, back again.

But how? I turned the pages, one by one. *Each* document – each clue – was now browned and crackly.

Each one was at least a hundred years old. Who had taken my more recent copies and replaced them?

"Epsilon?" I said. As soon as I spoke his name, I felt it in the air. That crackling. That strange energy.

I turned round, expecting to see him fully standing there. But there was just a warmth, and the faintest of strange shadows over in the corner. I peered at them, seeing the way they shimmered oddly.

"Epsilon." I smiled. "Why have you taken all my copies out and replaced them with the originals?"

His voice came from out of the shimmering. "I have not."

I turned back to the papers – lifted them up. "But you have! Look! All my copies, the ones I made last year! Every single document, replaced!" I held them out, showed him how crinkly and aged they were.

"What's going on, Epsilon?" I said. "Why on earth would you take these very pages from me last summer, so I had to make copies? Only to then take *those copies* and replace them with the originals again? It doesn't make sense!"

"Look closer," he said.

"What?"

The shadows shimmered. I felt as if he was laughing.

"Look closer. Are you sure these are the documents you call 'the originals'?"

I held them up, puzzled. "Of course they are!" I said. "Look – they're old and faded! These are the ones Sebastian left for me! You know they are!"

"Sebastian left them for you?" he said. "Are you sure?"

I stood there with my mouth open, wondering if he'd gone mad. But Bright Beings don't go mad. I tried again. "Look, Epsilon. You know as well as I do that Sebastian wrote these more than a century ago! He wrote them all down to help me. You saw what he'd written in his diary!"

I turned to the right page and read it out. "Listen! *This girl, Epsilon also says, I must assist when the time comes. But how can I help a girl from within a dream?* So he did it the only way he knew how. He wrote the clues down. He left them for me to find."

"There is one more thing he left you to find," said Epsilon. "Look in the first box."

"But – the boxes are empty. I emptied them myself."

His silence went on and on. Slowly, I put down the file – reached into the drawer. Found the little silver epsilon key and the first box. The box opened easily. Inside it – one last document. A diary page, written by Sebastian long ago. Slowly, I took it out. Unfolded it.

This is what it said:

Last night, the girl with the world in her hand came to me again.

It was the same as the other times – a dream that is not a dream. The first time it was on one of the little boxes in Epsilon's drawer. But this time I dreamed she was tapping and fumbling at the swan carved at my bed head. She tapped and tapped, and one of the swans glided out revealing a space hidden there! So as soon as I awoke, early this morning, I too tapped on the same swan. It opened. And sure enough there was another missive from her.

It is even stranger, this one, than the one she labelled 'The Key'. This one she has called 'The Riddle of the Two'. It talks about a feather'd bird with something hidden under the head and the breast and the wing. As usual, I cannot make it out. I do not know what she is trying to tell me.

Last week she left a map. I dreamed she was in the small library, poring over that huge book, THE CARTOGRAPHY OF LUME. In her hands she held two documents. So I went to the small library and opened the book. In between its pages I found them. The map. And a strange letter from Mama, in which she bids me go to a London solicitor if anything should happen to her.

How does this dream girl know where Mama has placed such a letter for me? It is as if the girl is trying to help me, trying to tell me how to piece all these things together. And what danger is Mama in? For I fear her strange affliction is getting worse.

All this is frightening me to a great degree. Epsilon tells me all will be well, so long as I trust him and trust in the name of the One he works for – Agapetos. But there are times I do not trust Epsilon at all. There are times when all I want to do with all this strange information is hide it. Bury it.

I may hide them all. Maybe in the pretty boxes in Epsilon's desk, with their tiny curly key. Lock them all away. The three documents she has left – the map, and 'The Key', and 'The Riddle of the Two'. The map and the strange letter I will just return to the heavy book. Likewise, 'The Riddle of the Two' I shall replace in my swan bed. I shall rest easier knowing they are all hidden away again for they unsettle me greatly. I know that I should persevere, should try to work it out. But I cannot. I am not gifted with the ways of riddles and ciphers.

Also there is the ring she wears in her nose. In ancient times, so Epsilon once told me, followers of Cimul and of the Ouroborus also wore a nose ring – it was their sign. Is there some link between her and the dark ways? I fear that Papa is involved in these dark ways, he and his visitors. There is always the symbol of the 'Borus on their mysterious documents. They read them closely, they mutter with their heads together, they stop speaking when I draw near. I mistrust them and their secrets.

So I will hide these things, I think. I cannot solve 'The Riddle of the Two'. I cannot solve any of it. I prefer to sit with Mama, as I did this evening. I sat at her knee in the candlelight and held my hands out while she looped her skein of wool over them. Then she slowly wound her wool into a ball, until less and less was on my skein and more and more was on the ball. She did not speak; her eyes were troubled and far away. But at least we were together.

So I have made my decision. I will ignore this latest message from the girl with the world in her hands. I will lock it all away, for to use it is to trust it, and that I cannot do.

So signed by my hand on this twenty-ninth of July in the year of our Lord eighteen hundred and ninety-four. Sebastian Wren, aged thirteen years.

As I stared down at it, tears came into my eyes.

"But I don't understand!" I wailed. "I didn't leave the messages for him! He left them for me!" The shimmering in the corner was growing brighter.

"So whose handwriting are the documents in?" he said. "Look closer." I looked again. Lifted the papers up, one by one.

Mine.

My writing on the shopping list – my attempts to copy Mum's hand, that funny writing she does when she's trying out a new pen.

The map I'd traced and filled in from memory – even down to adding that date in the corner – 1894. My carefully drawn symbols.

Mine. Mine. Mine. Yet there they were – *aged.*

I sat down, frowning. "Are you trying to tell me that Sebastian did not leave these for me? That Sebastian had *never seen* these documents – until I wrote them down?"

"Yes. Until you wrote them down. He dreamed of you each time, reading them, handling them. Then he found them the next day."

"But… I didn't *write* them – I just *found* them!"

"Yet they are in your handwriting – the way you write the Lumic symbols. They are in your handwriting. They always were."

"But only because I lost them! So I rewrote them. That's what these are, here in this file – my copies."

"Yet they are very old. Well over a century old."

Round and round in circles. Epsilon's light was growing brighter, but all I could do was stare down at the papers. My head felt like it was bursting. I shook my head and tried one last time.

"But, Epsilon – if I wrote them – if these three documents did not exist until I wrote them down... then – *where did the information come from?* Where did the rhyme come from, labelled 'The Key'? Where did 'The Riddle of the Two' come from?"

"Maybe you wrote those rhymes yourself?"

The shimmering grew and I heard it again – that fond laughter.

"But... even if I did – which I didn't – how could I have found them myself, found them old and faded? If I only wrote them *down* myself – later? How can Sebastian have found them a hundred years ago – if I hadn't even *written them yet? And where did the information come from?*"

There was no answer. I looked up. Epsilon's light shone out on to a picture on the wall. A round picture in a square frame.

The golden symbol of O. The One. The symbol of perfection.

The symbol of eternity. The One without beginning or end.

The One who *is* the beginning and the end.

The One to whom time is meaningless. The One who could do whatever he wanted with time. What had Mrs Shilling said, in the kitchen, a year ago?

"Time is nothing. Not to Him ... A glimpse in time ... What's time, I ask you!"

Quivering from head to foot, I stared up at that simple O.

Acknowledgements

My thanks go:

To Eunice McMullen and Katherine Tegen. To all the UK HarperCollins team – for your belief in *Epsilon* and your immense hard work for it. With real gratitude.

To William – for making me laugh at all the right times. For being so proud of me. *Sometimes, only you will do.*

To Catherine, Anne and Jan – for all that wonderful encouragement from the word go.

To Matt, Alex and Winona – for trying so hard. For all the cups of tea. To Christopher – for bringing me joy when I so needed it.

To Suzanne Davis – for extraordinary being there. And to Amy – for reading it first.

To staff, past and present, at Highcliffe Hotel, Sheffield – for letting me sit scribbling in various corners and for all the fun and banter.

To Andy – for always asking. For always caring. Likewise, Stuart, Tom and all my friends at the Highcliffe.

To Brigit – for reading the first chapter and telling me to get on with it.

There are two people who have literally made all this happen. So special thanks go to:

The ever-cheerful Robin. You wrote the flute tune that inspired all this. In addition, you sat for long days puzzling, thinking, reading aloud, being honest and saying, "It won't *do*!" You ruthlessly scrapped 45,000 inferior words! You strengthened me and brought inspiration aplenty. The fact that you cheerfully set aside so many weeks of your time at the age of thirteen is truly extraordinary. If I planted the seed for *Epsilon*, you were the watering can.

Finally, my husband, Greg. You have held me together when others threatened to crack me apart. All those bacon butties helped! How you ever put up with me and my haphazard working hours, I don't know. You have patiently read, edited and researched so many odd little things for me at the expense of your own work. You helped me see *Epsilon* as an antidote to the rubbish we were constantly dealing with. You laughed and cried with me during this time. What can I say of you? "A True Companion."

I am fortunate indeed.

Christine